SHOW ME DECEIT

Center Point
Large Print

Also by Ellen E. Withers and available from Center Point Large Print:

Show Me Betrayal

SHOW ME DECEIT

SHOW ME MYSTERIES – BOOK 2

ELLEN E. WITHERS

CENTER POINT LARGE PRINT
THORNDIKE, MAINE

This Center Point Large Print edition
is published in the year 2025 by arrangement with
Scrivenings Press.

Copyright © 2024 by Ellen E. Withers.

All rights reserved.

All characters are fictional, and any
resemblance to real people, either factual or
historical, is purely coincidental.

The text of this Large Print edition is unabridged.
In other aspects, this book may vary
from the original edition.
Printed in the United States of America
on permanent paper sourced using
environmentally responsible foresting methods.
Set in 16-point Times New Roman type.

ISBN: 979-8-89164-596-7

The Library of Congress has cataloged this record
under Library of Congress Control Number: 2025934473

To the readers of the first book of the Show Me Mysteries series, *Show Me Betrayal*. Thank you for your enthusiasm and support.

To Kristi Ponder, who cried happy tears when reading *Show Me Betrayal* because she was holding my dream in her hands. I pray every writer is blessed with friends and family who understand the importance of having
a dream come true.

Chapter 1

An Unrepentant Thief

The aroma of bacon and pancakes underscored my hunger. I scanned the crowd as casually as possible while making my way to the far end of the hole-in-the-wall diner. Thankfully no faces were recognizable.

I eased into the back corner booth—the best observation point, and no one could approach unnoticed. It also allowed me to spot anyone showing more than a passing interest in what was to transpire tonight.

Two hours later, I'd consumed a gallon of coffee and the breakfast special. Big T never showed, leaving me to fidget on a sticky table. The longer I waited, the more my fury grew. No one makes me wait. Highly disrespectful. The audacity. Big T had never been that brave before. Why now?

Fifteen minutes later, the bulge in the front pocket of my raincoat reminded me that something wasn't right. An envelope stuffed with that much cash wouldn't get away from Big T under normal circumstances. He'd always made it to our meetings, even if late, to claim his payment. We traded the goods he would steal for cash or drugs.

Big T wouldn't have given up the opportunity for this money. His addiction wouldn't allow it.

I scanned the diner one last time and accepted that he wasn't going to show. My stomach twisted. Something had gone wrong. Bad wrong.

Did he accidentally set off the alarm? Had someone seen him enter? Did he get arrested? A million different disasters could have prevented his appearance. Which one could it be?

He'd better not rat me out. I'll kill him.

Time to go. No use giving these strangers a chance to notice my presence. I threw down a twenty-dollar bill and walked out the door. The overstuffed envelope, still in my pocket, hit rhythmically against my thigh as I made my way through the parking lot and into my car.

The radio blasted rock and roll when my car started. The music that accompanied my earlier enthusiasm morphed into annoying noise. I punched it off and drummed my fingers on the dashboard.

Something bad kept Big T from showing.

The challenge was waiting for gossip or news reporting to unveil the reason.

Chapter 2

Kurt Hunter

Kurt Hunter pulled his sedan into the parking lot of the Audrain County Agricultural Museum and turned off his lights and siren. He was one of the first to arrive, and he expected to be one of the last to leave.

He strode toward the converted barn that housed the museum. As he approached, he scanned the lot for Hector Vega. Hector was his partner on this call-out. With Kurt's own lack of experience on the detective squad, he relished the opportunity to collaborate with the most knowledgeable detective in their department.

Patrol officer Randy Howard, short and heavyset, glanced over as he established a perimeter in front of the building. Once he had the traffic cones and crime scene tape in place, he approached Kurt. "That was fast."

"Pure luck," Kurt said. "Dispatch notified me of this suspicious death as Ross and I were heading to church. I barely slowed, handing him off to my parents."

With Hector still absent, Kurt asked, "What have we got?"

"Currently unidentified deceased Caucasian male. Approximately thirty to thirty-five years old. Found inside the museum by the cleaning lady. Her name is . . ." Officer Howard pulled a small notebook out of his uniform pocket. "Ah . . . one Josefina Delgado. Twenty-eight. Part of the cleaning crew. That's her van." He gestured to a beat-up white cargo van. "She's an employee of the cleaning service, not the museum."

"Did she touch the body?"

"I don't believe so. Her English is spotty. I suggest you wait until Hector gets here to talk to her."

Kurt nodded. "Did you touch the body?"

"Only to verify the man was deceased. He's face down on the concrete floor. No identification yet. Body's in the display room to the right. Enormous blood pool around him, and broken glass scattered everywhere. Also, a wooden and glass display case is broken into pieces nearby."

"Did he have anything in his hand? Or lying nearby?"

Officer Howard scrunched his face. "Like a tool or something?"

"Right. Something used to break in or break the display case?"

"Didn't see anything. I was looking to see if he was alive or dead. Could be underneath him or part of the mess scattered on the floor."

"I'll check that when the coroner removes the body. Any thoughts as to how he might have died?"

"My guess is the guy broke the display case and then somehow fell into the broken pieces or was pushed against the glass. If he was dumb enough to stand on the case, it might have collapsed under him. In any of those scenarios, if the shards of glass sliced into him, he could have bled out."

Kurt grimaced. "Exsanguination. An ugly way to die."

Officer Howard shrugged. "I'm only guessing. Someone could have shot him and I missed the bullet hole."

"You've been to more death scenes than I have. I trust your instincts and experience. At least until the coroner proves something else." Kurt eyed the exterior of the building. "Any cameras?"

"Not that I've seen. You best check with whoever runs this place. It's wired for a security system, but no alarm was chiming when I arrived."

Kurt pondered this. "Ms. Delgado should have disarmed any alarm if one was on when she arrived. I'll have Hector ask her. Curious how the deceased got in there without tripping it." He turned to the patrolman. "There was no alarm when she arrived, right?"

"Best I can tell, nothing was unusual until she spotted the body. Ms. Delgado called it in. 911. The station had no record of a tripped alarm here. I checked."

"Good man." Kurt pulled out his own notebook

and added this information. "Any nearby neighbors that heard an alarm?"

Officer Howard grinned and swept his hands outward. "Cows?"

"I'm hoping for a miracle."

"The nearest house is a mile or two away."

With a nod, Kurt tried another angle. "Know who the alarm provider is?"

"Mexico Security Service."

Great. Donnie Davis's company. Kurt and Donnie had been rivals in high school. "Could you please ask your officers to search for a parked, abandoned vehicle along Highway 22 or any dirt or gravel road offshoot?"

"You mean turn rows, city boy?"

Kurt smiled. "Yes, turn rows. Any drivable road or trail from town to here and from here to Centralia. If this guy was a thief, he parked near here and walked, or someone dropped him off."

"What about surveillance cameras?"

Kurt considered the pastures that surrounded them. "Have them identify any place along those routes that might have cameras. Residential and commercial." Kurt rubbed his neck. "Assuming everything took place last night, I don't know how much will be visible, but it would help to figure out what vehicle he used."

"Will do. Anything else?"

"Not that I can think of. You're doing a great job."

"Thanks," Officer Howard said. "Dispatch said the coroner requested the State Police forensic team to work the scene. He said it was beyond his capabilities."

This surprised Kurt. "Has the coroner even been here yet?"

"No, but he's coming."

Kurt studied the museum exterior. "He knows a medical examiner will be required, so he might as well call in forensics, too."

Officer Howard pointed to an approaching red truck with a camper top. "You can ask him about that right now." He turned back to Kurt. "About Ms. Delgado—"

Kurt noted the concern in the patrolman's voice. "What about her?"

"That woman is upset. So much so, she strikes me as being close to a mental breakdown."

"That bad?"

"I didn't make an official entry in my notes about her mental or emotional state. But she's not doing well."

Kurt glanced around. "Where is she?"

"I put her in my patrol car. Wrapped her in a blanket. She's mumbling in Spanish. It's obvious she's upset to have discovered the corpse."

"I'm glad you've taken care of her."

"But Kurt, if I write any of this down, I might have to testify about her state of mind. I'd rather testify about what I did when I arrived and let you address her mental state in your report."

"Got it. Thanks."

Kurt approached Officer Howard's patrol car. Ms. Delgado was, as Officer Howard described, distraught, with a limited ability to speak English. After a few minutes of questioning, Kurt sent her home and hoped she understood they would contact her with any further questions.

Kurt headed for the coroner's truck, where Anthony Cappelli was struggling to unload two enormous duffel bags of equipment.

"Tony, let me help you."

Tony handed one of the duffel bags to Kurt. "Officer Howard says this one is messy. And unique."

"That's what he's told me. I'd like to shadow you and let you teach me everything you know."

Tony had been the county coroner for over ten years. The state of Missouri had no requirement for medical training, but as an undertaker, Tony brought experience in anatomy, an ability to handle any situation involving human death, and an innate kindness for those left behind.

Tony patted Kurt on his shoulder. "How about I teach you to observe? That skill is the most important at a death scene."

"I'd like that." Kurt scanned for Hector, but there was no sign of him yet. "I was going to wait for Hector before going inside. But since you're here, I'll watch your processes."

"Perfect."

They stopped outside the entry. Tony pulled a high-grade digital camera out of his duffel bag, attached an elongated lens, and documented everything.

Kurt hurried back to his cruiser to grab a packet of plastic gloves and the small digital camera assigned to him. When he returned, they both shot photographs of the front of the building, then narrowed their activities to the two oversized plate-glass windows.

When Tony finished, he turned to Kurt. "These windows don't open and haven't been compromised."

Kurt pulled on gloves and checked the glass to be sure. "They're solid."

Tony switched lenses and took close-up shots of the locks on the doors.

Kurt did the same. "As Officer Howard said, no signs of forced entry on the front of the building."

Tony circled the building with Kurt trailing him, and both took pictures of every possible entry. Neither located any damage or suspicious marks on the exterior or spotted any cameras.

Kurt looked up at the roofline. "Before I leave here, I'll make sure no one came in through the roof."

Tony grinned. "Think we have a cat burglar in town?"

"Remember that burglary at the perfume

store a couple of years ago? They broke in from the roof." Kurt shrugged. "It was a one-story building. Even with two stories, we can't say there was 'no forced entry' until someone examines the roof or attic. We have to eliminate the possibility of roof access to the structure."

"See there? You're teaching me, instead of the other way around."

Kurt chuckled. "That will change the minute we get inside."

"Ready?" Tony handed him a pair of booties and a mask. "Outfit courtesy of the county coroner's office."

"Thanks."

When properly garbed, each man grabbed one of Tony's duffel bags. Kurt followed Tony as they crossed the threshold of glass double doors into the entrance lobby.

While Tony snapped pictures, Kurt glanced around. Although it had been several months since he'd been here, he noted nothing out of place. He'd brought Ross for a tour of the museum, and the items displayed in the entry were like displays they'd seen.

This museum had an excellent reputation for their exhibitions of antique farm equipment, combines, and tractors. Even though the information was more for adults, Kurt's seven-year-old loved anything on wheels and enjoyed his visit.

Kurt took pictures and noted the glass cases in the reception area were untouched. A magnificent antique cash register, possibly solid brass, was on top of a case. Several valuable antiques dotted the shelves inside. If the deceased's intent was to steal items of value, he'd overlooked these. Or the thief hadn't plundered this area before he met his demise.

To the left of the reception area was a glass wall and the door to a small gift shop. Tony checked the doorknob. "Locked."

They peered through the glass into the gift shop. "Appears untouched," Tony said.

Kurt pointed to the right. "The deceased is supposed to be in there."

Tony led the way into the exhibit room. Once beyond the threshold, he stopped and snapped pictures of the room. The dead man lay toward the back wall, to their left.

Although the building began as a two-story barn, this exhibit room was part of the renovations. The interior structure was a one-story framed room, paneled in reclaimed barn wood from the local area.

Kurt glanced at the concrete floor and the ceiling, covered in drywall and painted white. The only visible blood was the gigantic pool coagulating on the floor. As he stepped closer, the coppery aroma of the blood reached his nostrils and made his stomach queasy.

Tony turned to Kurt. "What do you see?"

"A dead man lying in a pool of drying blood. Broken glass, a smashed wood and glass case, along with knickknacks scattered everywhere."

"Give me details."

From his angle, Kurt examined the soles of the deceased's shoes. "The man is wearing a worn pair of sneakers. Gouges in the rubber. Cuts, too. They've had some hard wear." He squinted at the footwear. "It appears pieces of glass are imbedded in the soles." He then evaluated the man's pants. "Even with today's 'distressed' jean fashions, this guy's jeans are in poor shape. Those aren't fashion holes, they're wear and tear."

"Good. Step closer and tell me more."

Kurt examined the tattoos covering much of the deceased's neck and arms. "Various tattoos on the majority of visible skin. Not artistic. Low quality tattoos, like prison tats, but I'm speculating."

Kurt took another step closer, careful to avoid walking on glass shards. "The victim is wearing latex gloves. A professional thief, perhaps? He was concerned about leaving fingerprints."

"You're speculating again. Just the facts. Now tell me about the blood."

"Huge pool of blood. Only a few bloodstains outside of the pooled area." Kurt looked around. "The ceiling is clear of blood spatter."

Tony nodded. "With spatter being a type of blood pattern produced with force or motion, I'd guess there was no outside force." He glanced at the ceiling then down. "There appears to be some blood spatter on the floor, which could be from a fall. "We'll know more once the crime lab completes an inspection."

The exterior door opened. Both men turned to see Detective Vega striding toward them. Hector was an inch or two above six feet tall, but his thin, lanky build seemed to add several inches. God blessed him with bushy black hair, which added even more height to his appearance.

Kurt stepped back from the body. "Hi, Hector. Looks like we caught an interesting one. Tony's letting me follow him while he does his job."

"You've taken the perimeter shots? Checked for forced entry?"

"Yes, to the pics. No forced entry found, but I haven't been to the roof or attic yet."

Hector smiled. "You can't let go of the perfume store B & E, can you?"

"It was a clever method. It sticks with me."

With a gesture toward the dead man, Hector said, "This horrific scene is going to stick with you, too. I feel sorry for him and for us."

Chapter 3

Liesl Schrader

As Pastor Greg Woodson concluded the sermon, Liesl's purse vibrated against her leg. Her phone, set on "stun," was the guilty party, causing her purse to quiver.

Who'd call her on Sunday morning? They should know she was in church. She vowed to ignore the impolite person.

When the vibrations returned, moments later, she frowned. Might not be a rude person. Could be important.

Joey Bauer sat on the pew next to her. He turned his watery blue eyes toward her and raised his eyebrows in a "do something" gesture. Joey was elderly and mentally impaired. He lived in Liesl's garage apartment. She'd brought him to church this morning, which was their usual routine.

The congregation rose for the final hymn. Liesl grabbed her purse and fumbled in it until she pulled out her phone. Three missed calls. All from Kurt.

Kurt Hunter was a detective with the Mexico Public Safety Department. He was also the *former* love of her life. He was well aware she'd be in church now. An internal debate ensued. Something had to be wrong.

She hunched over to hide her movements and typed a text. By the time the congregation finished the hymn and resumed their seats, she had a reply.

She leaned toward Joey and whispered, "I need to call Kurt. Something has happened. Can you catch a ride home with someone?"

Joey nodded, unconcerned now the vibrating had stopped. He turned his focus back to Pastor Woodson.

Liesl half walked, half crawled to the aisle, excusing herself past the other occupants of the pew. She made her way at a snail's pace, restricted by the snug, A-line skirt she wore. At the aisle, she hiked the skirt high enough to allow her to quickstep toward the exit. Although many eyes followed her departure, only old Mrs. Franklin showed her disapproval. It was surprising to receive such an angry expression from a fellow parishioner.

She shrugged at Mrs. Franklin with an apologetic glance she hoped conveyed her regret for the disruption. Mrs. Franklin could use some work on her ability to forgive.

In the vestibule, Liesl shrugged into her hooded raincoat and stepped outside in the light drizzle. More April showers. Hadn't there been enough?

She called Kurt as she walked to her car. He answered on the first ring.

"Liesl. We need you."

He spoke in what she called "cop tone," which meant all business. "Your text said that. What's wrong?"

"You're on the board of the Audrain County Agricultural Museum, right?"

"Yes."

"Please come to the museum. I'll explain once you get here." Then he ended the call.

She frowned at her phone and quickened her steps toward her car. That man was so aggravating. Would it hurt to give her a hint about what was going on? Especially since he'd dragged her out of church?

Liesl worried for the full five minutes it took to drive across town to the western city limits on Highway 22. The rain remained a steady drizzle. As she neared the museum, she spotted the parking lot, full of emergency vehicles. Instead of fighting her way into the lot, she parked her red Trailblazer along the edge of the highway.

She grabbed her umbrella from the backseat pocket. Under the minute protection provided by her open umbrella, she tiptoed through the mud and gravel of the roadside. With gritted teeth, she vowed to make Kurt suffer if this expedition ruined her good high heels.

After scaling the long driveway, she spotted crime scene tape circling the entire exterior of the refurbished barn. She searched for a tall, brown-haired detective, but the only person in the parking area was Officer Howard. He wore a yellow slicker and had a plastic rain cap over his uniform hat.

Normally, she would pity him for being in the rain, but not today. Mrs. Howard frequently complained that he worked on Sunday mornings to skip church.

As he approached, Liesl smiled. "Morning, Officer Howard. Kurt called me out of church. He confirmed my being a board member of this museum, but he didn't explain anything."

The stocky officer maintained a neutral face. "I'm sorry to meet under sad circumstances, but I'm glad you and my wife are keeping in good with God."

Liesl raised her eyebrows. "We try."

He cleared his throat. "You said Kurt asked you here?"

"He did."

"I wouldn't want to throw you off the property as if you were some curious lookie-loo. Let me enter your arrival, and I'll get you past this barrier and out of the rain."

He pulled a small notebook out of his breast pocket and glanced at his watch before scribbling in it. Then he held up the yellow tape for Liesl to limbo. "Better hope they don't want to show you the crime scene. It's grizzly. I'll take you into the lobby. You can wait there while I get Kurt. Don't touch anything."

"Of course not."

Under the roof of the covered entry, Liesl shook out her umbrella. She hesitated to lean it up against the building if this was now a crime scene.

Officer Howard pointed to one of the two farthest columns from the door. "It's out of the way there."

Inside, the officer motioned for her to stay. He turned and disappeared into the display room on the right.

As she stood waiting, Liesl spotted a lanky man and a tiny woman, both decked out in jumpsuits identifying them as investigators with the State Police. They scurried around gathering and dusting things inside the gift shop.

Their presence gave her pause. Crime scene techs from the State Police? Officer Howard calling the crime scene grizzly? Something awful happened here.

Then it hit her. The museum board's chairman was out of the country for at least another week. Dr. Charles Barnes and his wife were gadding about in Europe to celebrate their fortieth wedding anniversary. They'd been planning this trip for over a year.

Kurt must be aware Dr. Barnes was unavailable, so he'd called her. She was on the museum's board of directors, currently in town, and a phone call away.

Officer Howard, as good as his word, produced Kurt, then tipped his hat to her and exited.

Kurt pulled off plastic gloves as he approached and placed them in his sport coat pocket. His face showed nothing but business.

"Thank you for coming, Liesl. It was a bother, but we need you." He reached inside his coat and withdrew a notebook and pen, flipping to a certain page on the pad.

She accepted his cop face—expected it under these circumstances. "I'm happy to help. What's happened?"

Avoiding eye contact, he hesitated before answering. "I'm going to ask some questions first, if you don't mind."

"I do mind." Liesl crossed her arms. In silence, she tossed him the best stink eye she could muster.

"I don't want to discuss the details we've found so far, as those details might influence your answers."

"I tell the truth. I can't imagine any circumstance that would cause me to alter my answers."

Kurt drew in a slow breath. "I'm sorry. I'm not trying to make you mad. Allow me some grace this Sunday. Please. This is a mess."

After a moment's hesitation, she took pity on him. She disarmed her stink eye glare and uncrossed her arms. "Okay."

"Who are members of the board of directors, besides you and Dr. Barnes?"

Her stomach turned. "Oh, no! Has one of the board members been hurt?"

"No. Nothing like that."

She relaxed and ticked them off with her fingers. "Patricia Sizemore, Paul Duck, Barbara Burson, Dr. Johnson, Mr. Van de Berg, Mrs. Whats-her-name from California—and Mr. Hardesty."

Kurt scribbled in his pad for a moment and then asked, "Which Hardesty?"

Considering the passel of Hardestys in town, Kurt's question was reasonable. "Thomas. He was a classmate of Aunt Suzanne's. He's the local farmers' representative for the board, even though he's mostly retired. His son Freddy handles most work on their place."

"That's a lot of people on the board."

"Nine. Not really, considering the average board size. Many boards have more, some who contribute a lot of money. On this one, Mr. Van de Berg and Paul Duck are generous patrons. Patricia Sizemore too."

"And your Aunt Suzanne?"

"I'm sure she was when she was alive. It was nice of them to ask me to fill her position."

"Who runs the day-to-day operations of the museum?"

She fought to contain her exasperation. "You already know the answer to that. Mark Detmeier."

Kurt ignored her annoyance. "Any idea how long he's been the curator?"

"Five, maybe six years."

"Has the board had any issues with him?"

"What issues are you talking about?"

"Misbehavior? Questionable accounting? Display items missing after inventory?"

Liesl frowned. "No. I've only heard compliments about his work. The museum keeps growing, getting donations, and has more visitors each year. He's doing his job well."

She studied Kurt briefly, checking that his hazel eyes were directed at her. "Mark's mother was one of Aunt Suzanne's best friends. I've been acquainted with the family since I was a child. Never hear any gossip about them."

Kurt chuckled. "Except that old Mrs. Detmeier had her car and keys taken away."

"True that. Some of Aunt Suzanne's landscaping was a victim of her unfortunate driving. I believe Nicole contacted her son after that incident." Liesl smiled. "I don't feel guilty, though. Mrs. Detmeier no longer had any business behind the wheel of any moving vehicle."

"Okay." He flipped a page on his pad. "Tell me about the security system."

Liesl gathered her thoughts. "Donnie Davis's business is the provider. The museum has alarms and heat sensors. The doors and windows should be armed. You're aware of those large carport-type buildings outside?"

"Yes."

"Well, they house the hefty antique farming equipment, but I don't believe they're wired. However, the expensive, sizable pieces of equipment have alarms. Something to keep thieves from loading them up and carrying them away."

"No cameras? Inside or outside?"

"I'm not aware of any. You'll have to verify that with Donnie."

"Who has a code to the alarm system?"

"You mean to get in after hours?"

"Yes," Kurt said. "After hours."

"Not me," Liesl said. "I doubt any of the board has that access, except Dr. Barnes. Again, you'd have to verify that."

"I will when he returns from his trip." He made more notes. "So you doubt any board member has a key, except Dr. Barnes."

"That's correct."

"Same with the alarm code?"

"Right. This is merely a museum. There would be no reason for anyone on the board to be here after hours. The curator should have access, but that's it, in my opinion."

"So, how does the cleaning crew get in?"

Liesl hesitated. "I didn't consider them. They must have a key and access to the alarm system. Unless there is some way they can disarm the system for cleaning without knowing the passcode."

"They may have issued her a separate code for one entrance. I'll check with the security company about that. What's their cleaning schedule?"

"Don't know, but I've never seen them during regular business hours. Mr. Detmeier will know."

They were both distracted for a moment as the crime scene crew moved from the gift shop to the reception area. Kurt waved Liesl away from the counter.

As she moved, she put her hand on his arm. "Please tell me what's happened."

He held up one finger. "One more area to discuss, then I will. Promise." He gave her a pleading glance before proceeding with his question. "What is valuable inside this museum?"

"You mean in historical significance? Or worth a lot of money?" She pointed at the brass register. "That beautiful cash register is worth a lot as an antique, but it could be worth more melted down for the brass."

His eyebrows rose. "You're thinking like a thief. The register is too massive for a simple 'smash and grab' theft. It would require at least two people to lift it. Also, you'd want a wheelbarrow or dolly to load it on before taking it to a waiting van or truck."

"It's heavy." She eyed the register. "You're right. Two people, minimum."

"Considering either historical or monetary value, what are the most valuable pieces?"

"Several of those antique tractors and combines outside. The ones with alarms."

He scribbled on his notepad. "And inside?"

She considered for a second. "My guess will be the Civil War items recovered from area farms. There are coins, buttons, belt buckles, sabers, ammunition—so many items. I can't list them all."

"Where are they housed?"

Liesl turned toward the display room. "They're in the shelves in there." She waved her hand toward the threshold. "The bookshelf-cabinet combination."

"On the north wall? With five or six levels of shelves and glass doors?"

"Yeah. They're antique, or nearly. They're called barrister's bookcases. In those really old ones, each shelf is a separate wooden piece with a glass front that opens. They stack on top of each other. Civil War memorabilia is kept in the locking shelves."

"So, if someone were to break the glass and climb on the shelves to get to the upper levels?"

She gasped. "The shelves aren't attached.

They'd slide right off if you pulled on them. Did one of the cleaning people do that and get hurt?"

"Well, someone got hurt, but it wasn't anyone from the cleaning service. A cleaner came this morning and found a dead man. He was most likely a thief and appears to have died from a fall."

Kurt turned to face her, his eyes searching hers. "I'm not trying to give the impression that his possible criminal intention here allows us to take this matter lightly. As a detective, I speak for the dead, no matter their motives or their occupation."

His need to explain this warmed her heart. "I understand. That's why they picked you to be a detective. You care about the victims. All victims."

"Exactly. You may have solved why he fell. If he was climbing up those shelves in the belief they were one bookcase, that would explain how he pulled a section down on himself."

Chapter 4

April, 1862
Mexico, Missouri

Enid Connolly

The gathering for worship Sunday morning was delightful for Enid. By her count, there were at least seven families and several soldiers from the Union encampment in attendance. The generous crowd filled the modest Fagan family home to its limits. Her pleasure at the increasing number of attendees offset the guilt she endured due to her attendance while her mother worked.

As the cook for Mr. John P. Clark, her mother's days off were a half day on Monday afternoon and a half day on Wednesday morning. Services had been sporadic throughout the war. Several of the established pastors had volunteered to serve as military chaplains, leaving itinerant pastors to cover much of central and northern Missouri. With services scheduled whenever a pastor came into town, her mother's duties almost always kept her away.

This morning's hostess, Mrs. Fagan, was a

heavyset woman with a kind personality. She led Enid into the gathering area and gestured for her to take a seat in the back row of stools and chairs, the usual seating area for women.

"Thank you, Mrs. Fagan. If someone else can use this seat, I'm happy to stand."

"Thank you, dear. If we need the space, I'll come get you." Mrs. Fagan patted her arm. "But it's more likely we'd need you to entertain one of the children."

Enid nodded. "I'm glad to do that as well."

As she waited, Enid fidgeted for a moment, viewing the crowd and murmuring greetings to those she recognized. She removed her gloves and the Irish lace scarf that adorned her head. Once the service began, there would be no tolerance for fidgeting.

If only Mother could have joined her. Word reached them yesterday that a pastor was in town, and the Fagans had volunteered their home for services today.

This morning, her mother pushed her out the back door of the Clark house and asked her to pass on her apologies for not being able to attend. Once she returned home, Mother would insist upon hearing all the details of the sermon, the hymns, and news from the attendees.

She'd been so eager to leave her own duties behind that Enid had walked all the way to the road in front of the Clark house before realizing she'd forgotten the location of services. She'd run back to her mother, who admonished her for not remembering. Enid apologized. Her mother brushed off her apology and returned to kneading dough.

As Enid scanned the crowd to gather details for her mother, she smiled at the sweet burbling sounds of the Kellys' newborn. Her coos mixed with the rattle of swords, belts, and other metal objects worn by the handful of Union soldiers in attendance.

The Union camp was on the western edge of town. They'd been in place there since last July. Mexico, Missouri's railroad connections were important in maintaining control of the railroad lines in the whole of northern Missouri. The problem was, many of the town's citizens resented the soldiers. Almost half of the citizens were Southern sympathizers.

Union soldiers didn't help matters by previously "commandeering" supplies and equipment from the citizens. Then they demanded loyalty oaths to the Union, sometimes at gunpoint. Colonel Grant put a stop to those things during his time in town. Now he was a general and assigned outside of the state to handle other war duties.

Most townspeople ignored the camp and the soldiers in it. Everyone hoped for a quick end to the conflict. Enid's wealthy employer, however, was a Union man through and through. This made Mr. Clark an object of derision with half the town and a hero to the rest.

Enid's musings came to an abrupt halt when she spotted a pair of bright green eyes staring at her. One of the visiting soldiers. He failed to glance away once she noticed, as acceptable etiquette would dictate.

Enid pursed her lips at his lack of proper manners. Because of his boldness, she held his gaze for a moment longer than she should have.

He seemed familiar to her. Red hair, green eyes. Perhaps he'd visited the Clark house before. Grant had been a frequent visitor for bourbon and a cigar. He usually brought several of his officers with him. Maybe this man had accompanied him there on one occasion.

Even after the service began, the soldier's green eyes kept surfacing in her thoughts. She admonished herself to pay attention to Pastor Fitzgerald and think of God and Jesus, yet she continued to consider this soldier. Those flashing green eyes signaled his intelligence while his countenance reflected a quiet dignity. She also liked that his hair was red, like hers, only his was a lighter shade. Did he have an Irish background too?

She darted a quick glance in his direction. This time, he was intensely watching the pastor, so she took a moment to study his uniform. His adornment differed from most of the other nearby men's.

What was his rank? Her lack of knowledge

regarding uniforms was infuriating. Especially when that lack of information kept her from understanding the Union insignia and the rank they represented. A household servant didn't have much need for such understanding. She called all soldiers *sir.*

Yet, curiosity ate at her. She'd like to know this rude man's rank. It would also be nice to spot a man of importance and be able to acknowledge his rank, even if he'd paid no attention to her.

At the end of the sermon, the worshippers were standing and singing a hymn when a commotion behind them caused heads to turn. A group of soldiers had pushed their way into the house. They filtered into the crowded worship space.

The hymn died on the lips of those in attendance as they processed the interruption. Confusion ensued.

One of the newcomers, with jet-black hair and muttonchops, approached the itinerant pastor. "I'm sorry for the interruption, sir. We need our soldiers. Now."

Pastor Fitzgerald spread his arms. "Of course, gentlemen."

The green-eyed man stood and barked orders to those near him. They moved quickly as the crowd parted to allow them to go. Enid saw Mr. Green Eyes steal one last look at her before leaving.

Enid shook her head. She must be acquainted with him somehow. She couldn't recall where they would have met, but she couldn't shake the feeling their paths had crossed.

Chapter 5

Enid Connolly

In the Clarks' spacious kitchen after church, Enid relayed all the details about the service and the abrupt exit of the soldiers to her mother, Mary.

When she finished her diatribe, Enid asked, "Don't you think they should have done something besides—leave? I think they owed an apology to the pastor. To merely up and go! In the middle of worship."

Her mother, warm from the fire and hard work, sat on a stool and fanned herself with a dishtowel. Her red hair, streaked with gray, began the day tucked neatly under her cook's cap. Now tendrils had escaped, thanks to all the bending, kneading, lifting and chopping she'd accomplished in so many hours. "Didn't you say the soldier who called them away apologized for the interruption?"

"I did. Nevertheless, don't you think those in attendance should have said something too? Instead of marching out the door, past all the worshippers?"

Her mother frowned. "There is a war going on. These things are to be expected."

Enid sighed and stalked away. Mama could

be so vexing at times. Always the practical one. Never ruffled. Enid had been mistaken to expect her mother to be offended when told of the soldiers' abrupt departure. As she left, she called over her shoulder, "I'll go get the jam out of the cellar."

Twenty minutes later, when she returned with her arms full of jars, her aggravation had disappeared. It had been scared out of her moments ago.

She placed the jars on a nearby counter. "I wish someone else could dig around in that root cellar."

"What happened in the cellar?"

Enid pulled herself to her full height, which was tall for a young woman, and puffed out her chest. "I about fainted when my hand brushed against a snakeskin on one of the lower shelves."

"It sounds as if the snakeskin hurt your pride." Her mother chuckled. "Did you remove it?"

"I did. Once my heart stopped racing. That encounter could have killed me."

"Stuff and nonsense. You are braver than that, my dear. You know snakes are attracted to the cellar during the heat of the summer. On a cooler day like today, they're outside curled under some rock. That skin may have been in there since last summer."

"I didn't think about that until I'd already

jumped a foot." Enid shook her head. "Why do they have to shed their skins and leave them around to scare us?"

"They want you to know where they've been. But the creature that shed that skin is long gone. He'd have been in there months ago."

Enid shivered. "I'd rather the creatures would have been somewhere else."

"Did you find the raspberry jam? I would like to use it in the icing for tonight's cake."

"I did. Since you forced me into that pit of snakes, I made the effort count for more than raspberry jam. I brought some strawberry and blueberry, too. I also discovered the jam jars in the cellar are getting low."

"Thank you. We'll have to use them sparingly until the berries are ready for harvest."

"Yes, Mama." She'd been helping her mother make and preserve jams and jellies since she was a child. It was a joyful part of her childhood. She'd assisted in the kitchen since her father passed away many years ago, and the help she provided was now routine.

Her mother cleared her throat. "One more thing. Would you mind shifting the kettle and giving the stew a stir? I'd like to sit here another minute or two."

Enid strode to the west end of the kitchen, where a fire had been burning in the massive fireplace since before daylight. She pushed wayward wisps of her auburn hair into the bun at the nape of her neck, grabbed a rag, and reached into the heat of the fireplace with care.

The kettle hung from an iron arm of the fireplace crane. The crane could be pulled or pushed, allowing pots to be moved toward or away from the heat of the cooking fire. Enid wrapped her hand in rags to protect it from the heat, then moved the kettle out from the fire. She lifted the lid, avoiding the steam, and stirred the contents.

"This mutton stew is cooking well, Mother. It appears and smells most appealing. I'm going to leave it a bit farther from the heat. You don't want it to burn."

Her mother smiled. "It does have an appealing aroma. I caught a whiff of it all the way over here. But it's the taste that's the test for compliments."

Mama had made sure Enid possessed all the skills necessary to run a kitchen and that she'd memorized all the best recipes. She wanted her daughter to be able to support herself if she didn't marry.

Marrying was not a likely option for a lowly servant like Enid, especially with a war going on around her. Some had predicted the fighting would be over after a few months, but it had been eight months, and the battles continued.

The clacking of shoes on hardwood floors alerted them to someone's approach. Both Mama and Enid scurried about the kitchen. It wouldn't do for either of them to be caught relaxing on the job.

Hurried footsteps crossed the formal dining room and continued across the porch that attached the kitchen to the house. Mrs. Clark swept into the kitchen, her normally calm demeanor flustered. She wore one of her beautiful day dresses, her dark hair layered in waves upon her head. She was a handsome woman and a kind mistress. "It smells delicious in here, Mary. A promise of a wonderful dinner tonight."

Mama curtsied and kept her head lowered. "Thank you, ma'am."

Enid turned from her busy work of rearranging jars and dipped in a curtsy. Mrs. Clark nodded at her, then returned her gaze to her mother.

"Mr. Clark has just now informed me some officers will join us for dinner tonight." Exasperation was clear in her tone.

"I've repeatedly asked him to give me more than an hour or two notice when he extends an invitation for someone to dine. We now have to feed several unexpected gentlemen. This is but another example of Mr. Clark's failure to listen to me. One day I'm going to ask you to serve raw chicken to our guests when he gives such short notice. Perhaps that will prove my point."

Mama's mouth twitched as she fought a smile. "Do you know how many extra are to be expected?"

"He said four. Or possibly five. No more than five. Can you save me, Mary? I don't want to be embarrassed. I want to appear the perfect hostess in front of these men. Whomever they are."

"Not to worry, Mrs. Clark. There will be plenty of food for all."

"Thank you, Mary." Mrs. Clark turned around, took a step, and then turned back. "I am so sorry for asking you to do more than you should. I'll make sure Mr. Clark rewards you for this. Either with coins or time off. You have my word."

"Yes, ma'am. Thank you, ma'am."

"I don't know why he insists upon treating us this way. I'm forced to come here and ask you to scramble. My apologies." Mrs. Clark stalked out of the kitchen.

Mother didn't speak until Mrs. Clark's footsteps reverberated on the wood floor of the dining room. "Oh my! Five hungry men."

"What can I do?" Enid gave her mother a pitying look.

"First, run out and tell Jeremiah I need him to wring the necks of two chickens. If you can pluck them and take care of setting the table, I'll make another dessert. Then I'll whip up some chicken and dumplings. Never met a man who didn't like chicken and dumplings."

"Will that be enough extra?"

"No. When you have the table ready, pull out the meat grinder. I think yesterday's leftover ham made into a ham salad, spread on fresh rolls, would make a good appetizer. Between the stew and the chicken and dumplings, there should be enough to go around for those eating in the dining room. The rest of us will have to get by on something else."

There must be something good about not getting to eat the food you've been cooking all day. Enid sighed. She just couldn't think what that might be right now. To not be able to partake in food that smelled so delicious now and would be even more appealing when they served it was a heartache.

When she'd taken the message to Jeremiah, she went back inside and moved toward the pantry. "Mrs. Clark didn't seem too happy about the prospect of more visitors." She paused. "It seemed like it was more than short notice. Is it possible she doesn't like these men?"

"It's possible. Being a local, she may be a Southern sympathizer. There are plenty here."

From inside the pantry, Enid called out, "That is a possibility." With an armload of dishes, she emerged and said, "When I'm serving the visitors, I think it's fun to listen to their talk."

Mother shot her a glare. "That's eavesdropping. Both Mr. and Mrs. Clark would be mighty upset if they were aware you were listening to their private conversations."

"Oh, Mother. We're invisible to them. It's as

if we don't exist. They act like the food courses appear like magic." She leaned against the doorframe of the pantry. "I'm so curious about the war. All the people who come here are important people. They have fancy clothes and fancy ways. They're the ones making the decisions that affect the whole country."

"Still, you should mind your own business. Mr. Clark might fire you if either one of them noticed what you were doing."

Enid shrugged. "I guess so. But since Mr. Clark brought you and me all the way from Illinois, I figure he likes you and your cooking. Too much to let it go."

"He is opposed to slavery. Coming to Missouri, where slavery is accepted, Mr. Clark wanted to show the people that you could pay for help. Have white servants. It's been a blessing he's been so kind to both of us since your father died."

"You've told me this before." Enid went into the pantry again and returned with more china. "I sure did like Colonel Grant. I wasn't invisible to him. He always thanked me when I handed him a drink or a slice of cake."

Her mother narrowed her eyes. "Was he too interested? Not a gentleman?"

Enid sighed in disgust. "Oh, Mother. He was a perfect gentleman. He treated me like a lady. I wasn't an invisible servant to him. I was a pleasant helper. Shame on you for even thinking that way."

"A mother has to protect her daughter from someone acting untoward."

"Well, Colonel Grant wasn't untoward. In any way." She looked at the plates in her hands. "These won't set themselves. When I finish, I'll do everything I can to help you."

"Oh, Enid. When you run to the carriage house for the chickens, let Jeremiah know we'll need him to help serve tonight."

"Yes, ma'am." She turned to do her mother's bidding, realizing she'd come up with a good thing about not being able to eat the stew tonight.

With the addition of these men, she could listen in on their conversation as she served them. Maybe they'd discuss how long they thought this conflict was going to last. Or something else interesting about the war and the world she couldn't explore.

Chapter 6

Liesl

At the Agricultural Museum, Kurt scratched more notes on his pad.

While he did, Liesl glanced toward the display room. "So the person died from a fall?" She grimaced and turned away. "How awful."

"Your information about the shelves makes sense. We can't say for sure until the autopsy." He paused as he studied her. "You okay? You're pale. Need to sit down?"

She blew out a breath. "I'm okay. This is such a shock. I need a moment to wrap my head around it."

"Would you be more comfortable sitting in my car?"

"No. I'm fine."

He put away his pad and pen. "I'm sorry to call you in for this, but we needed to talk to a neutral party before calling in Mr. Detmeier. I'm sure you understand why. Thank you for answering the questions."

"Did you know him? The guy that died?"

"I didn't, but Hector did. At least he recalled his street name. The dead man has a reputation as a thief. He's a known criminal, with a history of auto theft and B and E."

"Beanie?" She frowned. "What's that?"

Kurt smiled. "No. B and E. That's a law enforcement acronym for breaking and entering. It's second-degree burglary, a class D felony."

"Can't you speak English when you're talking to me?"

"Sorry. It's a habit. They're running his rap sheet right now. Once we get that, we'll learn more about him."

With worry flavoring her tone, Liesl asked, "Is anything missing?"

"I don't believe so. It appears the victim died before he got his hands on anything valuable."

"Need me to verify that?"

"Absolutely not. It's gruesome in there, and there's no need for you to have that death scene stamped on your brain for eternity. It appears he was alone, so likely nothing's been pilfered. When the scene's cleared, we'll gather the items that are scattered across the floor and ask Mr. Detmeier to do an inventory."

"If the thief was alone, then I'm still confused about how he died climbing and falling off the shelves."

"Our best guess is he wanted to get to those upper shelves. He might have climbed the lower shelves. There was no ladder around."

"I can explain about the lack of a ladder. The museum keeps the ladders in the supply closet. That closet is always locked. Some cleaning chemicals and such are stored in there. They could hurt children."

"I see." Kurt pulled out his notebook again and made more notes. "We found a hammer nearby, but he might have brought that with him. What about tool storage for this building?"

"Probably that same supply closet." She crossed her arms. "You think he used a hammer to break in?"

"Doesn't appear there was forced entry. Likely, the hammer was for inside use."

"Brought it with him."

"We think so. He could have smashed the glass and climbed up from one shelf to another. At some point, he pulled one of the upper shelves down on him. The glass cut him. He fell back onto the concrete floor and bled out."

"So it was an accident?"

"That's the theory. It could have been that he fell, the upper shelf fell on him and cut him, then he bled out. Either way, he was unconscious while he was bleeding. No smears or movements in the blood. The autopsy will tell us more."

"If he didn't break in, how did he get inside?"

"That's the problem. The alarm had either been disabled or wasn't set before this happened. He might have had a key."

Liesl grimaced. "An inside job." Now she understood his earlier questions.

The squeak of metal and approaching voices

caused both of them to turn toward the exhibition room. The coroner and a crime scene tech pushed a metal gurney into the reception area. On the gurney was a black body bag.

The coroner nodded at Liesl. "Afternoon, Liesl."

"Hello, Mr. Cappelli."

Kurt put an arm at the small of her back. "Let's get you out of here."

Aware of his touch, she pondered the meaning behind it. Was it a friendly gesture on his part or an example of unspoken feelings for her?

Within five minutes, Liesl was out of the museum, past the crime tape barrier, and tiptoeing back to her car. Escape was bliss. The fact she was slightly wet, hungry, and wanted—no, needed—to talk to Nicole spurred her onward.

When she reached her car, she shook her umbrella and slid inside. A glance at her phone told her she had enough time to drive through a fast-food place and still get to Nicole's open house before it was over.

Could she eat after this? She'd better try.

Although she'd questioned how food would sit in her stomach, it surprised Liesl how refreshing it was. Nothing like an order of french fries to make a stomach stop growling and improve a girl's mood.

By the time she arrived at Nicole's open

house and parked her car, the rain had stopped. This allowed Liesl to walk at a leisurely pace to admire the beautiful porch of the two-story Craftsman home Nicole was showing today.

The landscaping was fresh and colorful. The cheery flowerpots on the porch were inviting. Two rocking chairs and a table completed the homey atmosphere.

She rang the doorbell, then pushed open the door. Nicole's voice echoed from upstairs, along with other voices she didn't recognize. Liesl smiled, reassured that business was ongoing up there. Good for Nicole.

Her friend called down from upstairs, "Welcome. Show yourself around. We'll be down in a moment."

"I'll be in the kitchen," Liesl replied. Nicole would recognize her voice, making it unnecessary for her to rush downstairs. She was delighted Nicole was busy upstairs with someone interested in the property. Perhaps Nic could sell this beautiful home fast.

The aroma of cinnamon and, possibly, freshly baked cookies drew Liesl to the kitchen. She hoped a cookie-scented candle wasn't misleading her. Nicole used both options at open houses, depending upon her preparation time for each showing.

It was her lucky day. A plateful of snickerdoodles awaited her. Although they had cooled, they were tasty. Liesl helped herself to several before the peal of the doorbell alerted her to more visitors.

She hastily chewed her cookie and strode toward the front door. As she did, she called out, "I'll get it, Nicole."

"Thank you," came the cheery reply from the second floor.

When Liesl opened the door, she smiled and stepped back. "Justin. Please, come in." She restrained herself from giving him a hug, perhaps not the best choice for an open house event.

Justin was tall, blond, and fun. He crossed the threshold with a huge smile on his face. "What a pleasant surprise. You never mentioned you were in the real estate business."

His teasing delighted her. "I'd like to act like it's my new profession to throw your bantering right back at you. However, I can't mislead you. I came here to talk to Nicole, and I haven't even laid eyes on her yet." She pointed toward the ceiling. "She's upstairs with clients. But I can lead you to some cookies in the kitchen. That's pretty nice, isn't it?"

Blue eyes shone down at her. "The surprise of bumping into you is best. Cookies come in second."

Understanding their mutual appreciation for food, she took his comment as a compliment.

"You are such a sweet talker. As the temporary hostess, I'll take your coat."

He removed it, and she hung it in a nearby closet then turned to him. "I'm surprised you're here, too. If you don't mind me asking, are you in the market for a house?"

"Maybe. I'm enjoying my work and my life here." He took her hands in his and gave them a squeeze. "You're the main reason for that. I didn't believe I'd like living in a small town. Now that I've been here nearly a year, it's growing on me. I'd like to look for an affordable house. One that requires some DIY."

"I'll bet your job has taught you to fix many construction-related issues." Justin was the manager of Lumber City, part of a chain of big-box stores across the country.

He grinned. "Occupational hazard."

Liesl led the way to the kitchen while Justin surveyed the house. "I'd give you a tour, but Nicole is the professional. You'll want her to help you."

"From what I spotted in the listing, this is a candidate for me."

"I adore Craftsman houses. Especially ones like this, where the wood remains stained."

"Your house is lit. All that fine wood and craftsmanship."

She preened at his compliment. "I have to agree. Who doesn't love a Victorian?" Liesl offered the plate of cookies. "I can verify these are tasty. Extremely so." She brushed her other hand across the lower half of her face. "I might have crumbs to prove it."

He laughed and grabbed a cookie. He smiled his delight after it disappeared.

Footsteps on the staircase alerted them to Nicole's return to the first floor. "Be right there," she called.

"No hurry, Nicole," Liesl said. "I'm acting as your assistant."

They overheard Nicole talking near the front door to at least two women.

Liesl turned to Justin. "The professional is coming. When she does, I'll leave. Between the current people she's with and you, she'll be too busy to chat with me."

His smile vanished. "Don't go. I'm enjoying our cookie time."

She laughed. "That sounds like we're in preschool. If you want to spend time with me, as if our time together over your grilled steaks last night wasn't enough, why don't you come to my house after you finish here?"

"But you came here to see Nicole. Now I'm keeping you from it."

Liesl gave him a conspiratorial wink. "Before I leave, I'll invite her and her family over for dinner tonight. Stay and eat too. What do you think of that?"

"Perfect, except for one thing."

She frowned at him. "What?"

"I don't know what's on the menu."

She attempted a theatrical "evil" raising of her eyebrows. "Should I tell you? Or make you wait?"

"Tell, tell."

"Okay then. I'll text you when I figure out what I'm going to pick. With my kitchen remodel going on, no actual cooking will happen there for at least another week."

Nicole turned the corner and entered the kitchen. Her light green suit was the perfect color to highlight her brown skin and eyes. She'd pulled her soft waves of black hair into a professional chignon. "I'm so sorry. One of those ladies was Mrs. Fernando."

Liesl was instantly sympathetic. "Oh, my! Did she talk your ears off?"

"Of course." Nicole chuckled and turned to Justin. "She never gives you enough time between encounters to allow your ears to heal."

Justin ran his hand through his hair and smiled. "I don't know her, but I'm familiar with the type."

"Thank you, Justin." Nicole stepped up and shook his hand. "I like a man who gets my jokes." She then waved toward Liesl. "Did I hear something about food? Is Liesl still using her kitchen remodel as an excuse not to cook?"

"She is."

"No surprise there." Nicole smiled at Liesl before asking Justin, "You want a tour of the house?"

"I do."

To Liesl, Nicole said, "You're not here to buy a house, so do you need me?"

"What I came to talk to you about can wait." Liesl gave her a quick hug.

Nicole studied her face. "Not good news?"

Liesl shrugged. "No, but it will keep until later. Your outfit is stunning, by the way. I'll admit your hair is beautiful, too." Liesl had envied Nicole's hair since the day they met.

Nicole smiled. "You're so jealous."

"I'll own that too." Liesl gestured toward Justin. "Justin convinced me to invite you and your family over to my house for dinner. I have also invited your potential buyer."

"Wonderful!"

"You and I can find time to talk after we eat."

Nicole beamed. "That's terrific. It's been a busy day. With you handling dinner, I'll happily sit and listen to you forever."

"It's been a busy day for both of us. But I'll explain everything to you tonight." Liesl eyed Nicole's suit. "You are required to wear comfortable clothes. Dinner's at six, but you can arrive before that."

Justin gestured at his sweatshirt and jeans. "This okay?"

"Absolutely."

Liesl smiled and turned toward the front door. "Later, guys."

Chapter 7

Liesl

Liesl drove home from the open house excited about Justin's interest in owning a home. With his association in managing Lumber City stores, she'd figured he'd be on his way to a bigger store in a larger market in a year or two. Was his interest in buying a house proof he would settle down in Mexico?

How could he do such a thing when moving up in his company required frequent moves? He'd explained the way Lumber City handed out management promotions. Liesl added the topic to her list of things to discuss with Nicole that night.

The real question was what food to offer her guests. Finding a restaurant open on Sunday evening was a challenge in any small town. Mexico didn't differ from the norm.

Fast food was available, even food trucks, but not the cuisine Liesl wanted to offer her best friend, her best friend's family, and her boyfriend. She should ask Joey if he wanted to join them too.

One of the best restaurants in town, DeAngelo's, was closed on Sundays. Liesl couldn't resent this. The family reserved Sunday for worship and rest.

The restaurant was a family affair, and nearly everyone in the family had a role in the business.

With Italian out, Mexican was an option. Who didn't like salsa and chips, enchiladas, and tacos? After a moment's hesitation she realized, possibly Joey didn't. She'd have to ask.

She pulled into her driveway and admired the two-story Victorian that was her home. At the passing of her Great-aunt Suzanne who'd raised her, Liesl inherited this magnificent home. Some changes had been made recently, due to a fire that destroyed the garage six months before. Although the fire had been upsetting, it gave her the opportunity to rebuild the garage with an apartment for Joey Bauer, a family friend.

Joey suffered damage at birth and could take care of himself—to a point. He could not drive, but he cycled around town at an amazing pace. His reading and writing skills were poor, but he had an unbelievable knack for observation. Most food had to be provided to him, as he could not cook safely.

She pulled her car into her garage parking space and walked past Joey's bike, around to the addition. She hovered her finger over the doorbell before remembering Joey didn't like the noise, so she fisted her hand and knocked.

Joey opened the door, displaying his serene blue eyes and perpetual smile. "Hello, Liesl. Come in."

"No thanks, I just wanted to make sure you made it home from church."

"Yes, Dr. Johnson brought me home after taking me to Kentucky Fried Chicken for lunch."

"That was nice of him. I'm so sorry I had to leave before the end of church."

Joey shrugged. "You said it was important."

Anyone else would have asked why she left, but not Joey. Since he wasn't curious about the details, she didn't offer any. What happened might upset him. "I'm going to have company for dinner, and I'd like you to join us."

"No."

Joey always spoke the truth. Usually it was nice and polite, but occasionally, his responses bordered on rude, but he always said them in a respectful way.

She tried again. "I'm picking up Mexican food. Would you like me to bring you something here?"

"No, thank you." He glanced at his watch. "Tonight is Sunday. My British shows are on PBS. I'm having cereal for dinner."

Although Joey couldn't officially cook, cereal and milk were well within his preparation skills. "That sounds fine. Enjoy your shows."

"I will." He started to close the door and then reopened it. "Tomorrow is Monday, and that means Mrs. Zimmerman is coming."

"Thank you for the . . ." Joey shut the door in her face before she finished, off to whatever he was doing before she interrupted him. She smiled all the way to the house.

The Mexican feast was a hit. Better than Liesl imagined. With a plethora of spicy choices, the adults were happy.

Claudia, Nicole's five-year-old daughter, was a miniature version of her mother in personality and appearance, other than inheriting enormous brown eyes from her father. She stopped talking to eat her taco. Otherwise, words poured from her like a waterfall.

When she finished her food, the torrent of words began again. Once the adults realized they'd have peace if Claudia played with Barney in another part of the house, they encouraged this activity. This arrangement benefited Barney as much as the adults.

Barney, a beagle mix, was the same age as Claudia, and they played well together.

"Barney is looking better," Nicole said as she waved Claudia out of the room.

Liesl nodded in agreement. "His diet seems to be working. His original owner overfed him to the point his health was in danger."

Justin and Nicole's husband, Lee, enjoyed talking about sports. When they moved into the study to watch a ball game, Liesl and Nicole had the opportunity to clear the paper plates and food containers off the table and sneak away.

"Why don't we move our conversation to the sunroom?" Liesl suggested. "Claudia can play with Barney outside while we watch them from there."

They shared a smile.

"Claudia?" Liesl called. "Want to let Barney have a moment outside? Your mother and I are going to be in the sunroom. We'll turn on the outside lights for you."

Claudia came running from the front of the house. On her heels was Barney, his toenails clacking on the wood floors and his tongue hanging out from the exercise his play with Claudia generated.

"Watch me." Claudia tugged on Liesl's sweatshirt. "Are you watching?"

Liesl gave Claudia her full attention, which was a signal for Claudia to pirouette around the dining room. Barney tried to follow her every move.

Liesl turned to Nicole and whispered, "Does she ever stop moving? Or talking?"

"Only when she's asleep," Nicole whispered in return.

At a normal voice level, Liesl said, "Very nice, young lady. Now let's get you and your friend outside. You can do your ballet moves there as well. I'll bet both of you will like that."

When the four of them reached the back door, Nicole turned to the right, leaving Liesl and

Claudia standing at the door. Both watched as Nicole strolled down the hall.

"Where is Mama going?"

Liesl leaned over. "She's nosing about in the kitchen, where they're doing the renovations."

Nicole called out, "Oh, my. It is beautiful, isn't it?"

Liesl chuckled as she slipped a jacket on Claudia. "Of course. You helped me design it."

Once Claudia's jacket was secure, Liesl reached over to pet Barney, who waited patiently for his play pal to be ready. She turned her attention back to Claudia. "The two of you need to play inside the fenced area, okay? Your mom and I will monitor you from here."

"Yes, Miss Liesl." Claudia and the dog charged out the door and down the steps.

Liesl joined Nicole in the kitchen. She flipped a switch, and half the room brightened in white lights. "The electricians are coming back when the fixture for above the kitchen table comes in."

"That banquette is fabulous. Once they paint it, put the table in, and you get a light over it, they'll be finished, right?"

"Yes." Liesl was eager for the remodeling to be over. The place would look wonderful, and she'll be rid of the workers who invaded her home on a near daily basis. "Thanks for your help, Nic. It wouldn't have nearly the style and pizazz without you."

Fisting her hands on her hips in a Super Woman stance, Nicole said, "That's what I do. Drop gems of design knowledge when needed, and gems of life knowledge too. Otherwise, I assist you in your home purchases, as I'm a real estate professional."

"I wish I could use you to help me buy a house, but I'm all stocked up right now."

Nicole surveyed the area. "This is my favorite house in the entire world. I never want you to sell it."

"But it's too much for only me."

"How many times have I told you to use it as an events center? For wedding showers and engagement parties and fun, pretty gatherings. Charge for the private parties, and host free charitable events. I know how much you believe in giving back to those in need. This house is a beautiful way to do that."

Liesl turned off the lights. Nicole's idea of donating the use of the house for charitable fundraisers was a good one. "Are you going to keep nagging me about that?"

"If I don't nag you about something periodically, you'll believe you're not my best friend anymore."

Liesl smiled. "I'd never think that."

As they made their way to the sunroom, she and Nicole discussed the pros and cons of using the house for events. Liesl was going to have to decide about that soon, but not until the workers completed the kitchen.

Through the sunroom windows, they watched Claudia and Barney playing in the fenced backyard. When the house was originally built in 1883, there was a porch by the back door. At some point, the owners added screens to the porch. Eventually, Uncle Max and Aunt Suzanne tore down the old porch and rebuilt it as a sunroom, adding electricity, double-paned glass windows, and screens for the windows.

This was one of Liesl's favorite rooms in the house. There was nothing nicer than fresh air from open windows on exquisite spring and fall days. With spring beginning, she had many days ahead of comfortable breezes to enjoy.

Once she and Nicole settled into a matching set of chairs, Nicole turned to her. "So, spill already."

Liesl gave her the details about being pulled out of church and her interactions at the Ag Museum. Nicole made the appropriate noises of surprise and concern in the retelling of events.

When Liesl finished, Nicole asked, "So this may not have been a random break-in?"

"Exactly. Even though I was the one who spoke the words *inside job,* Kurt didn't jump to correct me. You know how he is when you speculate on something. He must have agreed with me."

"Even if the guy was stealing stuff, it's sad he died for his trouble."

"I agree. I feel sorry for him."

"Does Kurt know you're sharing this with me?"

"If he doesn't he's a fool, and Kurt is no fool." She shrugged. "He knows, even if he won't admit it."

Nicole frowned. "He didn't tell you to keep this whole thing to yourself?"

"Nope. He knows you're the only one I'd tell. That man knows we make a good team of investigators. Our work regarding Aunt Suzanne's death proved that."

"You're waltzing around the outside perimeter of his investigation. Like an expert witness or something. He needs your board experience to help with this case."

Liesl straightened in her chair. "I haven't been serving on boards long. Four months on some, five months on others."

"Longer than he's ever served."

"True. With our positive record helping him solve Aunt Suzanne's murder, he must understand he needs help for this. I mean, he called me immediately, didn't he?"

"That's a fact."

"He'll need more help. If this was an inside job, I'm his only trustworthy insider."

Nicole frowned. "If you get involved in this, please be careful."

"If someone associated with the Ag Museum board helped or is involved in this 'break-in without a break-in,' Kurt needs a reliable inside man to report on the actions of the other board members."

"Don't get carried away, Sherlock. You know he's going to keep your part in this as limited as possible. He won't want you in any danger. He loves you."

Liesl chuckled. "Oh, you hopeless romantic! The high school romance he and I shared ended with a proverbial screech of tires and a huge collision."

Nicole shot Liesl a side-eye. "So you say. But your return to town has reignited the old flame. For the record, I'm not a hopeless romantic. I'm a *hopeful* romantic."

"What about that cute man named Justin who's in the study and might be buying a house?" Liesl smiled. "I already have a boyfriend. I think Kurt and I haven't reignited the old flame as much as forgiven past transgressions. We're making a new start as friends." She held up her index finger. "Can't we agree to disagree about romance?"

"I suppose, girlfriend."

"Moving on." Liesl raised her eyebrows at Nicole to signal the end of that topic. "As far as this break-in, the other museums and charities in town should be aware of the issue. They should upgrade their security to prevent something similar from happening to them. Don't you agree?"

"No. Not yet, anyway. What if the suspected

insider serves on another board? If you warn them, you could be tipping them off to lie low."

Liesl pressed her lips together. "Good point. But I doubt the insider was a member of the board. After all, it could be an employee or someone in the cleaning service."

"I understand, but why take a chance if it *is* a board member? Why don't you and I visit Donnie tomorrow? He provides the security service for most of the local museums and charities, since his business mostly specializes in commercial ventures. We can use the break-in at the Ag Museum to inquire about increased security for other places in town."

"That's a great idea."

Nicole spread her hands. "If we ask about places we're connected to, he shouldn't be suspicious about the questions. It's natural for us to inquire about security for my real estate office and for you to inquire about the Butterfly House and the historical society."

"That beautiful home, Graceland, is part of the Audrain County Historical Society Complex," Liesl said, referring to a famous mansion in Mexico. "It makes me shudder to contemplate some thug breaking in there. John P. Clark built that home before this one was here."

"Your Aunt Suzanne adored Graceland. She proved that by serving on the board of the historical society for decades."

"She was a founding member of the Butterfly House too. She believed women and children in need should always have a safe place." Liesl's aunt had been a supporter of both nonprofits during her lifetime. Liesl had replaced her on both boards.

"You're so smart." Liesl smiled. "Once we ask about security for those, he won't suspect anything when I ask about Graceland. Since I'm on the board, it's natural I'd ask Donnie about security there, too."

"Exactly. Those are reasonable requests. Discussing security at museums you're not connected to may have to wait."

"Agreed. If you want to do that with me tomorrow, I take it you're not busy?"

"I need to stop at the office first thing, to check for any offers from the open house. I don't expect any, but you never know. After that, we can go together to visit Donnie. Then I'll swing by to check out Marc's progress on our little flip house."

Marc was Nicole's coworker at the real estate agency. "May I tour your flip house, too?"

Nicole shrugged. "It's a mess, but I'm happy to walk you through it."

Liesl stood to glance down the hallway that led to where they'd left the men. In a hushed tone, she asked, "Do you think Justin is serious about buying a house?"

Nicole chuckled. "Didn't I say a few minutes ago that I'm a real estate professional? I'm not releasing any information about a potential buyer's interest in a house I'm selling."

With a grin at Nicole, Liesl interpreted her statement as code for Justin showing a positive interest in purchasing something.

Did that mean he was seriously thinking about permanently relocating here? What would that do to their previously casual dating relationship? She'd think about that later. "Anything new in the Realtor business?"

Nicole lowered her voice to a whisper. "There is one rumor."

With urgency, Liesl replied, "Spill it! You know I won't say a word."

"I'd simply be spreading unreliable gossip."

"What other kind of gossip is there in a small town?"

"You've got me there."

"What is it?"

"Marc overheard from other Realtors that an entire city block might go up for sale."

"In town?"

"Yes. One block off the square, supposedly. The trouble with gossip is, we don't know which block is the one."

"Any guesses?"

"Everyone is guessing, but they haven't released anything solid. A sale like that would be huge. If I could be part of listing or selling that much real estate, I'd make enough in commission to shop for a beautiful old house like this." She waved her arm toward the front of the house.

"What does one do with a complete city block?"

"Depends. If it's full of buildings, an owner could rent out the spaces for businesses, if they're not already rented. If there is an area for parking, that would enhance the value of the property, since all town squares lack parking. I've always believed some lofts in the downtown area would be a fine addition. You know, space that single people, young couples without children, and artists would enjoy."

Liesl smiled at Nicole. "Such great ideas. I hope this rumor is true. It would be a successful expansion for the town and, potentially, for your pocketbook."

"I'm not getting my hopes up. If it's a block that needs work, it may take a long time to generate interest in a buyer who will remodel. Also, how many people can fork out a chunk of change to purchase a city block?"

"I'm sure you're right," Liesl said, keeping her face and attitude neutral. She didn't want Nicole to know yet that she was one of those people who *could* fork over that kind of dough. She changed the subject.

"Are you really okay with me tagging along to

peruse your flip house? I'd like to find out what you have planned for it."

Nicole reacted with delight. "I'd love to walk you through it. If Marc has a slow day tomorrow and it doesn't rain, he plans to rent one of those small front loaders to do landscaping work and knock down an old shed in the backyard."

Liesl chuckled. "Fascinating. Let's do it right after the visit to Donnie." She spotted Claudia approaching the back door. "Your ballerina has returned."

A moment later, Claudia came in with Barney trailing on the heels of her pink sparkling sneakers. "Can I have hot chocolate? It's cold outside."

Nicole rose from her chair and strode to her daughter. "Claudia, you don't ask for things when you're at someone else's house. That's not nice." She helped Claudia out of her jacket.

"Sorry," Claudia said, properly chastised.

Liesl walked over to them. "I'm the one who's sorry, sweetie. My kitchen isn't working. The only thing I can offer you is coffee, and you're too young for that. I promise to offer you something wonderful the next time you visit. Okay?"

Claudia smiled and ran down the hall.

Barney, instead of chasing her, waddled toward his nearby water dish.

Liesl pointed to the dog. "She wore him out."

Approaching footsteps that didn't belong to a tiny ballet dancer echoed down the hall.

Liesl turned to see Lee approaching. "Did you all get enough talk in for the evening? It's time for us to head home. My students deserve a happy social studies teacher and soccer coach tomorrow."

Liesl hugged him. "You're the best husband of a best friend a girl could ever have. Thank you for sharing your wife and daughter with me."

He grinned. "You know I'll do anything for a decent meal. Besides, talking and watching sports is always a good thing."

CHAPTER 8

LIESL

Monday morning, Liesl let Barney out in the backyard for his run. Although cool, it wasn't raining, and that was a blessing.

With construction over the past few weeks, Liesl was forced to rise at dawn to shower and dress. Her reward was to have coffee in the sunroom while waiting for the workers.

Coffee was an essential food group. With the kitchen remodel underway, she was prohibited from brewing any coffee there. To go without coffee was not an option, so she'd set up a temporary coffee bar in the sunroom.

With the comfort of her first steaming cup of java, Liesl sat and contemplated the rumor Nicole mentioned the previous night. The possibility of an entire city block offered for sale had kept her awake, tossing and turning, most of the night. Such a sale might be exactly what she needed to make her ideas come to life.

To ensure she didn't forget any of the creative thoughts sparking in her brain, she chided herself to write them down. She strode to the library she used as her office. It was another one of her favorite rooms in the house. With a fireplace and floor-to-ceiling bookshelves on three walls, it was cozy. A wall of windows was opposite the fireplace. She'd placed her desk there to make use of the natural light that streamed inside.

Her desk drawer held the laptop Liesl kept strictly for writing. She grabbed it and returned to the sunroom.

Since Aunt Suzanne's passing, she'd toyed with the idea of creating a community center to benefit the citizens of Mexico, Missouri. She wanted to take a portion of the immense inheritance she'd received and use it to form a nonprofit corporation that would act as a continuous gift to the residents of the area.

Would the rumor come true about an entire city block offered for sale? If so, she could do wonderful things for the citizens with it. She would donate the property to her eventual nonprofit organization that would operate the businesses.

The writer in her believed a combination bookstore and coffee shop would be the perfect addition to the town. Volunteers could run it, or perhaps an organization for the disabled.

Her fingers flew over the keyboard. What if her ideas about employees were combined, and the staff included both volunteers and the disabled? They could run the businesses together. With donated property, they could keep prices low and recycle all the profits to expand their services.

Any profit from fundraisers or donations, if those were added, might support projects for other charities in the area.

Barney's eager howls emanating from the backyard interrupted Liesl's meditation. Either the housekeeper or one of the construction crew had arrived.

The tall, straight figure of Mrs. Albert Zimmerman made her way across the lawn. She was a thin woman blessed with heaps of energy and terrific health for someone in her mid-fifties. Although she didn't necessarily love Barney, the housekeeper put up with him, and that was enough.

It had been a blessing to hire Mrs. Zimmerman as a dual housekeeper. She worked Mondays, Wednesdays and Fridays and took care of Liesl's house and Joey's apartment. The fact that she was a fabulous cook sealed the deal. Mrs. Zimmerman had been referred by Liesl's banker, Mr. Barnaby, who sang her praises.

Liesl crossed to the back door and opened it. "Morning, Mrs. Zimmerman."

"Good morning." The elder woman's smile faltered when she spotted the open laptop Liesl had left in her chair. "Have I caught you at a bad time?"

"No. I was making some notes on a potential project."

"Would you rather I start with Joey's apartment?"

"No. Please go do your thing. I'll sit here and

let the workers in. I can take notes on my project ideas while I wait for them. No problem."

Mrs. Zimmerman hooked her thumb toward the kitchen, her chin-length red hair laced with gray flowing with the movement. "That kitchen is going to be a dandy of a place for me to cook once it's complete."

"You did an amazing job cooking in a half-burned kitchen before the remodel. I'm sure the new appliances will only hone your talents."

New howls from Barney signaled an additional visitor. Liesl spotted one of the crew approaching. "Go ahead. I'll let him in."

Mrs. Zimmerman's face pinched, but she asked with an even tone, "How about I start upstairs? I won't be in anyone's way up there."

"Perfect."

Mrs. Zimmerman scurried down the hall, then called over her shoulder, "Give a shout if you need me. I'll be upstairs for about an hour."

"Thanks so much."

After letting in the worker and Barney, Liesl returned to the sunroom. The dog came padding up to her, and she gave him a quick pat before returning to her brainstorming project.

Mrs. Zimmerman had worked for her for nearly five months now. Even though everyone seemed pleased about the relationship, minor tension floated between them. Liesl wasn't sure where it came from.

Mrs. Zimmerman treated Joey like a prince but eyed Liesl occasionally with a slight frown on her face. It was as if she were a misbehaving child who needed supervision with a sharp eye. Joey adored her, and that was the most important aspect of her service. Yes, Liesl admitted she needed help to take care of such a massive house, but Joey needed to be happy above all other considerations.

The housekeeper surprised Liesl when she offered to iron their clothes. Who besides dry cleaners ironed anymore? With a three-day workweek, there was more than enough dirt and grime to keep the woman busy with cleaning, cooking, and laundry at the two residences. But when Liesl told her that no ironing was necessary, she'd received *the look*.

Perhaps the industrious Mrs. Zimmerman assumed she was lazy or something, since Liesl was taking a long break before returning to writing. Most people didn't understand how much time and effort it took to write a book. After the loss of a loved one, grief could interfere with the creative process too. Liesl had a notebook full of ideas, but no desire to develop them into a full manuscript yet.

During the initial interview with Mrs. Zimmerman, Liesl spotted pain in her eyes that most people wouldn't recognize. It was that sad flicker of grief from a missing loved one haunting her.

Liesl's heart hurt when she spotted it. Joey had noticed it too.

That settled the matter. God meant the three of them to be together. Mrs. Zimmerman relieved her stress and grief through all the hard work she performed. When she worked, the tasks somehow made her calm. She and Liesl needed more time to rub out the tension between them, but Liesl vowed to do whatever was necessary to keep Joey and Mrs. Zimmerman happy.

Back at her laptop, Liesl began enumerating the tasks required to make her dream center come true. The most important detail was still up in the air. Would an entire city block be offered for sale? How could she help make it a reality instead of a rumor?

As she pondered the possibilities, she chuckled. Aunt Suzanne and Uncle Max would have loved this possibility. They'd have adored all the subsequent ideas she'd added to it. It made her happy to do things they would have appreciated.

That settled it. She needed to pull off this crazy plan, if possible. She could sit and contemplate several alternatives for this dream project, but that wasn't being proactive.

After letting in two more workers, Liesl made her way into her office and pulled out her phone. She called Colette, the executive assistant to Sam Apple, who was customer service manager for Barston Investments. They handled a majority of

Liesl's inherited financial investments from their firm in St. Louis.

Colette answered her call with a chipper, yet professional, "Good morning, Liesl."

"Good morning, Colette. I hope you're having a nice day." Liesl pictured Colette with her hair smoothed back into her trademark bun at the nape of her neck, eyes warm and intelligent.

Colette chuckled. "You know Sam. He's been helping people since the crack of dawn."

The business belonged to Sam's family. Over the years, they'd developed a client base that stretched across the world. They worked around the clock if their customers needed them.

Liesl groaned. "Which means you've been at his side since the crack of dawn."

"Yes. I'm afraid that's true. It's a typical Monday. One of the reasons why I'm given extra vacation days." She laughed. "As much as I enjoy our talks, I assume you called to talk to Sam."

"To be fair, I enjoy talking to you, but I have some business to discuss with Sam."

"I'm so sorry, but he's currently on another call. Is it something I might handle?"

"Colette, you're always so kind to help." Although they'd only met in person a few times, they talked frequently. Liesl considered Colette more of a friend than a business acquaintance. "This may appear crazy, so I'm apologizing up front for this. I'm interested in developing a nonprofit corporation."

"No need to apologize for that."

"That's not the crazy part."

"Okay, sorry. Please continue."

"I'd like to get all the legal work going in time to make a purchase. A rather sizable purchase. An entire city block here in Mexico, Missouri, may go on sale soon. At least that's the rumor circulating through the real estate agents in town."

"So, merely a rumor?"

"My best friend is a Realtor, and the information is swirling around the agents in town."

"I'm following now."

"If such a prize goes on sale, I'd like to fund the purchase of it, anonymously of course, and develop several charitable businesses on the site. These businesses would also be nonprofit, charitable businesses to help the community."

"That sounds lovely, not crazy," Colette said. "We've had clients buy truly questionable things before, but a city block is not one of them."

"I'm sure the price per square foot comparing Mexico, Missouri to any large city in the country would make my purchase appear miniscule." Liesl chuckled. "Now I'm not experiencing so much guilt."

"Good. If you're okay with it, I'll explain the situation to Sam and he can get back to you about the details. Would you want to use a local attorney to draw up the nonprofit corporation, or one from here in St. Louis?"

Liesl considered this for a moment. "I'd prefer an outside attorney to handle the paperwork for purchasing the block. That way, no one in town would know I was behind the funding."

"How nice. I'm scribbling down some notes."

"Could this corporation also be used to purchase other things later on? Down the road, we might want to expand."

"I'll make sure Sam addresses these things when he returns your call."

"Please tell Sam this: If we can buy the city block, then my plan would be for a local attorney to handle the paperwork associated with the local business entities. Mr. Van de Berg can handle the legal paperwork for each of the individual nonprofit businesses I'd like to create to operate within the property. Even though Mr. Van de Berg can keep a secret, if a corporation out of St. Louis is the listed owner of the block, no one would have any reason to associate ownership with anyone in town."

"It would keep your interest anonymous."

"Correct."

"It's a good plan. Mind if I ask what businesses you plan to have?"

Liesl exclaimed, "I'm delighted you're interested. I'd like to start with a coffee shop and bookstore."

"Both new and used books?"

"Yes, if I could make that pay for itself. With no rent or overhead, I'd like it to cover the book expenses and salary for a few handicapped workers. I hope other workers would volunteer to keep the businesses functioning."

"Perhaps fill the walls and shelves with artwork from local artists? That would give them a place to display their work and sell pieces with a small commission for the nonprofit."

"What a wonderful idea, Colette. Thank you. Do you have any more?"

"I'll get back to you on that."

With a shared chuckle, they ended the call. In her happiness, Liesl turned a pirouette. She was stealing Claudia's dance moves.

Chapter 9

Enid Connolly

The dining room table setup looked good, Enid concluded, as she adjusted the glassware to make room for the soon-to-be-added table centerpiece. She stood back to verify the plates, silverware, and glassware were properly aligned.

Her mother entered the room at her usual quick pace. Enid guessed she was there to check the room and its condition.

"Enid, this is beautiful. But you set the table for eight. Do we not expect six or seven?"

"We do." Enid straightened a knife. "It evens out the table, which makes it more appealing. The fact that Mrs. Clark was put out about the late notice of guests made me wonder whether Mr. Clark reduced the actual count to keep her from being even more piqued."

"Wise of you." Mama nodded. "That is a good plan. Setting it for extras also ensures no last-minute shuffle will be needed to add another setting or two. Goodness me, we all understand it's faster to remove service than to place it." She turned and smiled at her daughter. "I'm sure it will be lovely when the flowers are completed."

"Thank you, Mother. I hope so." Enid glanced

around the room. "Do you think the room is warm enough? I can build a fire in the stove if it's needed tonight."

Her mother studied the stove for a moment and shook her head. "I believe the heat from the parlor stove will filter in here and be sufficient. Run on and get your flowers."

Enid hurried off with a smile. This was her favorite task of preparing the table. She secretly delighted in the times when Mr. and Mrs. Clark had guests, since it was her job to make the table presentable. No, more than presentable. Her assignment was to transform the entire dining room to make it appear respectable and wealthy.

To accomplish this, she reviewed what was available in the garden, then chose the right flowers and greenery. She worked with Mrs. Clark's silver bowl to make the perfect arrangement for the table centerpiece. The height had to be precise—not so tall that those in conversation would be forced to peer around it. Yet it needed to be attractive enough to catch everyone's attention. The second arrangement, in a longer silver dish, would grace the mahogany sideboard near the table.

Nearly an hour later, Enid completed and placed the arrangements. She was pleased with her work. It made her happy to make pretty things. Since Mrs. Clark didn't appear to be happy about the visitors, perhaps the flowers and their aroma would cheer her.

After she'd helped her mother with the food as much as possible, the time had come for Enid to assist with the guests. She replaced her now unkempt, everyday apron with her special serving apron. It was a fancy white one edged in a beautiful lace. Its sole purpose was to be worn while serving company.

She said a quick prayer of thankfulness when she found the apron ready to use. Her mother always insisted such things as uniforms and serving jackets be clean and starched immediately after use. She pulled it from the hanger in the pantry, lifted it over her head, and smoothed it down against the front of her dress. When she stepped out of the pantry, her mother frowned.

"Oh my. The apron is clean and crisp, but your hair won't do. Let me put it in plaits and perhaps twirl them into a bun at the nape of your neck."

"Do you have time for this?"

Her mother pointed her to a kitchen stool. "It must be done."

Enid had to admit that between all the work she'd performed in the kitchen, formal dining room, and the garden, her hair must be a mess. She was reminded of her childhood, sitting there as her mother's nimble fingers pulled and tugged her hair into submission. However, she was confident her appearance would be much more acceptable after this embarrassing session.

"There, dear." Mother stepped back to admire her handiwork. "You look a picture. All you need to do is pinch your cheeks."

As Enid did her bidding, Jeremiah entered the kitchen through the back porch.

"My, but aren't you pretty, Enid. Especially with those naturally rosy cheeks." He winked at her. He was a tall, middle-aged man with blond hair. Even though he teased, his smile revealed his approval of Enid's countenance and possibly her new coiffure.

Enid grinned at him. Jeremiah was like an older brother God hadn't given her in real life. "I wouldn't know what to do if you didn't make fun of me."

"Give me enough time tonight and I'll surely do it again." He turned to her mother. "Does my appearance meet your approval?" Jeremiah had traded his usual work clothes for a finely tailed suit and shiny, clean boots. "I even took a bath to rid myself of horse smells."

They all shared a chuckle. Jeremiah was an equestrian, and a horsey odor followed him everywhere. His knowledge about horseflesh was extensive. He was Mr. Clark's steward, carriage man, and all-around handyman. When there were special guests, Jeremiah fell into double duty as a butler or footman.

Mama shooed them away. "You two go now. I've got supper in hand."

Jeremiah extended his hand to Enid. "My lady."

Enid brushed it away and smiled at him. "There is no lady here. Save your fancy manners for the real lady of the house."

They made their way across the porch connecting the kitchen to the formal dining room.

Jeremiah paused for a moment and gazed around the room. "Looks beautiful."

"Thank you. It's my favorite part of working here."

"And it shows."

They continued through the dining room, turning right at the wide central hall to make their way to the home's entrance. Flanking the hall were two expansive rooms on each side. To their right lay the formal dining room and the parlor. To their left were the guest bedroom and Mr. Clark's study. Both sides of the house had a chimney, and each room had its own stove, which kept the house cozy during frigid Missouri winters.

The threshold of every room they passed included a handsomely carved wooden door topped with a transom. Stained glass, created and imported from the Czech lands of Bohemia and Moravia, decorated every transom in the home.

Enid was proud to spend time in this splendid part of the house, even if her role was only as a servant. The home was beautifully designed and decorated, built four years ago by Mr. Clark. The house still sparkled as if it were brand new.

She resisted admiring her apron in the low mirrors attached to some of the furniture adorning the hallway. Ladies checked their petticoats in these mirrors. If she tried to use one to check her apron, Jeremiah would tease her unmercifully.

Jeremiah turned to her when they were close to the entrance. "What time are they expected?"

Enid furrowed her brow. "I don't believe Mrs. Clark gave a time. She was far too upset about the short notice."

He shrugged. "Then we wait."

She and Jeremiah had worked this type of guest service, side by side, since the house was built. They each understood their role and executed it with pride.

Jeremiah would open the door to the guests, welcome them, and take their hats and coats. He would hand the outer garments to Enid. She would quickly, yet with grace, take the items up the stairs to the second floor and hang them in a wardrobe.

The house was built with few closets because each extra door incurred an additional tax. With Mr. Clark supervising the entire building process, he ignored Mrs. Clark's wishes for closet space. Instead, he appeased her with additional wardrobes.

Once the guests' outerwear was taken away, Jeremiah would lead them into the parlor. Having properly hung all the coats, Enid would run between the kitchen and the parlor, serving finger food to the guests. As she did this, Jeremiah would address any of the guests' other needs. Mother would keep the main meal warm until Mrs. Clark signaled to Enid she was ready for the dinner to be served.

Enid's musings were interrupted when voices filtered in from the front portico. Outside, Jeremiah's younger brother greeted the guests and led them to the front door. Caleb was taking over Jeremiah's normal duties tonight. He would care for any horses and carriages used by the visitors.

Jeremiah smiled. "Ready to run yourself ragged?"

She shushed him as she tried to stifle a giggle. "They might hear you."

Before the guests could knock, Jeremiah opened the door. Enid tried to observe the two guests as coats were passed to her. The flashes of uniforms she spotted made it clear the men were soldiers.

As the guests regarded the entry with admiration in their eyes, she made a run upstairs. Her return was timed perfectly to take the coats of the next two soldiers. She was startled when she spotted Mr. Green Eyes as one of the newcomers.

His eyes met hers and grew enormous with surprise. He nodded at her, giving her a slight smile. "Thank you, miss."

She refused to match his smile. With a quick curtsey, Enid turned to head back up the stairs, her face flaming with embarrassment. Why was he here? What was his name? She hurried through the task, hoping to listen to introductions and catch his name.

When she returned, the men were all in the parlor and Jeremiah was no longer monitoring the door. Likely, he'd been told all the guests had arrived. She turned and rushed to the kitchen. As much as she wanted to eavesdrop on the parlor conversation, her next duty was to serve light finger food.

When Enid entered the warm kitchen, she inhaled the enticing aroma of fresh bread and cooking meats. The heat from the fire and her work related to cooking reflected in her mother's red cheeks. "The guests have arrived."

"How many?" Her mother was putting the last additions on the second dessert.

"Four soldiers and Mr. and Mrs. Clark, although Mrs. Clark is still in her room."

Her mother gestured to the platter filled with finger sandwiches. "I hope the men enjoy these."

"They will. And with that extra dessert and the bread that smells heavenly, we'll be fine." Enid appropriated six small plates and napkins from the pantry, then lifted the platter, trying to balance everything with grace as she headed to the dining room. "With the chicken and dumplings you added, we'll have plenty of food, I promise."

When she reached the threshold to the parlor, she hesitated in the hallway as Mr. Clark was talking about the house.

"Thank you, Colonel. I'm quite proud of this home and helped design it. Its classic Greek Revival style reminds me of home."

One soldier asked, "Where was home, sir? If you don't mind the question."

"I was born and raised in Virginia. Even though I've lived in Kentucky and Illinois, it was my dream to build a home here that would remind me of my Virginia roots. I don't agree with their politics, but I find their architecture unparalleled."

At Mr. Clark's pause, Enid walked into the room. She offered the food to the men, careful not to glance at Mr. Green Eyes.

A stout man, likely the oldest soldier, asked, "Did you have any trouble obtaining the materials to build it?"

Enid surmised he must be the colonel from which Mr. Clark had received a compliment about the house.

"I ordered the lumber pre-cut to my exact specifications. Then it was brought upriver by steamboat to Hannibal, Missouri. From Hannibal, they hauled it here in wagons pulled by oxen."

"What about the bricks? Were they brought by steamship too?"

"No, the ground surrounding the Mexico area has some fine clay deposits, so the bricks were formed and fired here, on site. We used brace-framing and noggin for the exterior brickwork. I was able to build the two chimneys as well, thanks to the availability of the clay."

The colonel gestured to the fireplace mantel and wood stoves. "You were smart to incorporate the stoves into your fireplace. Very efficient heating."

"Thank you, sir. Missouri is a cold state in the winter. I learned of the usefulness of stoves when I lived in Illinois."

"And your trim work?"

"They planed the lumber at a nearby lumber mill, which supplied the trim for the stock molding, windows, sashes, and doors."

"Capital! With all your acreage here, in this small town, I'd imagined such a project would have been difficult to supply." He paused in speaking while Enid offered him the finger food.

She moved on to another soldier, this one with jet black hair and matching muttonchops. The man she dubbed "the colonel" asked another question.

"What about labor?"

"I was able to hire local workers and craftsmen from the area."

"Hired hands? No slaves?"

"That is correct, Colonel," Mr. Clark replied.

"The excellence of all the doors and your winding staircase shows the quality of the workers you employed, sir." The colonel gestured with an arm. "One day, when this war is over, I'd like to build a house like this." He chuckled. "On a much smaller scale, of course."

Mr. Clark shifted in his chair. "I've been told there is a plan for your command to use the female seminary as a barracks for some additional troops you're expecting."

The colonel nodded. "It's a fine brick building, and the school is closed because of the war. It would be a shame to let it stand empty when we need housing for soldiers."

When she reached the side of Mr. Green Eyes, Enid lost focus on the parlor conversation. She was too busy praying he would not act as if they knew each other. Now was not the time or place for him to acknowledge any type of acquaintance with her.

She needn't have worried. He helped himself to her offering without lifting his eyes from her platter. She let out her breath and moved on to others in the room.

At the entrance of Mrs. Clark, all the men stood. Jeremiah gave her a brief bow and walked toward her, extending his arm. Mrs. Clark took his arm and made her way to the center of the parlor.

Enid tried to curtsey with the platter and a plate in her hand, but it was more like a bob. Mrs. Clark took no notice of her as she surveyed the guests in her home.

Mr. Clark approached his wife and took her hand. When he did, she turned and smiled a dismissal to Jeremiah. He stepped back and away from them.

Mr. Clark beamed at his guests. "May I take a moment to present my beautiful wife, gentlemen?"

Mrs. Clark was formally introduced to the men, which allowed Enid to catch names and ranks as they were introduced. The colonel was named Michaels, and muttonchops was Captain MacTavish. A slight Scottish brogue was clear when Captain MacTavish offered his greetings to Mrs. Clark.

The man with a neatly trimmed beard and light brown hair was Captain Oliver. He had a pleasing look with a sparkle in his eyes.

Mr. Green Eyes was introduced as Lieutenant O'Malley, and his accent was from the North somewhere. Enid had only previously lived in Illinois, so this limited her ability to pinpoint his regional accent.

As the guests and the Clarks seated themselves, Enid tried to keep her face neutral. She fought back an expression of delight now that Mr. Green Eyes had a name. Had to be Irish with a name like O'Malley. She'd been right to assume his heritage matched hers.

Mrs. Clark settled into a chair, and Enid approached her with the finger food. Mrs. Clark placed a few morsels upon her plate then glanced at Enid. The lift in the woman's eyebrows told Enid that Mrs. Clark had not yet forgiven her husband for the late notice of dinner guests.

As she moved away to offer second helpings of food to the men, Enid imagined Mrs. Clark's attitude might contribute to an interesting supper conversation.

CHAPTER 10

ENID CONNOLLY

When Enid and Jeremiah returned to the kitchen to begin the dinner service, the amount of food Mama had managed to prepare for the guests tonight surprised them.

"I'm so proud of what you've accomplished here," Enid said. "You have nearly replicated Jesus feeding the multitudes."

Her mother grunted. "It's approaching sacrilege to compare my efforts to one of the miracles performed by the Son of God."

Jeremiah shot Enid a look of warning. He tried to lessen the damage done by Enid. "You must admit, Mary, you've put together an inspiring feast. Miracle or not, let's bless this food and work toward serving it."

They bowed their heads in unison as Jeremiah's deep voice resonated throughout the kitchen. "Bless us, Lord, and bless this food we are about to serve. Bless those that prepared it, and bless those that serve it. Let this bounty nurture our bodies to continue our service to You. Teach us to know by whom we are fed, and teach us to be thankful for all Thy gifts. Amen."

When Jeremiah finished, he picked up the massive soup tureen that held the mutton stew and nodded at the ladle. "Let's make your hard-working mother proud in our service of this feast. You get that ladle, Enid, and several of the other dishes. Let's load the sideboard first, then I'll start serving."

Jeremiah served the food at all formal dinners. Enid assisted him while he did so, bringing in the lighter platters and carrying out any empty containers. She also brought the dessert, along with teapots and coffeepots holding the beverages that would accompany it.

She made her way from the kitchen into the dining room and caught snippets of the conversation. This was her favorite part of having guests. Their lively discussions about local and national events educated her about the outside world. These dinners and any discussions she overheard provided a precious opportunity to learn about the life that occurred outside this house.

The main meal was still being consumed when Enid entered with the first dessert. She and Jeremiah would serve this after the guests finished the main course. As she made her way to the sideboard, her interest was piqued by a statement made by Lieutenant O'Malley.

Besides the sound of silverware on china, she overheard, "But sir, I have to disagree. With all respect, sir."

Colonel Michaels said, "O'Malley, it was

just luck for them. Pure and simple. You can't possibly believe there is someone acting as a spy in our midst."

Enid sneaked a quick glance at O'Malley as she scooted the cake plate onto the sideboard. Was he serious? The solemn look on his face made it appear so.

"I'm sorry to disagree with you, sir. Today was the second bushwhacking on one of our patrols in a week."

"You believe there was more to it than getting lucky at finding our patrols?"

"Yes, sir. It's like those Rebs know what we're going to do and when we're going to do it. Maybe that could happen once, but I highly doubt it could happen twice in one week."

Enid resisted leaving. She yearned to hear more of the conversation. Jeremiah was attending to Mrs. Clark, so he couldn't stop her from eavesdropping. She gathered a few empty platters from the sideboard so she'd appear busy and continued listening.

Someone else made a comment, "Well, sir, O'Malley has a point. So many suppliers come and go at our encampment. There could be a Southern sympathizer among them."

Captain Oliver said, "For example, there is one man, Hunter, making weekly deliveries at the camp. He's the most frequent visitor, including the growing number of peddlers we have now.

More are seen running around the camp each week."

Mr. Clark nodded. "I can vouch for the character and Union commitment of young George Hunter. He's out there at your camp once a week due to a demand from your army to have goods delivered."

Enid was acquainted with George. He was a friend. To hear his name included in this discussion concerned her. Were they questioning his character? She turned slightly so she could watch the conversation.

Captain Oliver asked, "Which one is he?"

O'Malley turned toward him. "He's the one with a pronounced limp. Delivers supplies from the mercantile."

"Is he the one who arrives in a wagon, stops at headquarters, and then goes on to the troop area?"

"Yes, sir. His delivery began with orders from Colonel Grant." After a pause, O'Malley added, "General Grant now, sir. Because they promoted him after he left us, I still think of him as colonel."

"George was wounded fighting for the Union, gentlemen," Mr. Clark said. "As soon as this conflict began, he enlisted. General Frost, a pro-secessionist, had taken over the Missouri Volunteer Militia."

Colonel Michaels said, "We are well aware of General Frost and his leanings."

"Of course," Mr. Clark said. "My apologies for mentioning that scoundrel."

"Were you going to say more about Hunter?"

"Yes. Our George traveled all the way to Illinois to join a Union-supporting unit. Wasn't long before he was so injured in a battle that they sent him home on a train, expecting him to die, but he survived."

Colonel Michaels turned to O'Malley. "That should be enough to put paid to this concern of yours, O'Malley."

To Enid, this statement by the colonel sounded more like a command than an observation.

The colonel turned back to Mr. Clark. "Thank you for vouching for him. I presume any other individuals who come to the camp have undergone a review process."

Enid glanced up to find Jeremiah frowning, and her face flamed. He'd caught her eavesdropping. She'd been too intent on the guests' conversation to notice.

She gathered the empty dishes and left the room as quickly as a servant could move. It was a shame her tattered dignity could not disappear as quickly.

Once the desserts were consumed, supper was officially at the end. The men retired to the parlor for cigars. With no women guests to entertain, Mrs. Clark excused herself. It was quick work for

Jeremiah and Enid to clear the rest of the dishes from the formal dining room.

Mama had cleaned the kitchen and finished most of the dishwashing while dinner was being served. She'd also laid out food for Enid and Jeremiah to enjoy once their duties at supper were finished.

They ate their thrown-together meal with delight while Mama sat in a nearby chair. Jeremiah rushed through his so he could assist the guests with anything they needed while enjoying their cigars. After he left, Enid took a bit more time with her food and then washed the last of the dishes and silverware. It was not her place to be in the parlor now that the men were having cigars.

At the sound of approaching steps, Mama got up from her chair and Enid stopped drying dishes. Neither was surprised when Mrs. Clark visited the kitchen before retiring for the night. Mrs. Clark frequently stopped in after supper to pass on compliments guests made about the food.

"Thank you for all of your hard work. The meal was a complete success. As a special treat, I'm giving all of you the afternoon and evening off tomorrow."

Mother nodded. "Thank you, Mrs. Clark."

"The time off includes Jeremiah too. I ask that you convey that good news to him once he's completed his duties tonight."

"Yes, ma'am, I'll take care of that." Enid was to assist Jeremiah with returning all the coats to the soldiers when they were ready to leave. He would be delighted with the free time.

"Perhaps the lack of food for tomorrow night's supper will teach a much-needed lesson to Mr. Clark." Mrs. Clark turned and left the room.

Mama and Enid exchanged glances.

When Enid believed it was safe to speak without being overheard, she moved near her mother, who was once again seated in the chair. "Do you think Mrs. Clark will receive her husband's anger over the lack of a proper supper tomorrow?"

Mama shrugged. "I'm not sure. We'll have to see what happens. He may be apologetic when he realizes how upset she is over this."

"Mrs. Clark is lucky to be married to the richest man in town, don't you think? Regardless of the age difference, she managed to make an advantageous marriage."

"Enid." Her mother's voice was icy. "That comment is uncalled for. It smacks of gossip."

Enid's face heated. "I'm sorry Mother. I understood I was stating something well known."

Mama pointed a finger at Enid. "It could be looked upon as if Mr. Clark was the one who made the advantageous marriage. He found a young and beautiful bride, who came with a fine dowry, thanks to her wealthy family."

"Wasn't there a scandal about her family?"

"So you want this gossip to continue?" Her face indicated Enid needed to answer in the negative.

Enid ignored the look on her mother's face. "I was a child when Mr. and Mrs. Clark married. Sorry if you consider this gossiping, but I'm trying to remember if there was something about Mrs. Clark's family being looked down upon. The information I asked about is not for passing on to someone else. I'm trying to establish the truth about something I was told long ago."

"There is doubt you were told anything about it long ago. It's likely you overheard a conversation you never should have witnessed. You have always been someone who likes to be in other people's business. That is a fault, not a virtue."

Enid tried to appear remorseful. It was a common situation for her, so she had a lot of practice working on a contrite face and posture. This was harder to do when she didn't feel she'd done anything wrong. Like right now. She was trying to confirm information, not spread gossip.

After a moment, her mother must have taken pity for her. She said, "Mrs. Clark's parents, Mr. and Mrs. George Muldrow, divorced when she was young. Mr. Clark told me that Mrs. Muldrow received this land in the divorce due to the fact it was originally part of her dowry."

"So it was the divorce that was the scandal."

"Again, none of your concern."

"Yes, ma'am." Enid dried the last piece of china and returned it to the pantry. As she exited, she pulled out the broom and began sweeping the floor, humming a gospel tune in an effort to change her mother's mood toward her.

A few minutes later, Enid asked, "So this home and the property belong to Mrs. Clark?"

"No. Mr. Clark bought the property from Mrs. Muldrow four years ago, in 1857. That was after she was his mother-in-law. Still not your concern."

"I must have been too young to pay attention when all this happened."

Mother harrumphed. "You're not paying much attention now, either, if you ask me."

Enid didn't dare confess that she'd been paying too much attention to the conversation in the dining room earlier in the evening. It had been awful to embarrass herself in front of Jeremiah. She was grateful he hadn't reported her activities to her mother. Another reason why she appreciated Jeremiah so much.

Mr. Green Eyes O'Malley was concerned about a spy visiting the Union camp. At least that was what she believed she'd overheard.

It had been startling to hear them talk about her friend. There was only one George Hunter in town, and he matched the description given at the table. He had a pronounced limp and was considered a local hero by townspeople on both sides of this war. And he was the one being discussed as a possible spy.

George, due to his Union service, had been chosen to deliver supplies once a week to the Union encampment outside town. Colonel Grant had established these deliveries when he'd put a stop to the army taking—stealing actually—whatever they wanted from the local citizens. To end the turmoil and violence that resulted from these acts, Grant ordered the deliveries to be made by a Union loyalist. They chose George to be that delivery man.

After a few months, some of the Southern-leaning local rowdies had kidnapped George in an effort to stop the supplies going to the Union camp. George had escaped and made them appear foolish. After that incident, the sheriff created a special deputy position for George. Whenever George delivered supplies to the army, he was now acting as a sheriff's deputy, which afforded him more protection against such raids.

If the Union camp had a spy, George wasn't the guilty party. His character was beyond question. He was a Christian man who admitted his Union beliefs but respected others who revered the secessionist plan.

Maybe Mr. Green Eyes O'Malley required information from a local. Would he listen to her? Maybe she could offer to provide background information about local people they suspected of being spies.

As a servant, she was nearly invisible. Someone in service to a family could go nearly anywhere, at any time, and they would think nothing of it.

Even Jeremiah understood this. He'd told her mother a few months ago when the army strung telegraph lines through town, "Telegraphs are a fine development, but the servant network was more reliable and faster."

Perhaps her position on the servant network would help O'Malley. If she offered to help and he accepted her offer, it would have to be a secret. If her mother found out, she'd be furious.

Enid considered those green eyes and decided she had to offer her help. But how could she communicate that offer?

Maybe she would cross paths with him again at church. She pondered that a moment and dismissed the idea. It could be weeks before another service would be held. Too long to wait when people's lives were at stake.

Perhaps she could slip a note in his coat pocket? No one would have to know. The problem with that idea was that she would need to sit down and write out a message on a piece of paper. She could never do that in front of her mother without being pelted with a hundred questions.

She studied Mama, who was falling asleep in front of the fire. The idea of sleep for the exhausted woman was the answer Enid needed.

She finished sweeping the kitchen and put the

broom away. When she exited the pantry, she said, "Mama, why don't you go on up to bed? You're tired from everything that you've done today."

Her mother straightened in her chair. "I can wait for you to go with me."

Enid shook her head. "There's no need for that. I'll be up as soon as I help Jeremiah with the guest coats."

With no further resistance, her mother stood. "Thank you, Enid. I appreciate all of your help today."

"Good night." Enid smiled as her mother climbed the steps to their sleeping quarters above the kitchen. Mama would be asleep in a matter of minutes. After counting to one hundred, Enid rose to search for an acceptable scrap of paper, ink, and a quill.

As she gathered the materials, she wondered what she should say. Would Mr. Green Eyes O'Malley find her actions too forward? Especially if she wrote about a conversation overheard through ill-mannered eavesdropping?

She ended her activities with a sigh. As much as she wanted to provide information to him, she didn't want to ruin his opinion of her. She returned the writing materials to their proper place, her mind racing. She'd have to figure out another way to help him. If God wanted her to help the lieutenant, He'd show her the way.

Chapter 11

Liesl

The original plan was for Liesl to pick up Nicole at her office, then they'd head to Mexico Security Service. However, Nicole had more Monday morning duties than expected, so Liesl agreed to meet her at Donnie Davis's business at ten o'clock.

Liesl's car rounded the corner near Donnie's business at the agreed time. She scanned the parking lot and found she'd beaten Nicole there. No surprise.

After she slid into a parking slot, Liesl stayed in her car, ruminating about stores she could add to her dream of the city block. The businesses must be of service to the community, but only needed to turn a small profit. They needed to compliment the other businesses, serve the community, and clear enough to pay for themselves.

Liesl loved Colette's idea of adding consignment sales by local artists. She considered art supplies. Might be something to stock. With the Missouri School for the Deaf nearby in Fulton, the bookstore should include braille books and audio books for the blind, selling them at cost.

Her stomach growled, which made her think of food. Could she add sales of the best doughnuts in town? She pulled out her phone and made a note about the art supply idea and Ralph's Bakery. She'd wait to contact him until her idea transformed into a reality. Everyone loved Ralph's doughnuts and all of his other baked goods. That might be a better draw than a coffee shop.

Ralph's current shop was only open in the mornings. She could ask him to provide goods for the bakery for afternoon and evening treats. Or, if he wanted to open a satellite bakery, she would have him donate his rent to the nonprofit.

She admonished herself for getting lost in the details. She only needed ideas at this stage.

She glanced around the parking lot. Still no Nicole.

What about a tearoom? Or a room available for meetings? Nonprofits could meet there free, while "for profit" businesses would be charged a small fee as a donation.

Liesl deliberated about Nicole. If this city block came up for sale and she purchased it through a nonprofit corporation, she'd have to confess her ownership to Nicole. She'd want Nicole to be the real estate agent on the sale. It was time to tell her more about her inheritance.

Would people want tables for something besides conversation? Liesl typed a reminder about the possibility of having several game tables where people could play checkers and chess while they drank coffee and munched on a doughnut. Who could resist such a place?

She could sponsor a writing club. Actually, clubs. One for younger writers and one for adults. They could have classes on writing memoirs, short stories, and other topics.

Joey would be a perfect person to interview about what he'd like in a community center. It would need to be fitted with automatic doors for those in wheelchairs and doors with a delay to close, so people with a slow gait wouldn't be knocked over by a closing door.

Maybe a place for teenagers to hang out. *Always a great thing for our youth.*

As her dreams for the center kept expanding, Liesl realized she would need to involve a trusted banker and a good accountant to help her make these ideas reality. She added talking to Mr. Barnaby and her accountant cousin, Gretchen, on her list of things to do if the purchase happened.

Liesl spotted Nicole's red Chevrolet Suburban sliding into the parking lot. She turned and waved at her, then stuffed her phone back in her purse.

When both women were out of their cars, Nicole strode toward Liesl. "I'm so sorry I'm late."

Liesl frowned. "No need to apologize. I just spent ten minutes brainstorming in my car."

"Brainstorming about what?"

"I'll explain later. But I appreciated the time to sit and reflect in absolute solitude."

"Are you keeping secrets from me? That isn't allowed. This *reflection* of yours better not get me in trouble."

They shared a smile.

"I hope to tell you about it soon. In the meantime, we need to figure out how to get information out of Donnie without alerting him to our investigation."

"I've got that covered. Follow my lead."

Liesl held the door for her diminutive friend. Nicole was small, but she was mighty in personality and brains.

A teenaged girl staffed the reception desk. She peeked at the visitors between two enormous monitors. "May I help you?"

Nicole crowded the desk area and leaned in to the only space not covered in monitors. "I'm Nicole Smith, with Smith and Sharp Real Estate Services."

Nicole waved a hand toward Liesl. "This is Liesl Schrader. She's on the board of directors of The Audrain County Historical Society and the Butterfly House. We need to speak with Mr. Davis."

The girl's eyes widened as if she was nervous. "I'm sorry, but Mr. Davis is with someone right now."

"How long will he be?"

The girl focused on the top of her desk. "I'm sorry, but I don't know."

"That is unacceptable. We need answers. If Mr. Davis can't help us, then perhaps you can—" Nicole read a plaque on the desk. "Miss Simpson."

The girl's head jerked up, her eyes enormous at this suggestion. "Oh no, ma'am. I'm not the real receptionist. She's Miss Simpson. I'm a Vo-Tech student. Courtney Brown. I answer the phone and take messages when the real receptionist isn't here."

In case Nicole's plan was a "good cop-bad cop," ploy, Liesl stepped to the desk to play the good cop role.

Using a kind tone, Liesl asked, "Is it possible for you to get a message to Mr. Davis? Perhaps send him a text to let him know we're here? Both of us are current customers and friends. I'm sure he'll want to see us."

Courtney considered this request.

Nicole piped up with, "If that's the best you can do, we'll have to be satisfied with that."

Resisting the urge to elbow Nicole into silence, Liesl added, "I'm sure he'll want to see us. Why don't you send him a text?"

Courtney's wariness increased. After a moment's hesitation, she reached for her phone and typed in a message. "Mr. Davis will not appreciate being interrupted when he's talking with the police, but I have sent him a message."

Nicole stiffened. "The police?"

Liesl and Nicole's eyes met as they shared an unspoken dread.

Courtney's phone beeped. "He said for you to wait. He'll finish soon."

Nicole, now deflated in spirit, walked beside Liesl as they made their way to nearby chairs. Nicole hissed, "Kurt will be angry."

"No doubt." Liesl struggled to conjure an excuse for their visit with Donnie. "We are here to beef up our own security."

"Donnie would fall for that, but not Kurt."

"What if we say we're afraid our properties will be targeted?"

Nicole shook her head. "Your home, garage, and the garage apartment already have the highest security Donnie can offer. As far as my business goes, what valuable things are in a real estate office? Our clients' personal information? Can't you come up with a good excuse on the fly?"

"My excuses may be weak, but you haven't contributed any suggestions."

The sound of a door opening and approaching footsteps interrupted their bickering. Both women turned to identify the person approaching. Kurt was making his way toward them, Donnie on his heels. They rose from their chairs.

Kurt glowered at Liesl and Nicole for a moment then assumed a neutral expression. "Good morning, ladies. What a surprise to bump into you here."

Liesl let his sarcasm flow over her then struggled not to feel ashamed. "Good morning, Kurt. We're out and about on some volunteer business."

He stared at Liesl for a moment. "Nothing related to the incident at the Ag Museum?"

Nicole and Liesl squirmed under his gaze until Nicole, in a brilliant move, ignored Kurt's question and strode over to Donnie. "How are you doing today, Donnie? Good to see you. I'm here about my office building security."

Donnie towered over pint-sized Nicole, forcing him to stoop to give her a hug. "You're as pretty as ever, Nic. How's Lee?"

Kurt turned his back to Donnie and Nicole and aimed his green eyes at Liesl. "When you finish with your 'business' here, will you call me? Or send a text? I need a favor."

The request surprised Liesl. "Sure."

"I'd like to talk to you about it as soon as possible."

Feeling guilty about being caught at Donnie's place, Liesl said, "Of course. I'll call you when we leave here."

"Thanks. Come to the station. Bring Nicole if she has the time. She'll need to be part of this, too."

"How about a hint as to what this is about?"

His eyes shot to the girl at the reception desk. "Not a chance." He turned and walked out the door.

Kurt could be so infuriating. Being forced to wait for information would drive her nuts. She saw him try to mask his displeasure about their presence. Must be some favor. He rarely hesitated to show her his displeasure.

Why hadn't she spotted his cop car in the parking lot? Had she been too focused on her brainstorming? Nah. More likely it was due to this building being within walking distance of the police station.

Liesl turned her attention to Donnie. She approached and smiled her sweetest smile at the tall man with the beer belly waist.

He ran a hand through his receding blond hair. "How can I help you ladies today?"

Liesl raised her eyebrows at Nicole, signaling her to take charge.

Donnie regarded one, then the other. "Are you here about the Ag Museum too? Kurt told me not to discuss it with anyone."

Nicole patted Donnie's arm. "No. It's about security for my real estate office."

"Then let's go to my office."

They followed Donnie down the hall and entered a room that had papers strewn everywhere, as if it had been ransacked.

Liesl gasped. "Did Kurt do this?"

Donnie's face reddened. "No. It always looks this bad." He moved papers from one chair in front of his desk. The other chair was clear, presumably cleaned earlier to provide Kurt a seat. "Please, take a load off."

Liesl ignored Donnie's crude remark as Nicole launched into a sales pitch to convince Donnie her office needed security. They discussed options and made an appointment for him to inspect her office the next day, to make a plan for her with various levels of security.

When it was Liesl's turn, she asked how to improve security at the Butterfly House, a shelter for displaced women and children. Then she turned his attention to the Audrain County Historical Society buildings.

"You know, Donnie, I'm worried about Graceland too." There was no need to mention what occurred at the Ag Museum. Donnie understood her reference.

Graceland Mansion was the name of the primary structure of the Audrain County Historical Society Complex. John P. Clark designed the home in Classic Greek Revival style and built it in 1857.

"Donnie, as a board member of the historical society, I task you to come up with some options for security improvements. Right now, do we have anything for security?"

Donnie held up a finger. "No. But there are heat sensors throughout the house, the kitchen addition, and the attached museums."

During the long history of the house, the

separate kitchen and a connecting porch had been demolished. Additions to the structure included a wing with a modern kitchen and classroom, and a wing containing the Cauthorn-Stribling Library, the American Saddle Horse Museum, and the Fire Brick Museum.

"Graceland needs interior and exterior cameras, plus alarms for all doors and windows," Liesl said. "Would you do an inspection and give me an estimate for the cost of those upgrades?"

"Yes, ma'am."

"What about getting the cost to add these options to the other structures at Robert S. Green Park?"

"You mean the church, the country school, and the Green Stables?"

"Yes."

"They all have heat sensors too."

"The school and the church need alarms for all doors and windows, right?"

Donnie's face brightened and he jotted himself a note. "Of course. That would be an additional increase in security." He could not hide his delight in this opportunity.

Liesl was happy to confirm the current security for Graceland and the Butterfly House. Their conversation also confirmed there were no internal cameras at either of those entities. This placed Graceland, with its antiques and special displays, in the bull's-eye for a theft.

When they left the office, Liesl was confident Donnie was unaware they'd obtained the information they wanted.

Outside, she turned to Nicole. "That went really well. It's a fact we need to upgrade the system in Graceland. Whether the Butterfly House needs it depends on how much an upgrade will cost."

"I agree."

Liesl pointed to her car. "Hop in. We need to discuss something."

Nicole opened the passenger door and slid in, her face perplexed. "Is it what you were reflecting about?"

Liesl chuckled. "No. It's about Kurt. When you were talking to Donnie, he asked me to call him. He needs a favor. He specifically asked me to bring you. He wants us to meet him at the station."

Nicole shuddered. "This doesn't sound good. You sure he wants me too?"

"I'm positive. You hungry? I think we need to grab some food. This may take some time. I don't want my stomach growling while he's talking to us."

"I could eat, that's for sure."

"How about I call him and say we're on our way and picking up food? I bet he'd be happier, and might forgive us for pumping Donnie for information, if we bribed him with food."

Nicole grinned. "I'd rather consider the food

a peace offering. What about picking up some kwikis from the food truck?"

"He loves those."

"Make the call." Nicole reached over and buckled her seat belt. "We can leave my car here. After we talk to Kurt, bring me back and I'll lead you to my cute flip house."

Nicole and Liesl entered the public safety department station with the aroma of barbecue sauce and corn dogs rising from the sacks they carried.

The desk sergeant waved, so Liesl headed over to greet her. "How are you doing, Roxy? Seems like I only bump into you here. We need to find a better place to meet."

Roxy stood and leaned over her desk, eyeing the bags. "I'm guessing those are not for me."

"I'm sure we can find one with your name on it," Liesl said.

Roxy laughed and her blonde ponytail bobbed as she did. "I'm teasing. My uniform is snug. The salad in the break room refrigerator is enough for me. Thanks anyway."

Nicole reached into one of the bags and extracted a wrapped corn dog. "You can thank Kurt for making a huge order. He'll never miss this one."

They shared a smile. Roxy called Kurt to tell him about his visitors, and they enjoyed a casual conversation until Kurt materialized.

Liesl expected him to take them to the break room to consume the goodies, but he took them down a hallway, into an interview room.

Nicole scanned the small room. "You'll have to forgive me. I picked my outfit this morning thinking I was going to visit a business. I didn't realize I needed to dress for an interrogation."

Liesl tensed, sending a frown in Nicole's direction as she placed her food bags on the table. Kurt might not appreciate Nicole's sense of humor right now.

A grin crossed Kurt's face. "I'm sorry about this lunch location, but we need a room with complete privacy."

Liesl gestured toward the two-way mirror adorning one wall. "That mirror isn't private."

"I have a solution." Kurt left the room and returned moments later. "I locked the adjoining room and covered the other side of that mirror. No one can listen in or watch us."

Liesl pushed a bag of fries and kwikis toward Kurt. "Why all the privacy?"

"We need your help. But what we discuss must remain secret."

Chapter 12

Kurt

Kurt, Liesl, and Nicole had finished lunch when Hector Vega, Kurt's partner, joined them in the interrogation room.

Hector acknowledged both Nicole and Liesl, then took a seat next to Kurt. "Did you save any for me?"

Kurt looked at his watch and tapped it with his fingers. He refused to admit relief at Hector's appearance.

"Glad you could drag yourself in here, regardless of the time." He then pointed to a half-eaten container of french fries. "Care for a fry? You lost out, buddy. Liesl gave your kwiki to Roxy."

Hector grabbed the container. "Don't mind if I do." He rounded up a couple of packages of ketchup and squirted it on the fries. Before he filled his mouth, he asked, "What did I miss?"

"While I was being courteous enough to wait for my partner," Kurt spotted the sparks in Liesl's pretty eyes and pointed at her, "this one has been wounding me with evil eye rays due to my lack of explanation."

With a note of impatience in her tone, Nicole added, "This one is about to do the same thing."

Kurt smiled. He wished he could be ashamed of how much he enjoyed teasing these ladies, but that wasn't going to happen.

Before he formed a neutral reply, Liesl leaned across the table.

"Hector is here now. Proceed. You have our attention, and you're killing us with suspense."

Hector snickered but gestured for Kurt to take the lead.

"We are officially asking for your help. Hector and I had an idea, and we need your help to pull it off."

"Kurt's right," Hector said. "It's associated with our investigation of the death of the man discovered inside the Ag Museum."

Liesl's eyebrows nearly flew off the top of her head. "An active investigation? You want us to help you with an *active* investigation?"

Hector grunted. "You're not investigating. Kurt and I will investigate. We need your help with a special project."

Kurt interrupted Hector. "We need you to get us inside the historical society. In the door of Graceland. Literally."

Nicole turned to Liesl. "Have they banned them?"

Liesl grinned. "Not yet. Or rather, I should say, not that I'm aware."

Hector shifted in his chair. "This is unusual, but please hear him out."

"Unusual? That's an understatement." Liesl turned toward Nicole with a smile. "Do you find this *unusual?*"

Nicole widened her eyes at Liesl but stayed mute.

Kurt tried to regain control of the conversation. "Liesl, you're the only board member in this town we can trust. This might have been an inside job at the Ag Museum. We need you to get us inside Graceland, with no one discovering we're there. Graceland will be their next most logical target, and we want to implement an aggressive reaction."

The women hesitated. They seemed suspicious.

Nicole feigned surprise and turned to Liesl. "I never dreamed this would happen."

Liesl grinned. "Me either. Now you can't tease me about being Sherlock anymore. We'll be real investigators."

Kurt held up his hand as his face flushed. "Hold it right there. Again, no investigation. I mean it." He addressed his remarks directly to Liesl. "We need your access. If you'd just let us explain."

Liesl crossed her hands on the table. "Go on. We're listening."

"This theft might have connections to a structured criminal organization. The possibility of another hit at a museum in town is likely. It could be out of town, but Hector and I believe with the failure of the theft at the Ag Museum, they'll try another local target." He gestured for Hector to take over.

"The museum with the most valuable items is the Audrain County Historical Society's main building. Graceland."

Liesl turned to Nicole. "What did I tell you? It's the most likely candidate for a theft."

Kurt held up his hand. "Let us finish. There are several expensive pieces inside that museum. In addition, the security hasn't been upgraded."

Hector cleared his throat and said, "Several board members of the Ag Museum also serve on the board of the historical society. That crossover gives us pause. If it was an inside job at the Ag Museum, that person could also be associated with the historical society."

"It makes sense," Liesl said. "The inside person could be a board member, or an employee or volunteer. Several people serve on both boards. Patricia Sizemore, Dr. Johnson, Mr. Van de Berg, and someone else. A woman. I can't remember her name." She turned to Nicole. "That woman from California. Marc sold her a house when she moved into town a few years ago."

"Do you mean Mrs. Constantine?"

"Yes. That's her. She's new to both boards, actually. Newer than I am, which is saying something."

"What is her first name?" Kurt deciphered the blank faces of Nicole and Liesl and continued,

"Okay. That won't be hard to figure out." He jotted a note about Mrs. Constantine being new to both boards. As a detective, even with limited experience, it bothered him that Mrs. Constantine wasn't a long-term member of either board. He'd ask Hector for his take.

"Let's talk about each board member. Hector and I will do background checks, but I want your opinions." He turned to Nicole. "Yours too. You don't have board service with these people, but you've conducted business with them." He viewed his notes. "Let's start with Patricia Sizemore."

Liesl frowned. "She was a suspect in Aunt Suzanne's murder and we were wrong about her. It seems disloyal to suspect her actions again. I can't imagine Mrs. Sizemore being involved with a theft. She's been a participant on both the Ag board and the historical society board for decades. At the Ag Museum, she's the gift shop buyer and coordinates the volunteers who work there. She's saved them a lot of money by not having anyone on the payroll. The shop has constantly pulled a considerable profit, because she uses her own money to buy about half of the gift shop items."

"I can't imagine her as a suspect either," Nicole said. "She's not the type to work well with others, no matter who they are. She is a rich, nosy lady who holds herself above everyone. Associating herself with thieves and poor people is simply unimaginable for her."

"I agree, she wouldn't mix with criminals or be part of the criminal hierarchy or mastermind," Liesl said. "Mrs. Sizemore contributes time and money for the women and children at the Butterfly House. She was a wonderful friend to Aunt Suzanne. Now, she's trying her best to be nice to me and that's a sizeable stretch for her."

Kurt scribbled on his papers and kept his face neutral. In his opinion, they were spot on about Mrs. Sizemore. "What about Mr. Van de Berg?"

"On both boards, he doesn't volunteer much time, but he sure donates his money," Liesl said. "He doesn't have much personal knowledge about agriculture, but he brings legal and contract experience to that board. There are some grants he's helped write, and that brings in additional funds. Same with the historical society board. He offers free legal services and grant writing help."

Kurt turned to Nicole. "And your take on him?"

"He drives me nuts by never arriving on time. As a real estate agent, I work on a schedule. Whenever he's the attorney handling the real estate or representing the estate of someone, I have to allow extra time since he's going to be late."

Liesl nodded. "She's right."

Nicole continued. "That said, I have no complaints about his character. He donates money. He was raised by a single mother and they had little money. His childhood made him a magnificent philanthropist. He's one of the most generous people I've ever known."

Kurt wrote this down. "What about Mrs. Constantine?"

Liesl considered for a moment. "She's older than me, but considerably younger than Mrs. Sizemore and Mr. Van de Berg. I don't care for her strange haircut, but I suppose it's a stylish holdover from her time on the West Coast. She's been at every official meeting since they placed her on both boards."

Kurt turned to Nicole. "Do you know her?"

"Only through my business associate, Marc. He spent time with her when he sold her a house. He complained about her being fussy, but that's not uncommon. I'll ask him some specific questions about her and let you know what he says."

"Don't make him suspicious," Kurt warned.

Liesl reached for her phone and scrolled through her emails. "I can't find them right now, but I can check my emails with the board meeting minutes and see what I can remember about her."

"That would be great. If there were any discussions about security, things like cameras, or upgrades, we'll want all the details." Kurt decided to start digging into Mrs. Constantine's background. She was an unknown entity. He consulted his list. "The last member of both boards is Dr. Johnson."

"I love that man," Liesl said. "He tried to save Aunt Suzanne and alerted us to the possibility she was poisoned. He doesn't make many of the meetings, so he's another one who donates more money than time. Even with his busy schedule, he's great to volunteer on festival days and always brings his medical bag."

Kurt turned to Nicole. "What's your take?"

"I like him. I appreciate his volunteering as a doctor at the Butterfly House and the homeless shelter."

"I forgot about that," Liesl said. "He also came from a poor family and helps others who are struggling."

Kurt and Hector looked at each other but remained silent.

"What?" Liesl asked.

Hector shrugged and waved at Kurt to continue.

"The man who died at the Ag Museum had been living at the homeless shelter. We will not ignore the shelter connection between those two."

Liesl straightened in her chair. "There must be a lot of people in the homeless shelter. They come and go. Who knows when Dr. Johnson was last there?"

"I understand," Kurt said. "We'll check into it. No one is jumping to conclusions."

"I'll hold you to that," Liesl said. "Any more

information about the man and how he died?"

Kurt opened a file folder. "You know I can't discuss much. His criminal history is extensive. He was on parole for B and E, plus receiving stolen property."

Liesl turned to Nicole and said, "Cop-speak for breaking and entering."

Nicole nodded at Liesl and then turned toward Kurt. "Do you have any idea what he was trying to steal from the Ag Museum?"

Kurt glanced at Hector.

Hector shrugged. "If we're right about him climbing the bookcases, we think he was after some of the Civil War memorabilia on display in the top shelf."

Nicole asked, "You're sure his death was an accident?"

"That's how they've ruled it," Hector said.

Liesl nodded. "Thanks. I'm glad he wasn't attacked or anything."

"The man's street name was Big T," Kurt said. "His legal name was Theodore Sims."

"His occupation was being a criminal, according to his rap sheet," Hector said. "Almost every one of his arrests is related to theft. The autopsy showed he was a long-term alcoholic and probable drug user."

Nicole frowned. "So why do you think he had help breaking into the Ag Museum? Couldn't he have been working on his own?"

"Since Big T died at the scene, it revealed clues that indicate this was an inside job," Kurt said.

"Ms. Delgado from the cleaning staff didn't think anything about the alarm not being active when she arrived," Hector said. "She says it happens a lot in commercial cleaning. People leave work and forget to set the alarm or don't set it right."

Liesl frowned. "So, I'm confused. The cleaning crew aren't considered suspects anymore? A commercial cleaning service would have cleaning contracts all over town. I know for sure that Graceland has a commercial cleaning service. We've discussed their contracts during board meetings."

"As far as the Ag Museum goes, there were two people scheduled to work that day," Kurt said. "We confirmed the other employee was ill. I saw her, and she wasn't faking. Ms. Delgado and her absent coworker have both been cleared as suspects. Someone gave the thief the code, but it could have been other cleaning service staff, an Ag Museum employee, or a volunteer."

Nicole turned to Kurt. "We need more information. What is the rest of the story you're not telling us?"

Hector and Kurt exchanged looks, and then Hector explained. "We're concerned the theft might be a means for a group to fund drug or gun smuggling, or even human trafficking."

Liesl held up her hand. "You say *group*. Is that related to your speculation that several people are involved?"

"Yes," Kurt said. "The likelihood more than one person was involved seems solid. Big T was a petty criminal. This attempted heist smacks of planning and associations. Whether this is a group pulling heists to fund drugs, guns, or human trafficking is pure speculation on our part. It's the reason we're taking this so seriously. Also, it's why we've come to you instead of asking the museum director, to assist us in quietly placing an officer inside the museum for several nights."

Liesl shifted in her seat. "Someone is going to wait inside a museum until a thief comes? That may take a long time. Is that necessary?"

"Yes," Hector said. "We believe it is."

"How do we get you inside?" Liesl asked.

"It might be as easy as an unlocked back door, or unlocked front door with a diversion planned elsewhere, so everyone's attention is focused on the distraction."

Nicole shared a look with Liesl. "Between the two of us, we can handle that."

"Or the officer who is staying enters with a group and we hide them," Liesl added. "Doubtful anyone would notice someone stayed behind when the rest exit Graceland."

"You are not to tell anyone about this operation.

Understand? Only those of us in this room, and our commander, will be briefed about it."

"I'm upset this might be one of our friends," Liesl said. "Someone who's supposed to care about the museum might be the one hurting it."

"We feel the same way," Kurt said. "It's upsetting to consider someone who's supposed to protect and serve may be in on it. A lot of groups hire off-duty police officers as security guards. So, until we can eliminate police involvement, we have to keep all possibilities open."

Nicole tapped on the table with her index finger. "What you need is a reason for them to break in to Graceland. Entice them to plan it there."

Liesl studied her. "I'm confused. There are plenty of valuables inside Graceland. Kurt mentioned to me how a thief takes into consideration how easy the item is to steal, such as its size and weight. Graceland has several small and valuable items."

"I'm talking about something a thief can't resist," Nicole said. "Something new and alluring. Like a new collectors' item or similar valuables that acts as bait. A new donation, or a fresh display of something both expensive and easy for a thief to carry."

"That's genius, Nicole," Kurt said. "Baiting them to come where we want them to come, when we're ready for them to appear."

Liesl turned to Nicole. "Do you remember I inherited Civil War era coins from Aunt Suzanne?"

"Vaguely."

"They appraised as more valuable than I imagined. There were several Civil War era coins, and one gold piece. It was from the nineteenth century but prior to the Civil War and the most valuable of the coins. Anyway, I hid them somewhere in the house. In a very safe place. The place I chose was so safe, I haven't bumped into them since."

Nicole laughed at her. "You mean you lost them?"

"No," Liesl seemed exasperated with her friend. "I've merely misplaced them in a very safe place. That's all. I'll remember where they are. Eventually. When I find them, we can use them as bait."

Nicole rolled her eyes. "When you find them, we can advertise an open house or showing. It would help to talk about the display, getting publicity in the newspaper and on the radio."

Kurt shot a grin at Hector. "Assuming Liesl can find them in the 'very safe place' she used."

"You're still a sweet talker, Kurt Stephen Hunter," Liesl said with acid in her tone.

"Big T was likely after the Civil War memorabilia at the Ag Museum," Hector said.

"Maybe they won't be able to resist something similar on display at Graceland."

"That reminds me." Kurt wrinkled his brow. "My father had a display of some family coins from that era. I haven't seen them in years. I'll have to ask him about those."

Hector lobbed a question to Liesl. "What happens when someone offers to loan or donate a special display to a museum?"

Liesl hesitated, appearing to mull over the question. "I'm not sure. I guess you'd contact the director and offer to display the items. If I use the words *historical value,* the director will be beside himself to display them to the public."

Kurt added, "Assuming you find them in their very safe place."

Liesl stared bullets at him. Then, in a low tone through gritted teeth, she added, "Trust me. I'll find them."

Hector said, "What's the director going to do after that? Once you've offered them for temporary display?"

"Probably ask for them to be examined by a Civil War expert or historian for an idea of their use and the history of such coins."

"How long would that take?"

"I imagine a week or two."

Kurt pointed at Liesl. "When you find those coins, in their very safe place, Hector and I will have some specific input for you about offering them for display."

Liesl bared her teeth, making Kurt squirm. "When I find them, *in their very safe place,* we can have another *fun* meeting outlining your specific requests related to the board meeting."

Kurt's phone pinged. He read the message and then turned to Liesl and Nicole. "We're going to have to end this. We have something we've got to do."

Kurt showed the text to Hector, then he turned back to them. "No investigation, you guys. None whatsoever."

Liesl and Nicole exchanged a message in an unspoken language Kurt couldn't decipher.

"Did I miss the meeting where you two were appointed special deputies?" he asked sarcastically. "No. That's because you have *not* been appointed special deputies."

Nicole and Liesl remained silent, staring daggers at him.

Kurt ignored their hostility. "Remember what I said?"

Liesl gave him a fake smile. Uh-oh. He'd received that look before, and it was only displayed when she was angry.

"It's engraved on my mind," she said.

His face flamed. "Your sarcasm is unwelcome."

Liesl shrugged. "Appears to me, you and Hector are the ones asking for a favor. Perhaps more honey and a little less vinegar would sweeten your request." She stood, swiftly followed by Nicole. "We're leaving now."

Hector opened his mouth, but Kurt signaled him to silence. Instead, the men rose and studied Nicole and Liesl as they left the room.

Kurt called after them, "Thanks for coming and for bringing lunch."

The only response was the sound of high heels clicking on the floor.

Hector spun to him and grinned. "That went well, don't you think?"

"Your sarcasm is also unwelcome."

Hector chuckled. He clapped Kurt on his back. "May I suggest we call this operation Honey and Vinegar?"

Hector's laughter reverberated down the hall, leaving Kurt and his embarrassment alone in the interrogation room, clearing away the detritus from their lunch.

Chapter 13

Liesl

Liesl stalked out of the police station with Nicole scurrying to catch her. When they reached the cool air outside, Liesl spun to Nicole. "I'm so angry at Kurt right now. I'm grateful for this cold air; otherwise, I might burst into flames."

"You have every right to be angry. Kurt's teasing was funny at first, but he pushed it way too far."

"True that." Liesl sighed. "Count me out for a tour of your flip house today. I need to extinguish this fire in my brain. Kurt all but begs us for a favor, but then he throws insults at me simultaneously. My brain is fried. I've got to go home and start searching for that *very safe place* I hid those coins."

"I understand." Nicole added, "When you find them, take a picture of the hiding place. Send it in a text to Kurt, showing him how safe they were. Maybe we can all laugh about it then."

"Great idea. You're a genius."

"I am." Nicole beamed.

"Modest, too."

Nicole preened. "I admit I need to work on my modesty. That's hard to do when you're always right."

"I wouldn't know." Liesl chuckled. "You've lifted my spirits. Thank you. Your idea about bait really was genius. The right suggestion in these crazy circumstances."

"I had my Super Woman cape set on *invisible* in that meeting, but we could tell it was working, couldn't we?"

Liesl smiled. "You were awesome."

"Your cape was on as well."

"We were both quite impressive."

"Thank you. How about tomorrow for touring my flip house? I'm expecting another slow day at the office."

"Sure. Call me." Liesl turned to walk to her car.

Nicole strode after her and called out, "Hey. Drop me off at Donnie's work so I can pick up my car."

With a grimace, Liesl turned. "See? That is what I'm talking about. I'm so upset I forgot you rode over here with me."

Nicole laughed and walked around to the passenger side of the car.

After she dropped off Nicole, Liesl paused her car in the parking lot of Mexico Security Service and added a note to her nonprofit ideas. At the police department, when talking about Mrs. Sizemore and her gift shop contributions to the Ag Museum, she'd realized Mrs. Sizemore was a great resource.

Liesl decided to approach her to manage the

bookshop of the community center, or ask her to train someone to run it, if the community center came to fruition. Mrs. Sizemore was an expert at making the Ag gift shop profitable. Her help could make this community center work.

While she drove home, Liesl's phone rang. She was so focused on remembering the location of the Civil War era coins, the sound startled her.

The call was from Sam Apple, her investment counselor at Barston Investments. "I'm sorry to take so long to get back to you, but I have the information you wanted. Is this a good time for us to discuss it?"

"It's perfect," she said. "I'm in the car and need to take my mind off another issue, so chatting with you is perfect."

"Fine. Let me start with your conversation with Colette. She explained your desire to form a nonprofit and to use an attorney from St. Louis, so I reached out to several we use."

"Isn't one attorney enough?"

Sam chuckled. "Absolutely. What I wanted was one of our usual people to do it quickly. The first one I approached couldn't commit to a short timeline, but the second choice was delighted to help. She's an excellent contract attorney, and you'll really enjoy working with her. Her name is Cynthia Dugan, but she goes by Cee Cee."

"Thank you so much."

"If she's acceptable to you, I'll send her contact information. You can call to discuss the details."

"Thank you."

"Cee Cee will handle the nonprofit incorporation and will create it so the owner-slash-incorporator, which is you, will not be listed in any public document. She understands that, as the main donator to this charity, you want to remain private."

"That's perfect, Sam."

"I'll provide Cee Cee documents to verify your funds came from a legitimate source. In your case, that legitimate source is your inheritance. I will also verify the charitable nature of the business. These things are necessary for keeping your name out of the paperwork."

Liesl squirmed in her seat. "What about the fact no city block exists yet? Is that a problem?"

"Cee Cee plans to describe this as a nonprofit dedicated to community service. There will be no need to get into the weeds of details about your plans. She says she should be able to get it filed within a few days."

"Thank you so much." Liesl sighed as her mood lifted.

"It's my pleasure. It should be fast, even though it may take several days to gather the paperwork and file. I'm glad to give you this news." He coughed and then added, "I like your idea of buying a city block."

"I'm glad you support my crazy idea. I hope it's affordable and actually listed for sale. Right now it's just rumors."

"Where there is smoke, there's fire. I'm confident the rumors will prove true."

"About the money transfer and stuff. How will that work?" she asked.

"No money needs to be taken out to start the nonprofit, except for a nominal sum. We'll fund the purchase of the land once the property goes for sale."

"If it's listed."

"It will be. I'll call you to discuss the funding when that happens. Same with paying the legal bills."

"Excellent. Thank you."

"Is there anything I can help you with regarding the other problem? The one you wanted off your mind?"

"What skills do you bring to finding lost objects?"

She'd barely finished her question when his laughter reached her ears.

"I suggest you take that up with Colette. I can't find my way out of a paper bag."

CHAPTER 14

FEBRUARY, 1862
AUDRAIN COUNTY, MISSOURI

THE SPY

The chill of the dark night reached into my bones. The moon, hidden behind cloud cover, made it a near perfect night for a clandestine meeting. If only it wasn't so cold.

Would anyone be there? More than one? Or just a waste of time? When I'd let word of a Yankee spy seeking secessionists filter through the haze of a smoke-filled saloon two weeks ago, it had been done with a light touch. Perhaps too light? Three nights later, I dropped hints of a secure location for passing information. Then I left a note in the secure spot last night requesting a meeting—all steps necessary to gather the group I need.

Twenty hours later, in the middle of a frosty night, I crunched through frozen meadows toward the meeting spot. Would the plan work? There were no guarantees anyone would show. If they did, would they greet me with bullets or a handshake? When you were in the heart of a state with as many rebels as pro-Union men, wouldn't someone show up?

When I neared the banks of Davis Creek, my pace slowed. I heard no crunch of footsteps and saw no flicker of golden hues from candlelight or lamplight. I made a loop around the exterior of the shed that was once frequented by fishermen and trappers. No sign of anyone. Perhaps no one was coming.

I pushed the door of the shed, and it responded with a creak as it swung open. A musty smell assaulted my nose. I stepped inside and momentarily allowed my eyes to adjust to the cavelike blackness. When I could make out shadows, the silhouettes of three figures came into focus. Two tall, one short.

I hesitated only a second then spoke the agreed word. "Grayback."

The only response was the sound of boots shuffling on dirt.

When the cool barrel of a pistol touched my neck, I stiffened. Prickles of fear erupted across my body. I struggled to stand still with this weapon against my skin. My instincts screamed *run*.

I held up a hand in the darkness. "Easy, fellows. I'm one of you."

A nasally voice from my right asked, "What makes you think you're one of us? Why should we trust you?"

"If you're sympathetic to the Southern way of government, then it's best you hear me out."

The men murmured until one barked, "Talk."

Where to begin? I had to build trust but couldn't convey the whole truth. The fact that I killed a man for the opportunity to be a spy is none of their concern. "I didn't plan to become a spy for the Confederacy. My only strategy in life has been to claim a significant inheritance."

I hoped I had their attention. "But the wealth didn't pan out. Circumstances forced me to make the best of a situation that trapped me behind enemy lines. You see, I'd traveled to attend my grandfather's funeral."

A gruff voice asked, "You got a Yankee grandfather?"

"I've got a dead grandfather. No idea where his loyalties lay."

"Go on," Nasally Voice demanded.

"The telegram about his funeral arrived in a timely manner, but it took too long to travel from South Carolina to Massachusetts. I missed the funeral but was there for the reading of his will. It was a fool's errand. All I received was one gold coin and twenty acres of land."

The men smirked. At least they were listening.

"I sold the land to my cousin's husband. They wanted to scratch out life on a farm in that unbearable cold weather. The additional coins in my pocket from the sale were welcome. With money, albeit less than I deserved, I intended to return to South Carolina. Then the war started at glorious Fort Sumter!"

The men rumbled their agreement.

"I found it impossible to secure a ticket for my journey home. The outbreak of war shut down travel by rail or coach for all but the military."

I licked my lips. A swig of water would be welcome, but the gun's touch reminded me to stay put.

"An opportunity presented itself while I was trapped in Massachusetts."

Pressure of the barrel against my neck increased. "Go on," said the man holding the pistol.

"I'd be more agreeable about talking if you'd lower that weapon a bit."

"Not a chance."

I cleared my throat. "You don't need the details about my situation. What you do need to consider is that I'm prepared to reveal inside Union army information to Southern sympathizers brave enough to act upon it."

"What if they identify you? You willing to hang for treason?"

"Each day, my face reflects whatever emotion is expected. Humor, horror, fear, or whatever is called for. Once I can pass on information, I doubt they'd even suspect me. It's likely I won't go undetected forever, but for now, it's a noble feeling to have a mission for the South."

"Can we trust you?"

"You'll have to decide that among yourselves. After all, I am trusting you. You either trust me and take the information, or figure out another plan."

The men discussed my proposal among themselves.

Although they questioned how I got into this position, I'd never tell them the details of an opportunity placed at my feet when a Union colonel walked into a saloon where I was indulging myself. He looked kin to me, other than the Yankee uniform hanging on his shoulders. We shared the same hair and eye color. The same erect bearing. Both of us carried too much flesh on our frames.

He intrigued me. So when I went up to the bar to refill my drink, I invited him to join me. He was a talker and said he was from Maine, visiting relatives in Massachusetts on his way to a new command in Missouri.

This man willingly imparted the details about his old assignment and new assignment. I listened for hours. The more he drank, the more he shared. With the military training I had in South Carolina and the information he so eagerly shared, I hatched a plan.

Here was a man going to a new unit, where he was unknown. He even showed me his papers that he kept in the breast pocket of his uniform. As he yammered, I verified no one else in the saloon was paying any attention to us. It was easy to entice him outside with the offer of more drinks at another watering hole.

Outside, I pulled off his jacket before slitting his throat. I needed that uniform and all of his paperwork to take over his life. He stared at me in drunk and dying confusion as he slid down to the cobblestones. I dragged him to a nearby stable and covered him with straw. That gave me time to skip town before they'd smell his carcass.

His life and his uniform have been a perfect fit, but for the boots. I exchanged them for an appropriate size at the quartermaster's tent when I reported for duty.

The men interrupted my musings with another question.

"No one suspects you might be a spy? You have an accent that labels you a Southerner. We can't work with someone about to be revealed as a traitor."

"I have legitimate papers and a reasonable explanation for my accent. Not all soldiers for the Union have lived their entire life up north. My commanders swallowed the history I fed them, and no one suspects anything different."

Nasally Voice asked, "How long them papers and explanations gonna work for you?"

I pulled out my knife, pointing it against the chest of the man who held the pistol against my neck. When he moved back from the slight stab, I pushed the gun from my neck. He then stepped back to join the other two.

"Let me leave you with this. I'm a ranking officer, and the men feel I'm supporting them. That I care for their welfare. My favorite trick is to speak of my 'homeland' and watch them nod and agree with what I say. They don't know my 'homeland' is the land of their enemy."

I strode unimpeded to the door then turned and said, "It's been a pleasure, boys. You know how to get ahold of me if you want the information I'm offering."

Chapter 15

April 1862
Mexico, Missouri

Lieutenant Cormac O'Malley

At the Union Army camp of Northern Missouri, Cormac O'Malley stood inside one of the officers' tents within the headquarters area. The officers' camp, situated on high ground, provided a panoramic view of the surrounding area. With the ability to observe long distances and their proximity to the railroad lines, the Union Army hierarchy had found the perfect place for the encampment. The rest of the Army's forces were set up in squads, in rough formation, in a nearby valley.

Cormac chose this tent, usually occupied by Captain MacTavish, due to its unobstructed view of the road leading into camp. Luckily, the tent was temporarily uninhabited for the afternoon, as the upper-level officers were meeting. He was pleased to hide from the prying eyes of most inhabitants of the headquarters area. Anyone who outranked him might perceive that he was loitering, rather than protecting the camp's inhabitants.

From his position, he could see anyone or anything approaching the camp's entrance. He watched town resident George Hunter making his way through the officers' part of the camp. Hunter and his escort, Sergeant Samuels, then rode Hunter's supply wagon down the hill, to the enlisted area.

A few nights earlier, Mr. Clark had vouched for Hunter's loyalty to the Union during a supper held at the Clark home. Mr. Clark was a resident with the reputation of an unquestionable Union loyalist and supporter of the army and its officers.

Regardless of what anyone said, Cormac was not acquainted with Mr. Clark or George Hunter well enough to trust either of them. He was going to rectify this lack of information. Once enough information was gathered, he would make an informed determination of their loyalty.

Cormac saw another officer approach and realized he would be spotted if he tried to leave the tent. As the officer grew closer, Cormac recognized his commander, Captain Oliver.

Why was he coming to this tent? It wasn't his. Could he be searching for him? Cormac stepped farther into the tent to allow passage for his captain to enter. Had Captain Oliver switched tents with Captain MacTavish for some reason?

Captain Oliver entered and recognized him. He halted, as if frozen in place, and stared at Cormac, who straightened to attention.

"Morning, Captain," Cormac said.

It distressed him to observe his commander's reaction. Captain Oliver was usually an easygoing, unemotional type of leader. He frowned then barked, "What are you doing in here, O'Malley?"

Cormac's face flushed. His commander was angry, and rightly so. "I was observing that man from town, Hunter, making his delivery to camp."

"Why? What concern is he to you?"

"I'm still of the opinion we have a spy in our midst, sir."

"Even after Colonel Michaels gave you everything but a direct order to stand down on the subject?"

The captain had also attended the supper at the Clark house and heard Cormac questioning the safety of allowing the peddlers and suppliers in camp. Their host had given a positive evaluation of George Hunter, and they all witnessed their colonel's flat dismissal of Cormac's concerns.

Cormac studied Captain Oliver for a moment. The tone in the captain's voice gave warning of impatience and intolerance of his concerns. Yet Cormac couldn't dismiss his apprehension about the issue.

Although Oliver was Cormac's superior, they'd shared an affinity with one another since their assignment to this unit. Cormac was happy to serve a man he could respect. He risked his captain's ire to express his position on spies. But he wanted to explain what he understood about the possible spy situation, so he made a leap of faith.

"Yes, sir. Sorry, sir. I'm convinced the issue has not received all the attention necessary when the lives of our men are in danger."

Captain Oliver rubbed the back of his neck. "I'll give you three minutes to convince me more attention to this issue is necessary. Prove to me that the colonel's belief there are no spies among us might be based upon flawed intelligence and I'll allow you some leeway for investigation. Now, state your case."

Cormac blinked at his captain, surprised at being offered this chance. He took a deep breath.

"If there is a spy or a spy network among us and we ignore the possibility, we are allowing our entire encampment to be blind. This would also leave us exposed to any number of threats against us. Inside information is the lifeblood of war. Ignoring these dangers would make it easier for the enemy to attack or use intelligence against us."

"Continue." Captain Oliver folded his arms across his chest.

"We are in an area where nearly half the residents are Southern sympathizers. To be prepared, we have to anticipate the possibility there are those who could be spies and intelligence gatherers. Our enemies would celebrate any intelligence gained about this camp, then they'd use it to harm us."

Cormac studied Captain Oliver's reaction to this, but his face remained expressionless. He pressed on.

"No one suspects malfeasance except me. No one is scouting for suspicious activity. At the dinner party, Colonel Michaels said that someone must have investigated the peddlers before they were allowed into our encampment. However, the way he stated it made me believe he doesn't know the answer. Have we investigated them? I don't know the answer to that."

Captain Oliver nodded. "I agree. The colonel's statement was more a question than a declaration of fact. I've not been briefed on any investigation related to peddlers or others entering camp. It's almost giving them a free hand to plunder information and valuables."

Cormac took heart that his captain agreed. "I don't believe anyone is gathering or has previously gathered intelligence related to the frequency of raids, including whether they could relate those raids to enemy communication or knowledge. The notion makes me sick to my bones. What if someone is out there spilling secrets to the enemy? I believe there is a threat. But I can't prove a threat without intelligence on the subject."

"What is your plan of action?"

"Ah . . . I'd like to gather information about all of our delivery people and peddlers, such as who first allowed them access to the camp, when it started, how often they visit, and how long their visits last."

"Sounds fair," Captain Oliver said. "A logical plan."

"I want to track all of our reconnaissance missions and collect information about their success or failure. How much time, on average, passes from the time a mission is planned until it is implemented? Does that allow enough time for information to be passed to the rebels?"

"Good plan. What else?"

"There have been rumors that information is leaking out of the camp. We've had soldiers killed because of a surprise raid while on a mission. I'd suggest last-minute changes to the missions, to throw off those who received any previously leaked information."

Captain Oliver held up a hand. "If you can identify a spy, do you want to intercept him? Or identify him and then feed him false intelligence?"

Cormac considered the question. "If it's something as simple as a peddler, then we bar that peddler. We can restrict our dealings to those who offer necessary goods and services outside of the camp boundaries."

"Are you thinking of some type of delivery station outside the camp?"

"Yes. Transactions could happen there. Peddlers wouldn't observe anything inside our camp, which would immediately reduce their information. No counting of soldiers, cannons, horses, estimating of firearms and other munitions, and such."

"Go on."

"If they aren't around the campsite, they also won't have the ability to see our squads working and training. They won't witness officers discussing plans for raids or be able to easily identify who each officer is. They won't overhear when we're planning to reconnoiter an area. If a horse needs the local farrier, then take the horse to the farrier rather than allowing the farrier access to the entire camp."

"It's a good plan, but what if it's not a peddler?"

Cormac frowned. "That's the possibility that hurts the most. If one of us is a spy, sir, then I want to catch him in the act. Arrest him. Charge him with treason. Have him in a military tribunal to face the decision from some of the men they were putting in danger."

Captain Oliver strode to a trunk at the end of the cot and picked up a rolled parchment, likely a map. When he returned to the front of the tent, he stopped in front of Cormac. "Did you ask MacTavish if you could use his tent?"

Cormac hung his head. "No, sir."

"If you're going to use a higher ranked officer's tent for spying, you should get his permission. MacTavish might not appreciate you loitering in his personal tent."

Cormac's face heated. "Yes, sir. But this is a perfect example of the problem. I don't know who to trust, so I don't want to explain what I'm doing."

"But you explained your mission to me."

"You're one of the few I do trust."

"I'm placing you on special assignment for thirty days regarding this issue," Captain Oliver said. "You will report your findings each day directly to me and only to me."

"Thank you, sir."

"I'm not finished." Captain Oliver paused and pulled at his ear. "You will not write anything down unless it is in some type of code not easily read. Anything written will come to me, and I'll keep those notes. If anyone asks what you're doing, tell them your orders prohibit you from elaborating. They are to take their concerns to your commander. I'll handle them from there. Is that clear, O'Malley?"

"Yes, sir. Thank you, sir."

Captain Oliver pointed a finger in Cormac's face. "Not a word about this to Colonel Michaels. Nothing. Do you understand?"

"Yes, sir."

"Colonel Michaels might consider your actions to be disobeying an unspoken, but implied, order. Not a word. That is an order. Do I make myself clear?"

"Yes, sir." Cormac saluted.

When Captain Oliver left the tent, Cormac sighed in relief. He wasn't sure if his captain was pleased with him or furious about the whole situation. Either way, Cormac was happy with the outcome. He smiled, anticipating the opportunity to investigate his concerns.

This security breach might be related to the actions of Colonel Ulysses Grant. When Colonel Grant was assigned to this camp, he'd come in and put an immediate stop to the forcing of locals, at gunpoint, to swear their loyalty to the Union. He also stopped the military from seizing local property and supplies. The halting of the troop's power of seizure ultimately led to George Hunter delivering supplies to this camp.

Cormac had done his best to stop Colonel Grant from sanctioning these weekly deliveries. He'd gathered his courage and spoken to the colonel regarding his concerns about an unknown person from town making deliveries to camp and the possibility of establishing an outside delivery station.

Colonel Grant had listened to him but seemed to ignore most of the points he tried to make. The only consequence his impassioned speech brought about was the insistence of a "loyal Union man" providing the deliveries.

Now Colonel Grant was gone, moved to St. Louis and beyond, promoted to brigadier general. Cormac was grateful Captain Oliver was going to allow him to investigate the locals who had unfettered access to their military operations.

His next step was to define a plan of action. How did one spy on a spy? Such skills hadn't been taught to him, but he was determined to make a success of it.

Who among us is a spy? Is it George Hunter? One of the other frequent peddlers? Or one of the soldiers inside the camp passing secrets to the enemy?

He must figure it out.

After making a mental list of the most important things to investigate, Cormac set off to find Corporal Danny. He had personally witnessed the corporal talking with George Hunter, the driver of the supply wagon, on several occasions. There was no real reason for so many conversations between the two, unless they'd sparked a friendship. Danny was assigned to a regiment located in the valley area, and Cormac found him relaxing near his tent.

When Danny noticed Cormac's approach, he pushed some things into his pocket and came to attention. "Sir. Can I help you with something, sir?"

"At ease, Corporal. I was looking for Sergeant Samuels. I saw him and that fellow making a supply delivery today."

"Yes, sir. They made that delivery. I was in charge of the squad unloading headquarters' supplies. Actually, I volunteered for the duty so I could talk to George Hunter, the fellow who does the delivering."

"Why would you want to talk to him?"

Danny pulled a small carving and folding knife out of his pocket and held up a rough whittling of a quail. "Why, sir, he's a mighty fine whittler." Danny's face lit up as he spoke. "Private Martin and I like to whittle. We were convinced we were some pretty fine whittlers until we saw what Hunter can do."

"So, he's shown you some of his work?"

Danny grinned at him. "That man! He makes beautiful things. It's the finest whittling I've ever seen. So lifelike when he does animals and birds. He's showing us how he does it."

"He's teaching you?"

"We can only grab a minute or two when he's here, but he's been kind enough to show us a new trick every time he comes. There are some fascinating things that he's learning us. He's making sure we do it proper and such."

"What do you know about Hunter? Besides the whittling."

"He was in the 16th Illinois Infantry before he was mustered out due to wounds."

"Why did he join the 16th Illinois? Wasn't there something closer?"

Danny shook his head. "Their governor has secesh leanings. He refused to raise troops from Missouri to serve in the federal army. So George went all the way to Illinois to enlist."

"He has a serious limp. Does he say anything about that? Something that bad sustained in battle might make a man hold a grudge."

"I don't get that impression from him." Danny shrugged. "When he was wounded, they put him on a train with his discharge papers in his pocket. I got the impression the army didn't expect him to survive the trip home. It doesn't appear to have made him bitter. Instead, he acts grateful to be alive. As if he wants to get on with life."

"Does he ask you any questions about what we're doing? Like what our plans are or how many soldiers we have?"

"Nope. We just talk whittling. If you're like us, we don't want to talk about nothing else."

The quarter moon provided marginal light this evening. Stars winked from their heavenly posts while shadows stretched black and gray tendrils across the field in odd patterns.

Earlier in the evening, Cormac had listened to the songs of the crickets mixed with the music made by camp musicians. There was one fiddler, two buglers, several who played a harmonica, and drummers of all ages. Truth be told, the best drummers were the young boys, but they had plenty of practice.

At this late hour, the music was gone and campfires were dim, burned down to ashes. Only pickets roamed the perimeter. A perfect night for spying.

Cormac made rounds to all the sentries, ordering them to be on alert this dark night. He told them to pass that caution on to their replacements when they arrived. They must be vigilant. There were enemies outside the perimeter of the camp, to be sure.

As he walked back to his own tent, he considered the possibility that the enemies he'd warned the men about might be *inside* the camp. Hiding in plain sight inside the encampment's boundaries. Whether inside or outside of the camp, they were the enemy. He vowed to find them.

Chapter 16

Liesl

Liesl was in trouble. When she made the offer to use her inherited coins as bait for thieves, she'd forgotten how well she'd hidden them. After Kurt had teased her unmercifully about her hiding them in a "very safe place," she would do nothing else until they were back in her hands.

She'd brought them home from a meeting at the bank with Mr. Van de Berg and Mr. Barnaby. After Liesl located the key, they'd opened a lockbox belonging to Aunt Suzanne. Now she needed to locate the missing coins. Even though she was tired from the stressful day, she remained on the hunt.

With all that occupied her mind at the time she received the coins, including whether someone had poisoned her aunt, she'd hidden them. Where? That was the problem.

Liesl turned to Barney. "We need to start upstairs. I believe that's where I went that day with my arms full of sacks from the bank."

Barney wagged his tail.

She petted him and led the way upstairs to the bedroom she'd had since childhood. Although Aunt Suzanne had passed almost six months ago, she had not moved into the main bedroom.

She'd grown up in this house. That bedroom had always belonged to Uncle Max and Aunt Suzanne. It was still too soon for her and Barney to claim that space. One day. Not now.

Uncle Max was her father's uncle, which made him her great-uncle. Aunt Suzanne was officially her great-aunt by marriage. Liesl's grandparents had passed before she was born, so Liesl's father had asked Uncle Max to be her guardian. Uncle Max and Aunt Suzanne stepped in to raise Liesl after her parents' tragic car accident when she was a toddler.

Thanks to the fact that she still used the same bedroom she'd had as a child, even though her memory was vague, the coins must be hidden there. She rifled through her chests of drawers and, coming up empty, turned and opened the closet doors. Where were they? *They have to be in here somewhere.*

She laughed out loud when she found them in an old pair of boots at the back of the closet. Those coins remained untouched, nestled in the toes of her old boots, a copy of the appraisal still in the bag. Fantastic!

When she held the coins and ran her fingers across their indented surfaces, she longed for their history. How did they come into the family's possession? What had they meant to her aunt and uncle? Was it possible they'd been in the family for a long time?

Uncle Max's family arrived in the country prior to the Civil War, but Aunt Suzanne's family came from England in the 1880s. Could they be from Uncle Max's family? That side of the family was her side.

It was hard for her to fathom the fact that she had no official blood relation to Aunt Suzanne. Regardless of the DNA, Uncle Max was her father figure, and Aunt Suzanne was her mother figure.

Liesl suspected Uncle Myron might know the history of these coins. He was Aunt Suzanne's brother. Although he wasn't officially an uncle to her, she loved him and had always called him Uncle Myron.

She called Uncle Myron a week earlier than their usual bimonthly call. He lived in California, so the time difference benefited her. He was a creature of habit and went to bed early. At eighty-five, he deserved a good night of sleep.

After they exchanged pleasantries, she said, "I need to pick your brain about something, Uncle Myron."

"Well, there's not much brain left for you to pick, but you're welcome to everything I might still have."

She imagined the smile on his face as he teased her. It made her grin. "There's actually two things I want to talk to you about, and both came out of Aunt Suzanne's bank boxes. Her banker, her lawyer, and I had to do an inventory of her lock boxes to settle her estate."

"Okay."

"One item we found is your father's gold pocket watch and the fob that connects to it. Could you tell me, why did Aunt Suzanne have those? Sentimental things like that usually go from father to son."

"Well, the explanation is embarrassing." Uncle Myron blew out a breath. "I founded several businesses that were successful. Then I invested in a dot-com company, a fully online company. When the bottom fell out of the dot-coms in the 2000s, I packed up the watch and mailed it to Suzanne."

"So you wouldn't be tempted to sell it?"

"I was afraid I'd have to file for personal bankruptcy and didn't want the banks to get their hands on a family heirloom. They'd only consider it as a gold watch and fob to be sold to repay my debts."

Liesl was startled. "Was that legal?"

"I hadn't filed bankruptcy yet. It wasn't illegal for me to give it to her. Suzanne would never have been a part of anything that even smelled like it might be illegal."

"You're right."

"In the end, I didn't have to file bankruptcy. As an entrepreneur, your livelihood rides on a tide. You can't predict when the tide may turn again.

I didn't try to get the watch back to keep it safe."

"But you've been so successful for so many years, Uncle Myron. You never asked her to return it?"

"Occasionally I'd think about getting it back to give to my son, but I never acted on it."

"You've got Trey and Young Tom to consider. A whole legacy of the father-to-son inheritance of that watch."

"Young Tom lives the California life. He's thirty-nine years old and a surfer 'dude.' He wouldn't appreciate it."

"Well then, start with Trey. What is he now—about retirement age? He'd appreciate the watch. Either way, I'm putting it in a box, insuring it, and mailing it back to you."

"I'm not sure Trey would cherish it like he should."

Liesl considered this for a moment. "I have another option. You could approve of me putting it on temporary display at the historical society or another museum for now. They would research the watch and its history. The public would admire it, which might make Trey appreciate it more. When he understands its value historically and sentimentally, then I'll mail it to you to give to him."

"But I gave it to Suzanne."

Liesl laughed. "And now I'm giving it back to you so you can pass it down. All of you share the same name, so the initials on the watch are even more special since you're all named after your father."

"You're right." Emotion filled Uncle Myron's voice. "Thank you, Liesl, for such a precious gift."

"It's a re-gift, and I'm happy to return it to its rightful owner. When you pass it on to your son, make sure he appreciates the fine man who originally owned it and the man who owns it now."

"I'll do my best to make him understand."

"Now for the other question. There were some coins in the lockbox. One was gold, and several were from the Civil War era. Do you have any idea where they came from?"

"You mean, were they from my side of the family?" He paused. "I don't believe so. I don't recall any talk about coins or seeing them at the house, either displayed or brought out to admire."

Liesl sighed her disappointment. "I hoped you might remember something about them. Could they be from Uncle Max's side of the family?"

"Max's people were already here during the Civil War. I'm sure of it. They were farmers back then and are still farmers now, so I figure you'd better talk to your Schrader relatives."

Liesl considered her plethora of Schrader relatives. Gretchen would be the most fun to talk to, and she was a history buff as well. She might know some of the family history. Liesl would start with her.

"Thank you, Uncle Myron."

"Has a trial date been set for Doreen?"

"No. The wheels of justice are barely moving right now. They're still providing information to Doreen's attorney related to her prosecution. Kurt says it will take months, maybe even a year or two, before they set a trial date."

"Contact me when they do. I plan to be there every day. I want her to see my face in that courtroom. She killed my sister."

Liesl dreaded coming face to face with Doreen again. Their last encounter involved Doreen trying to kill her. She shivered and then gathered her courage. "I'll be right beside you. If they will let me be in there, that is. I'll be a witness. I may have to stay outside the courtroom until my testimony is over."

"Well, I'll be there. You join me when you can."

"Thank you, Uncle Myron. We need to be there to represent Aunt Suzanne if this goes to trial, but Kurt mentioned they might offer a plea deal."

"What kind of deal?"

"They haven't shared any details about it. Kurt said we'd get the chance to approve it before they'd offer it."

"Good. I feel better about it."

"It was a tremendous relief to me too. I don't

want her walking free. There are times a jury feels there wasn't enough evidence presented for a guilty verdict. A plea deal would ensure she'd remain behind bars."

"Then I shall pray for a plea deal."

At her bedtime, she received a call from Nicole. At this hour for a call, Nicole must have something on her mind.

"Huge congratulations on finding the lost coins."

Liesl laughed. "Did you like the text and picture? They were never lost, merely stashed in an excellent hiding place."

"That's right. Kurt will have to apologize, since you found them in record time."

"I had help from an expert. Colette is the assistant to my financial advisor. She's also a Renaissance woman. So many skills. You, Miss Wonder Woman, need to meet her, the Renaissance woman. We'll have to plan a girls' trip to St. Louis."

"You know I'm always game for a girls' trip."

After a moment of chitchat, Nicole said, "I'm sorry, but I'm going to have to put you off on our planned visit to my flip house tomorrow. I got a call from someone moving into town. They want me to show them every house on the market within their budget, and they want a drive-by of all the elementary schools and churches. It's going to take an entire day."

Liesl responded to the excitement in Nicole's voice. "You go, girl. Don't worry about me. I'm glad you have this opportunity."

"Thank you. Now that I've changed your plans, what will you do tomorrow?"

"I offered to research the board meeting minutes and send them to Kurt and Hector, along with my impressions. They'd appreciate it if I got those in as soon as possible."

"Aren't you still mad at Kurt?"

"Of course, but I'm not mad at Hector. I don't want to punish him when Kurt is the one I'm angry with. Besides, if it will help the case, I want to do it. Another opportunity for them to be indebted to me."

Chapter 17

An Unrepentant Thief

When my cell phone rang, I reached for it then hesitated when I saw the name of the caller. My gut clenched. Best to face this head-on and try to mitigate the damage.

"Hello, Boss."

There was a pause before he spoke. When he did, it was sharp and to the point. "You've got one minute to explain why I don't have the money you owe me."

"Sorry. One of my people died. On the job. The police are involved."

"And how is this my problem?"

"It's not," I said. "I'm transferring the money today."

"Should have been fixed yesterday. Don't make me call you again."

Once he disconnected, I held out the phone. It took restraint not to throw it against the wall, as anger vibrated through me.

The fact that I'd been scrambling to pawn items of value to make this payment went unappreciated by the boss. At least I had enough to transfer the money now. But that didn't solve the problem of next month's shipment and payment.

How did Big T manage to get himself killed on a theft job? My anger over the situation made me want to put my fist through a wall. Did Al Capone have such trouble with his men? Did Frank James have issues like this with Jesse?

Although I was furious about the situation, I had to admit sharing some of the blame for hiring the wrong person for the job. Or, I should say, for the unsuccessful job. At least I didn't have to pay him, so that money was going toward the transfer to the boss.

I'd been exposed to the public in that diner for at least an hour and a half, waiting for Big T to appear. All the time I spent, risking identification and nosy people wondering what I was doing there, he was either dead or dying. All that risk for nothing. Nada.

Now the police had a death investigation related to the *someone* found inside that museum. The cops would ask a million questions. A thug like Big T had no business in there. Thanks to the media coverage, everyone knew about it now.

I strode to the window, paying no attention to the view. How was I going to escape being associated with this mess?

Big T's name had been withheld, pending notice to his next of kin. Maybe they'd had trouble identifying him? Nah. He was a career criminal. They were having trouble finding any kin, more likely.

Did he have a heart attack in there? Did someone discover him and kill him? Nothing in the newspaper about the cause of death.

Would law enforcement figure out how he got in? Maybe they'd already figured it out, or would figure it out soon.

My plan with clues to make it look like a normal break-in was to be put in place *after* the theft occurred. All those clues were to be set up to make the police believe it was a simple burglary. I needed to know where Big T was in the plan when he died.

Without this information, I was forced to sit and wait. Every second I had to act unconcerned, while I worried about this broken link in the chain. Would it result in the demise of my entire criminal network? *Not if I can help it.*

Until this nightmare, everything was smooth sailing. The people I hired provided a routine supply of goods, and I paid them in return. Thanks to this mess, I'd have to come up with a new plan to get them the money next month.

In the meantime, I was left to worry if there were any ties between me and Big T. I'd have to plan my next operation even more carefully.

I need someone smart. Someone with skill and cunning. Perhaps the only person with all the qualities to carry out a plan without a flaw was the person reflected in my mirror.

I would search for a skilled thief who had half

a brain. If I couldn't find one, then I'd have to do it myself.

Now, time to make the money transfer. I picked up my briefcase and headed toward the back door.

This money should keep the wolves off my back for a while.

Chapter 18

Kurt

Kurt had laughed aloud last night when a text from Liesl pinged his phone. A picture of old coins lined up in front of a pair of women's boots, plus a photograph of the appraisal, accompanied the text.

She had to zing him about her discovery. It was well-deserved. He'd been unpleasant yesterday. His effort to set aside nervousness and attempt humor failed.

The value of the gold coin surprised him. Any thief would be interested in stealing it.

Kurt wasn't surprised that Liesl didn't answer when he called her this morning. It was her passive-aggressive way of punishing him for making her mad during their meeting yesterday.

He waited an hour to see if she would call him back. With no return call, he sucked in a breath and tried a second time. This time, she picked up.

Her tone was cool. "Yes, Kurt?"

"Thank you for finding those coins." He hesitated, but she made no move to reply. "I'm being sincere as possible for the snide cop that I am. I mean it when I say I appreciate your search for them, finding them, and letting us use them for a setup."

She didn't say anything for a moment, and he visualized her face in a frown, unwilling to accept praise from him when she was still mad.

"You're welcome," she replied stiffly.

It was harder than he'd imagined. He tried Plan B.

"I owe you a huge apology. Yesterday, I was rude. My only excuse is that both Hector and I are flailing around on this case. The answers we need are eluding us. I'm sorry. I shouldn't take my frustrations out on you."

"No, you shouldn't. Neither should you have teased me mercilessly about those coins."

"You're right. I'm sorry about that too." After a moment of silence, he pressed on with his idea for the rest of Plan B. "How about I treat you to some of your favorite food? To make it up to you."

After a pause, Liesl responded. "I'm not sure Justin would appreciate us having dinner together."

"Wait. You didn't let me finish. I want to include Ross in this. My investigation has kept me away from him too much."

"I would be delighted to see Ross."

Kurt noted she did not include him in that delight.

"What did you have in mind?" she asked.

He smiled. Ross and food were an irresistible combination for Liesl.

"Would Justin object if it was actually both of the Hunter men taking you to dinner?"

"I'm not sure. But I do know Ross would enjoy coming here and playing with Barney. Why don't you bring him and some food over here?"

"If you're not busy, could we do it this evening?"

"Sure. Suits me."

She was thawing. "So the next question is, pizza or lasagna?"

"What would Ross like?"

"He loves both."

"Were you thinking DeAngelo's for the lasagna?"

"Yes. Unless you have changed your mind about DeAngelo's lasagna."

Liesl chuckled, which lifted his guilt. She was forgiving him. "Never. Lasagna it is."

"What time?"

"Anytime it suits you fellows. I've been digging through my email, locating all the past board meeting minutes. I'm copying them into two files—Ag Museum and Historical Society. I'm tagging the Butterfly House minutes, so if you want those, I can give them to you tonight."

"That's terrific. I don't think the Butterfly House is on their thievery radar. Since it's a safe house for women and children, I doubt there's anything there worth stealing. Am I wrong?"

"I agree. It's not a museum with priceless objects on display."

"We can discuss more about the board minutes tonight."

"We also need to discuss how I should offer the coins for the museum to display."

"Yes. We can do all that."

"Be aware I have carpenters banging and painters painting until five o'clock most days."

"That's fine. We'll arrive later than that. What about Joey? Do you think he'd like to join us?"

"Doubtful, but thanks for including him. I'll ask him."

Kurt chuckled. "Whatever Joey wants is fine with me. See you between five thirty and six. I'll be the one at your front door standing beside the eager seven-year-old boy."

"Perfect. I'm in great need of a hug from an eager seven-year-old boy."

When Kurt hung up, he shook off a twinge of guilt for offering his son as a token of peace. Not enough guilt existed to make him regret his actions. He would do whatever necessary to get back into Liesl's good graces.

That evening, Ross ran up the porch steps as fast as his lanky legs could carry him. "I'm ringing the bell, Dad. Your hands are full."

Kurt couldn't argue. He juggled bags loaded with lasagna, salad, and garlic bread, careful to avoid a spill on his clothes.

The afternoon and evening had been a tight

race with time. He'd collected Ross from his after-school care, showered off his cop day, and change into jeans and a sweatshirt before they'd left to pick up dinner.

Liesl's doorbell was an antique brass bell built into the massive front door. Visitors twisted the brass knob on the outside to make the clappers hit the brass bells attached to the inside of the door.

It took all the force Ross could muster to twist the knob, but he was successful. He and Kurt exchanged a grin when the sound of success dinged from inside the house, followed by Barney's unique combination of howl and bark.

"I hear Barney," Ross said.

"He's going to be excited to see you, buddy."

Liesl opened the door, and Barney shot onto the porch, jumping on Ross's legs, while Ross tried to pet his squirming body.

"Barney has lost weight," Kurt said.

Liesl smiled. "Over fifteen pounds. I'm so proud of him. He enjoys his walks, even though I've been drawing out the distance and increasing our speed. He only tolerates his diet dog food, but it's paid off. He's becoming model thin."

Kurt laughed. "I wouldn't go that far, but he's certainly a new dog. See all the energy he has?"

They stood and observed the giggling boy wrestling with Barney. Kurt's heart filled with love. A child playing with a dog was one of the best sights in the world. Did he need to get a dog for Ross? He'd think about it. But how could they care for a dog? His work hours were long and unpredictable.

He glanced up and saw Liesl observing him. He winked at her. "I have something to discuss with you. Later. When little ears aren't around."

Liesl reached out and took a bag from Kurt's hands.

Ross's head popped up. "Are you saying I have little ears?"

Kurt turned to Ross. "Seems like you have *big* ears."

"Come in, you guys. Instead of ears, think about your stomach and nose. The food smells delicious. Let's eat." Liesl led them to the dining room, then she turned to Kurt. "Do we need to secure your pistol?"

"Yes."

Kurt and Ross followed Liesl as she escorted them into the library to lock his weapon in a built-in, small locking cabinet on a bookshelf. Once accomplished, she led them on a quick tour of the kitchen renovations, before returning to the dining room and the food.

After dinner, Liesl suggested Ross and Barney play in the backyard. Both boy and dog accepted this idea with enthusiasm.

Kurt insisted Ross wear a jacket and had Liesl turn on the yard lights.

"While they are busy, I want to go over the board minutes I've gathered," she said. "If you think Ross is okay out there without us watching him, I'd like to spread out in the library."

Kurt opened the back door. "You stay inside the fence, okay? Liesl and I will be in the library when you're ready to come in."

"Okay, Dad," Ross replied.

Kurt then followed Liesl back to the library, which was his favorite room in the beautiful old house. With ample bookshelves, a fireplace, and a wall of windows, the room was cozy. When she turned on the electric fire, the orange glow made the room warm and comforting.

Liesl walked to the desk near the windows. "You didn't want the Butterfly House's information, right?"

"Correct."

"I've only been on these boards for a few months, but Aunt Suzanne served for years. She kept all the records from her board duties."

"That's terrific."

"When I took over her desk, I moved her contents to file boxes and put them in the attic."

"Becoming a hoarder like your aunt?"

Liesl smiled. "You'll be glad I have that skill." She waved her hand over the desktop stacked with papers. "I dug out the file boxes and found minutes from the last seven or eight years for both the Ag Museum and the historical society."

"What did they say?"

"I didn't scrutinize the records but did flip through them. Our generation prints nothing, but Aunt Suzanne's generation printed everything. You won't have to chase through computer records and get a warrant or anything. I'm handing you years of records. I don't know that I'll ever need them, but please return them when you're through."

"No worries. I'll make copies and return the originals."

She grabbed the stacks and handed them over. "Do you think these will help?"

"They won't hurt." He held the papers for a minute. "Could I get a folder or a sack for these?"

"Of course. Sorry."

While she searched through the desk, Kurt asked, "What was your general impression about these minutes?"

"Nothing made my skin itch. They include a discussion from several years ago related to the security system for the Ag Museum."

"How long ago?"

"Six years? Seven? They put in the alarms on the building and the heavy exterior equipment. Exactly what's in place now, if I'm right about the current system. They had bids from two companies and went with Mexico Security Systems."

"No cameras discussed?"

"No." She handed him an expandable accordion folder. "But I could have missed it. I did a quick review."

"Donnie Davis won the bid. You said there were bids from two companies?"

"That's right."

"What about the historical society?"

"They only have heat sensors, I think. I don't believe they have cameras anywhere. They discussed where those sensors were to be in Graceland and the additions."

"Any exterior cameras discussed?"

"Not that I found. Why wouldn't either of these museums discuss cameras when they were upgrading security?"

"Could be they were expensive. Or images were not very clear due to early technology."

Liesl frowned. "It wasn't *that* long ago. I could have missed camera references. Double-check me."

"Will do. Thanks so much for doing all this."

Liesl held up a hand. "I have a suggestion, but I don't want you to think I'm investigating."

Kurt's face burned. "I apologize again for being rude about the investigation issue. All suggestions from you and Nicole are welcome. I mean it."

"One of your best resources, if you can eliminate her as a suspect, is Mrs. Sizemore. She's difficult to deal with. She's a prickly personality. But there's nothing wrong with her mind, and she remembers everything. She'd provide 'insider' details, such as who on the board resisted various security upgrades."

Kurt sighed. "She's a troublesome personality. So stiff. She comes across as judgmental too. I always feel inadequate in her presence."

"I agree with you, but the lady from California . . . Uh?"

"Mrs. Constantine."

"Yes." Liesl frowned. "I don't know why I have trouble with her name." She ran her hand through her hair. "She's not from Mexico proper, but she grew up around here. And you can bet Mrs. Sizemore knows her background."

"As far as Mrs. Constantine goes, the worst we found was unpaid parking tickets from the San Diego area." He shot her a serious look. "You can't share those details. That's confidential."

A peal of laughter erupted from Liesl. "Then why did you tell me?"

He joined her in laughter. "I can tell you. You can't tell others."

"Let's go sit down." She gestured toward the chairs near the fireplace. When seated, Liesl said, "Do you have results from a background check on Dr. Johnson?"

Kurt shook his head. "No comment."

"Playing by the rules, huh?" She changed the subject. "One person at the historical society sees everything that goes on there. Adam. Adam Miller, the maintenance man."

Kurt searched for the right thing to say. "No comment."

Her eyebrows rose as she stared him down. "What's your problem with Mr. Miller?"

"You know he had a criminal record at one time, don't you?"

"No, I didn't. But I can tell you I've known him my entire life."

"How's that?"

"Mr. Miller was a friend of Uncle Max. Uncle Max didn't hang out with anyone dishonest. If Adam Miller was a criminal, he must have given it up decades ago."

"His issues were in the past."

Liesl pulled a face at him. "Don't you believe a leopard can change his spots?"

"Yes. I believe it can happen. Though it's not real common, people change. I am one of those leopards."

Confusion crossed Liesl's face. "I don't understand."

"I wronged you when we were dating, and it broke us up. That action resulted in Ross. You're doing your best to put it behind us. We're friends again. I'm grateful for that. I wish you knew how much it means to me."

"For years, I held on to all the hurt and the pain. It was beyond time for me to move on."

"I admire you for doing that." He hesitated and then plunged ahead. "I admire most everything about you. No one else has made me feel what I feel for you."

Liesl reached into a pocket and dabbed at her tears with a handkerchief. "Don't forget that I'm currently dating a nice man. Trying my best to move on with my life."

Her reaction surprised him, and he rushed to add, "I'm glad you're seeing someone. I want you to be happy. Once I had Ross, life was worth living again. I've dated some women. It's not fun being the odd man out in a group of couples. So I've dated, but I've never gotten over you."

The slam of the back door signaled the return of the other guest in the house.

Liesl called out, "We're in here, Ross."

"Coming, Miss Liesl."

Kurt stood, holding the file folder under his arm. "I don't want to chase you away because I confessed I'm not over you. I'm happy we're friends. Overjoyed to be friends. Thanks for that."

Ross ran into the room, followed by Barney. He spilled words into the valley of their silence, oblivious to the previous conversation. When he ran out of descriptive words about his time outside with Barney, he threw himself into the chair Kurt had vacated by the fireplace.

Kurt frowned. "Don't mess up the furniture,

Ross. Did you check for dirt on your pants or shoes?"

Ross examined his pants. "This chair is so old I don't think you could tell if I messed it up."

Kurt sucked the air out of the room. "Ross. That was rude. You don't call someone's furniture old. You apologize."

Ross slipped off the chair, smacked the seat twice with his hand, then turned to Liesl. "I'm sorry."

She stood, walked over, and gave Ross a hug. "Like father, like son. This dinner is part of an apology from your father."

Ross grinned. "He got in trouble too?"

Liesl nodded. "As for the furniture, it's time for an upgrade in here. After the fire, I had to replace some pieces in the living room, but I did nothing in this room. What kind of furniture would you like?"

Kurt frowned at the direction of the conversation, but Liesl held up a hand to halt his comments.

Ross glanced around. "I'd like a small table," He pointed to a corner. "Over there. A place where we can do puzzles and play games."

"Anything else?"

"The furniture is old, but I like the fluffy chairs beside the fireplace and the long couch. Maybe replace them with new stuff, but the same?"

"I understand," Liesl said. "I'll get it done.

Thanks for your decorating advice. Is it okay if I ask Miss Nicole to help me?"

Ross smiled. "She knows a lot about houses."

"Yes, she does. Interior stuff, too, like furniture and paint color. I need to upgrade the upstairs den, too."

Kurt asked, "Have you moved into the owner suite? You are, in fact, the owner now."

Liesl's face filled with pain.

He regretted his words. "I'm sorry. I didn't think."

"Honestly, I've considered it and I'm not ready. One day. I promise."

"Call me when you're ready. I'll help you pack, clean, and move stuff in and out. Your Aunt Suzanne would want you to use that bedroom."

"You're right. She would."

Later that evening, Liesl and Kurt sat on the "old" couch with Ross nodding off, his head on Kurt's lap. Barney's light snore sounded from his resting place in front of the fire.

"What do you think about me getting a d-o-g for someone?"

Liesl sucked in a breath. "Someone would like that very much. Love it, in fact."

"My worry is taking care of it. I'm away from the house all day. A puppy can't handle that."

"Then do what I did. Adopt an older d-o-g. One that can have a d-o-g-g-y door. That way, they can let themselves out when nature calls. Otherwise, it lounges around the house."

"I'll check into that." After a pause, Kurt added, "I really am sorry about the way I treated you at the station."

"You should be."

He smiled and held up a hand. "Wait. You interrupted me. Give me a chance to state my complete apology."

"Pray continue. At no time would I want to cut short an apology from you."

"I'm new to being a detective. Joking was a method to hide my nerves. It makes me nervous to ask you to do something possibly dangerous."

Liesl studied him for a moment. "You think this potential criminal group is dangerous?"

"Yes, I do. Some people will do anything for money. Hurting or killing someone who gets in their way is always a possibility."

"Do you know if they're connected to the stuff you mentioned, drug sales or human trafficking?"

"No. Greed seems to be their primary motivation, but that's my gut feeling. I have no proof. The next likely target will be Graceland. Hector and I wanted a way to get inside without involving you, but we failed to come up with another option. You and Nicole are the only people we're certain are trustworthy."

"We're happy to help."

"Not after yesterday's smart remarks. I know you well enough to bring you your favorite foods, then top it off with one cute little boy. To calm the waters and ask for your forgiveness."

She poked him in the arm. "You're telling all your secrets."

"Here's another one. I miss our verbal disputes. The ones where you and I would go *mano-a-mano* over our opinions about everything. Movies, food, the worth of cars, other people's relationships. Everything."

"I can't believe you think of those as something special."

"Our 'battles' were fun. You argued your opinions well, and we usually ended up laughing about whatever we were arguing over."

"True. I can't argue about that."

He rolled his eyes at her poor joke. "Since losing you, that's not in my life anymore. We were partners."

"Yes, we were."

As he looked into her eyes, he experienced an overwhelming desire to kiss her. With tenderness, he brushed a stray lock of hair behind her ear and then maneuvered in for a kiss. A soft caress that conveyed his feelings.

She didn't pull away until Ross rolled over in his lap.

He patted Ross, then said quietly, "I'm sorry to have caused you so much pain. I've hurt too, with no one to blame but myself."

She touched his hand that rested on Ross's back. "It's in the past."

He shifted so their hands were palm to palm, then he laced his fingers with hers.

She looked down at their entwined hands and didn't pull away.

Chapter 19

Lieutenant Cormac O'Malley

Cormac woke the following day energized by a mission. He shaved and dressed in a hurry, not bothering with the mess tent. He headed straight for the stables.

Horses and mules were important to an army, and they needed horseshoes and other care. Today he would observe those who tended to these animals, whether they were from inside or outside of the camp.

He worked his way cautiously around the stable yard, talking to various men. He took great care not to let his actions raise anyone's suspicions. Killing two birds with one stone, Cormac gathered information from anyone who had taken part in a mission outside of camp. He casually asked about their success or failure and encouraged the men to give him honest answers. Most of the men seemed to trust him and were forthcoming about their experiences.

Not one man attributed the missions' success or failure to the enemy knowing where they were going to be. They told Cormac about situations he wanted to investigate further. There could be more than what the men imparted if a spy network was factored in.

After he'd interacted with the soldiers for about an hour, a middle-aged man pulled up in a wagon. This man was not part of their army, and no one accompanied him from the main gate. Cormac frowned. Exactly what he feared. This man had unfettered access to the camp.

Cormac also took note of the man's physique. Muscles ran from his hairline, which was starting to gray, down through his body. Muscles that never seemed to end. With broad shoulders and back, thick upper and lower arms that ended in sausage fingers, the man resembled a bear.

The muscled stranger carried tools as he approached one of the men, and they shook hands. Within a moment, the soldier was leading a horse to him.

Those sausage fingers were able to calm the horse, trim his hooves, and shoe him in minutes. Impressive, but draft horses used for the wagons were generally a calm breed.

Cormac speculated on how he would deal with a high-spirited horse. The officers used them on missions and travel. Mules and donkeys rounded out their current livestock inventory, used as pack animals. On rare occasions, they used oxen to pull their cannons and other heavy weaponry. Their unit was not a calvary unit, but they used horses for scouting, trips to town, and on reconnoitering assignments.

He waved over one of the men who handled the livestock to question him about the farrier. He learned the man's name was Duncan Wilson, and he didn't live in Mexico. Rather, he farmed some acres between Mexico and Moberly, where he maintained a herd of horses and mules.

"Have you seen him in any other area of the camp?"

"No, sir. You sure can't miss him if'n he did go somewhere else."

The soldier made a valid point. Duncan Wilson, due to his size, could not slip in and out of anywhere without being noticed. His bulk also kept him from being nimble. He shifted his weight from side to side as he walked, like the animal he resembled.

Later in the day, Cormac followed another civilian who seemed to be making himself comfortable inside the camp. The man was a craftsman in leather. He was peddling all types of leather goods, including belts, bridles, reins, stirrups, and harnesses. He would see the camp's artillery due to his task of sizing the harnesses that hitched the mules and donkeys to it.

Cormac watched the leather craftsman being led out of camp by one of the sergeants. He'd speak to the sergeant privately and request that the leather worker be accompanied at all times within the camp. He'd located rules outlining the procedure, but the camp had grown lax about enforcing them. He'd also talk to Captain Oliver about improving the administration of these rules and others that protected the camp's secrets.

Later than night, Cormac walked from campfire to campfire. As he made his rounds and questioned the men, he was heartened by the pride they took in their jobs, their missions and assignments. Morale was good.

Who in this camp could pull off the role of a spy? How was the spy getting the information on their missions? Cormac needed to determine which men had been on a mission that wasn't fired upon. The enemy wouldn't fire on a squad that included their informant, would they? Such information might lead him to the culprit.

He would gather records telling which men and officers were associated with each mission. Then he'd interview the men casually, asking what they remembered about each ambush. Cormac could say the officers were trying to learn from each incident. His goal was to find out every bit of intelligence possible, without giving any indication he was searching for a spy.

He would have to keep an eye on vendors, peddlers, the farrier, and any tool suppliers. Gunpowder and military supplies came directly off the railroads, which was one reason General

Pope and his command were assigned here. They were guarding the railways, which shipped munitions, boots, uniforms, hats, pistols, and rifles to the camp.

Cormac did not know the source of every vegetable and piece of fruit for their meals. Were they purchased from local farmers? He would have to find those answers too.

That afternoon, reporting to Captain Oliver, Cormac snapped to attention and feared his nervousness was visible. While he gave his verbal report, he struggled to calm his shaking legs, which made standing at attention difficult.

"What's wrong, O'Malley?"

"Sorry, sir. My investigation is taking longer than I expected. Lives depend upon me getting the information, and it's slow to gather."

"At ease, O'Malley. I've added to your pressure by ordering you not to write anything down. If there is a spy here, written notes might endanger you. You're making good observations, and you're forming a plan of action."

"Begging your pardon, sir, but I need some type of code. I'm not sure I can keep all of this in my mind."

"You have an incredible mind, but I will agree for you to make up some type of secret code for record keeping. Keep it simple. Associated with people or things you can relate to that would be meaningless to someone else. If the spy should happen to read what you've written, he must not realize it's a code. Do you understand?"

"Yes, sir."

"Your life may depend upon it. Dismissed."

When Cormac exited Captain Oliver's tent, he saw Colonel Michaels standing in a group of other officers. He watched the colonel for a few minutes. The simple act of questioning Colonel Michaels's actions could be considered an act of treason. Yet, Cormac continued his observation.

The man seemed as normal as one would expect for a colonel.

Why had Michaels dismissed his concerns about outsiders being in the camp? Was he distracted by other concerns? Could he be a man promoted beyond his capabilities? Or part of a spy ring?

When Colonel Michaels looked over and frowned at him, Cormac's gut twisted. Did he see a twinge of hatred in the colonel's eyes? Or were his nerves getting the best of him?

Cormac strode quickly away. He could not call attention to himself with the colonel. Nor with anyone. Not while he was investigating.

Chapter 20

Enid Connolly

Once again, Enid was attending worship services while her mother was working. It was odd to have services on a Friday morning, but Pastor Fitzgerald had surprised his parishioners with his offer of one more service before moving to another town along his regular circuit. He couldn't wait until Sunday to do it, so the Jennison family offered to accommodate everyone in their home, and they quickly spread word of another opportunity to worship.

Her mother had allowed Enid to escape her duties to attend but couldn't see her own way clear. Enid was convinced Mama worked too hard, and she'd offered to switch places since it was her mother's turn to worship. Enid could take care of the cooking duties. However, her mother wouldn't allow it.

The Jennison home was filled with Union soldiers, and they were mostly dressed alike. Nearly half of the service passed before Enid picked out Lieutenant O'Malley, otherwise known as "Mr. Green Eyes," among them.

Didn't they have their own chaplain? Not that she was complaining about them, but it seemed odd to her that the number of worshipping soldiers grew every time there was a service. Why were they here? Who was telling them about these services?

Guilt panged Enid. The Lord would want her to share her service with everyone alike. Crowded homes for services might prod the congregation to move forward with building their own church.

She said a quick prayer, asking God to put her and Green Eyes together if He wished her to assist the lieutenant with information about the trustworthiness of local people. If she could help prevent attacks on the Union squads by providing that, she would be contributing to the cause.

She was well aware of the allure of this handsome man. With her red hair, she was drawn to others who shared the same hue. Nevertheless, such a man wouldn't be interested in her. He was from a far-off place. Most likely, he would return to his part of the country one day if he survived the war.

Did he have a sweetheart waiting for him at home? Enid took a deep breath and willed herself to be patient and pay attention to Pastor Fitzgerald.

When the sermon concluded, the Kellys' newborn let out a wail that caused the congregation to chuckle. Since Mrs. Kelly sat next to her, Enid stood to help her get the squalling child out of the room. When they reached the kitchen, Enid suggested Mrs. Kelly take a chair near the fireplace to nurse the baby, then went to the pump and pumped a glass of water for her.

With mother and baby settled, Enid stood on the threshold between the kitchen and the living room to observe the end of the service.

At the conclusion of the final prayer, she turned to make her way back to Mrs. Kelly. A voice called out, "Enid?"

She spun around and realized it was Mrs. Jennison calling her. She waved a hand in her direction as she struggled through the crowd. What did Mrs. Jennison need from her?

When Mrs. Jennison drew close, Enid realized that Lieutenant O'Malley trailed behind her. Did he have something to do with Mrs. Jennison calling her? Her face flushed at the thought.

"Miss Enid Connolly. It is my pleasure to introduce you to Lieutenant Cormac O'Malley. They assigned him to the Union encampment west of town under the command of General Pope."

Enid bobbed a curtsey. Cormac, she contemplated. *That's an Old Country name, for sure. Could be he is Welsh instead of Irish.* Both nationalities had a propensity for red hair.

Mrs. Jennison turned to Lieutenant O'Malley. "Miss Connolly works with her mother, Mrs. Mary Connolly, at the home of John P. Clark. Mrs. Connolly is their cook. Miss Connolly assists her mother in the kitchen."

Cormac bowed and then smiled down at her. "I had the pleasure of enjoying a fine dinner at Mr. Clark's house a few nights ago. Miss Connolly worked hard to make sure those of us in attendance received a good meal and good service. Thank you for the introduction, Mrs. Jennison. I'm honored to become formally acquainted with Miss Connolly."

Mrs. Jennison turned her attention to other attendees, which left Enid in a panic at her departure. When she glanced at Cormac, he smiled at her. This turned her anxiety into an unexpected shyness. She'd never been introduced to a man her mother didn't know. What should she say? Or should she speak at all?

"I hope you don't find me too forward, Miss Connolly. I noticed you at an earlier service. Then, when I saw you at the Clark house, I was flustered as we'd not been formally introduced."

His unwavering attention made her forget everyone else in the house. "So nice to meet you, Lieutenant O'Malley. It was my pleasure to serve you at the Clark house."

"I noticed all those in service at the Clark house are white people. At least, everyone working the evening I was a guest. Mr. Clark does not appear to own slaves. Is that correct?"

"Yes, sir. Mr. Clark does not believe God intended for any man to own another man, woman, or child."

"Is this why he is considered a loyal Union man?"

She nodded. "That is at least part of it. The men who visit appear to accept that he is loyal. Most women are not privy to such conversations."

"But you are by serving the guests throughout their visit to the home."

"Generally, that is true."

"Do you believe he is a loyal Union man?"

Enid stared at him for a moment. Was this man asking for the opinion of a mere woman? A servant and a woman?

"Please." He lifted his hands. "I'd like to hear your thoughts."

"In this town, we have Unionists and secessionists," she said. "Only a handful of citizens refrain from expressing their opinion. I would place Mr. Clark firmly in the Unionist category."

He lowered his voice. "That is a great help to me." Cormac shuffled from foot to foot, then returned to speaking in a normal volume. "Is it possible for me to call on you sometime? Perhaps take you for a walk?"

She furrowed her brow at his suggestion.

"With a chaperone accompanying us, of course," he added.

She wrung her hands, then became aware of what she was doing and forced them down at her sides. "I can't say whether that would be acceptable. No one has ever called on me before."

"I understand. Then it would be my pleasure to meet your mother, the wonderful cook. What about your father? I should introduce myself to him as well."

Enid shook her head. "My father passed to his reward when I was young. If you come and meet my mother, I imagine she'll want more information about you, but she'll feed you nice pastries or cakes when she questions you."

He smiled, revealing evenly spaced white teeth. "I look forward to it. Perhaps after your mother has been properly introduced to me, she will consent to my calling on you. When would be most convenient for me to visit with her?"

"She is off Monday afternoons and Wednesday mornings. Otherwise, she works in the kitchen of the Clark house. You can come to the kitchen door if you wish. Stop by anytime it suits you."

"I hope my own schedule will rapidly lead me to the door of the Clark kitchen. Good day, Miss Connolly. It was a pleasure."

He made a slight bow.

"Good day, Lieutenant O'Malley."

He turned and joined the other soldiers, who were talking to Pastor Fitzgerald. When Enid walked into the kitchen, her face flamed again when she discovered half of the women in town had been listening to their conversation.

As their gossiping tongues converged on her, Enid thanked God for the lieutenant's interest, even if only to pass him the bits she overheard at the Clark house. Perhaps she could provide information to him that will help save lives.

Three days later, as Enid was kneading bread dough, men's voices drew near the kitchen. Mr. Clark had guests and business acquaintances in the house frequently, so she didn't think twice about it. Many of his guests asked for a tour of the extensive gardens and surrounding grounds.

Caleb, Jeremiah's younger brother, opened the kitchen door and called, "You have a visitor, Mrs. Connolly."

"Mother's in the garden, Caleb. Would you run and get her? I'll make myself presentable for company."

Enid was up to her elbows in dough, so she walked to the wash basin to clean her hands. Many women from town popped by on occasion, so why hadn't Caleb announced the name of the visitor? Odd, actually.

She was curious to identify her mother's visitor, so as she wiped her hands, she turned toward the door. Once she recognized Lieutenant O'Malley, she gasped.

Cormac removed his hat and bowed toward Enid. "It is such a pleasure to be in your company again, Miss Connolly."

Although surprised, Enid was excited to see him again and have a chance to admire his tall stature and fine manners. When she realized she was staring at him, she put down the towel and moved toward him.

"Good afternoon, Lieutenant." Enid waved at her apron. "You must excuse my attire. Cooking can be a messy occupation."

He bowed to her. "With great rewards for those lucky enough to sample your completed wares."

She chuckled. "You, sir, are a man who has clearly kissed the Blarney stone."

He was forming a response when her mother entered the kitchen with an apron full of greens from the garden. Cormac spun on his heel and stepped over to assist her.

Enid's mother, after being thoroughly charmed by Lieutenant O'Malley, allowed the lieutenant to stroll with her daughter around the grounds of the Clark home. Caleb, following three paces behind them, was not pleased with his assignment until bribed with a slice of pie upon a successful conclusion.

Enid and Cormac walked side by side in silence for a moment. The yeasty aroma of bread was in the air, thanks to her labors. That fragrance mixed with a slight scent of cedar from the trees surrounding the house. Did he appreciate the aromas? She could not bring herself to ask.

She considered taking his arm, but he had not offered it, perhaps to keep her mother happy by maintaining a respectable distance between them.

To break the silence between them, she settled on giving him a compliment.

"I've never known my mother take to someone as fast as she has taken to you," Enid said. "It must be the uniform."

Cormac chuckled at her joke, verifying that he possessed a pleasant sense of humor. Enid had previously experienced his personality as a serious soldier at church and the dinner party.

"I believe I've accomplished my mission today. My aim was to make a positive impression upon your mother, without seeming insincere."

"You succeeded."

He smiled down at her. "I must confess that, as a man who is half Welsh, only half of my heritage would kiss the Blarney stone. The Irish half."

"I figured that red hair of yours put you somewhere near my people."

"It was your hair that first caught my attention." Cormac gestured toward it. "The moment I spotted it, I wanted to meet you. That day in church, when my unit was called out of the service was the second time I'd been able to admire you. Then God played a trick on me and placed me inside the home where you work. Once again, I could admire, but society dictated that I say nothing."

"When did you first see me? Not during church, when your unit had to leave?"

"No. I delivered a message to Mr. Clark from

Colonel Michaels before that. I spotted you in the garden near the house. The sun was setting." He smiled. "You and the garden captured my attention."

"I recognized you in church, but I couldn't remember where I'd noticed you before." She glanced up at him. "I believe I saw you when you delivered that message. Briefly, perhaps. I was in the garden searching for flowers and believed someone's eyes were upon me. When I looked up, you turned and walked away."

"It embarrassed me that you'd caught me staring."

Enid chuckled. "Mrs. Jennison seemed ready to burst with excitement when she realized your desired introduction was to me."

"That day, you said you've never had a suitor to call?"

"True."

"Are the local men blind?"

It was her turn to chuckle. "I'm but a servant. Even though I am a good cook, that skill hasn't tempted any suitors."

"You give me hope that I might be considered suitable to call."

"This type of conversation must take place with my mother."

"Then I shall discuss it with her." He stopped and turned to her. "But only if you desire further acquaintance."

She blushed. "You need to become more acquainted with me. I have many faults. Upon closer examination, you might find I have too many."

He smiled and motioned for her to walk again. "I know you are a hardworking woman who loves God and loves her mother. With these attributes, I happily anticipate being introduced to each and every fault."

"Here is a fault," Enid said. "Before Mrs. Jennison formally introduced us, I eavesdropped on your dinner conversation. I overheard you asking about George Hunter the night you were a guest of Mr. Clark."

Cormac shrugged. "It would be natural for you to be aware of such a conversation when you're serving guests."

"This is forward of me, but George and his sweetheart are friends of mine. He is a loyal Union man. He doesn't possess the ability to hide his feelings. His reactions are displayed prominently on his countenance."

"That is a good thing for you to pass on to me, Miss Connolly."

"A group of rebels kidnapped him this past December, but he escaped."

"Is that so? I was not informed of that incident. Who were the kidnappers?"

"A group of rowdy locals. Young men that are Southern leaning. They were in jail for weeks and recently had a hearing, then a trial in front of our circuit judge. They were all sentenced to prison for various amounts of time. Some of them are out now. Causing trouble again."

"Thank you for telling me your thoughts about George. I appreciate your opinion, and I'd like more information about others who visit the camp. Would you consider helping me with that?"

"Who are you inquiring about?"

"Anyone visiting the camp. Especially someone who makes you uncomfortable or acts suspicious in some way."

"I'll do my best to help you," Enid straightened with pride at her actions. "If I'm not familiar with them particularly, I can ask others about them. What information do you need?"

"Their names, which way they lean in this conflict. The impression they make on you and other people in town. But I have to ask, why would you do this? What is your interest?"

"A man can join the fight to save the Union, but a woman can only watch the men march away. They leave us to sit on our porches. We can knit socks and roll bandages. I'd like to take part in actively helping the Union. To give you information about townspeople is easy for me and might help you and the Union Army."

He patted her hand. "You are full of joyful surprises, Miss Connolly. I'm delighted the Lord brought us together."

Chapter 21

Liesl

After all that happened with Kurt the previous night, Liesl was glad to have something to do in the morning. Nicole had phoned and asked to meet at the flip house. It was a welcome distraction for Liesl's swirling mind and her heart filled with churning emotions. She needed to pray about Kurt and define her feelings. What was God's plan for them? What kind of relationship should they build?

She wanted to tell Nicole about the kiss. But was she ready to receive Nicole's opinion about it?

And what about Justin? Was he putting down roots in town to be with her? If so, what were her feelings about that? Her feelings about him?

No, she needed to set aside some time to contemplate her feelings about the men in her life before she got Nicole involved. She had enough going on with her own thoughts without adding Nicole to the mix.

Besides, Liesl anticipated what Nicole would think about Kurt. She'd say, "I told you he still loved you."

That girl was always right.

She drove to the west side of town and parked near the little bungalow Nicole and Marc had bought. The business partners occasionally purchased a house in need of repairs and "flipped it" to return it to the market to sell. It was a win-win. The house became marketable and rose in value, as well as increasing the property value of nearby neighbors.

Liesl looked it over. With peeling paint, dilapidated siding, and landscaping out of control, the little house had a spooky vibe going. It was more someone's nightmare than a dream house, but she'd never say that to Nicole. Who was she to judge?

Nicole could make something beautiful out of almost anything. Given time, sweat equity, and some money, Nicole and Marc would get this ready to sell and could turn a profit.

Liesl spotted her friend in the side yard, waving her toward the back. The drone of a mower or other piece of equipment seemed to be coming from there.

Shouting over the noise, Nicole said, "I'm glad you could come here today. Don't you love it?" She gestured toward the house.

Liesl chuckled and shouted back, "The word *love* is a bit strong. Ah . . . perhaps *potential* is the descriptor I'd use. As in, 'This house has potential.'"

"Always a writer."

Liesl cut her a sly glance. "Guilty. However, it does have potential. So, 'Lead on, Macduff.'"

"I don't know what that means."

"It's a butchered phrase from Macbeth. Originally, the phrase was, 'Lay on, Macduff,' which meant 'go ahead and fight with me.' I prefer you forget the fighting and lead me to whatever you want me to see. I'm curious about the noisy equipment back there."

The noise level rose as they walked to the back of the bungalow. Liesl struggled to keep her face neutral as she observed the house's condition and its forest of a backyard. What seemed broken down and damaged to her was an opportunity for Nicole.

Nicole had a gift in conjuring magical transformations of houses. As her best friend, Liesl supported those renovations. Super Woman Nicole would come out as a winner with the house, because flipping was one of her superpowers.

Marc was riding inside a miniature piece of construction equipment. It had a scoop on the front, and Marc manipulated it by pushing and pulling levers. He maneuvered the machine to push brush and overgrowth into an enormous pile.

Liesl waved at Marc. To Nicole, she asked, "What is that thing?"

"A skid-something. Whatever it is, it's working great. He rents it from a friend who hauls it on his trailer. His friend needed the trailer for something else. Today was the first day he could deliver it here."

They stood and watched as Marc finished clearing the brush and overgrown shrubs from the backyard. Then he turned the machine toward a ramshackle wooden shed.

"Is he going to knock down that shed?"

"Yes," Nicole said. "Before it falls down and hurts someone."

They stood transfixed as man and machine crushed the shed. In a matter of moments, there was nothing but debris. Using the oversized bucket on the front of his equipment, Marc scooped it full of detritus and then drove it over to the brush pile. On his third or fourth scoop, he pulled up dirt and something else. Something resembling a group of brown sticks.

Why were there so many sticks in the dirt under that old shed?

Nicole and Liesl stared at them until Nicole screamed and jumped back, as if in fright.

Startled, Liesl stepped closer to the scoop, and as she approached, she waved for Marc to stop.

He cut off the engine and scrambled off. "What's wrong?"

"I don't know. I'm trying to figure it out." Liesl couldn't spot anything in the scoop that was scream worthy. She strode back to Nicole to calm her down and divert her attention. She put her arm around her friend's shoulder. "Nic, what is it? Marc and I don't understand."

At that moment, Marc let out a yelp of surprise. "Oh, no!"

Liesl turned to see his face twisted in horror.

"What is it?" Liesl asked, in an exacerbated tone. "A snake?"

Marc turned to her, horror still painting his face, and pointed to the brown sticks clinging to the teeth of the bucket. "Bones, I think. Human bones."

Liesl focused on the edge of the bucket. There were scraps of old, moldy leather alongside the brown sticks.

Not brown sticks.

That was a boot, and those were bones of a human leg.

She almost screamed, "Call 911."

Marc stared at her as if she spoke in a foreign language.

"Do it, Marc. 911. Tell them we've found human bones."

Marc blinked at her then nodded and pulled his phone out of his jeans.

Liesl stepped between Nicole and the bones, with her back to the grisly sight. Nicole remained pale, and now she was sweaty. Was she going into shock?

"Why don't we sit down?" Liesl glanced around for somewhere to sit. Spotting no lawn furniture, she said, "Right here. In the grass. It'll be fine."

Nicole looked weak but didn't move.

Liesl pulled her down to the ground, so they were both in a sitting position. "Now, lie down."

Nicole lay back without question, moving in slow motion.

"Slow, deep breaths, Nicole." Liesl grabbed her friend's legs and hauled them into her lap. "Slow breaths." Nicole's feet were not high enough over her head, so Liesl placed one foot on the top of each of her shoulders.

Marc was arguing with the emergency dispatcher. "They're too big to be dog bones . . . Could they be horse bones? . . . Lady, how many horses wear leather boots? We found a pair of those along with the bones."

Liesl waved to Marc as he continued the debate. "Ask them to send an ambulance. Nicole's going into shock."

He gave her a thumbs-up. "We need an ambulance or a paramedic . . . No, not the person we *dug up,* but one of us who found the bones is going into shock." He continued by giving specifics about Nicole's age and general health.

Nicole's feet remained on Liesl's shoulders. Liesl patted her at intervals, keeping Nicole's focus on her. She searched her memory for anything else she could do.

Lee. She needed to get in touch with Lee. After fishing her phone out of her purse, she called the high school office.

The secretary who answered Liesl's call was a friend, and she listened to her urgent ramblings, promising to hunt down Lee and arrange for him to call her for more details.

A moment later, an approaching siren lifted Liesl's spirits. Help was coming.

A lanky patrol officer rushed to Nicole. "Is she hurt, Liesl?"

Liesl recognized the officer as Dennis Bates. He'd been a class behind her and Nicole in school. "Dennis, I think she's in shock. She seems better since she's had a few minutes on the ground with her feet up."

"The ambulance will get here soon. I was closer." Dennis pulled gloves from his pocket, pulled them on, and then kneeled on the ground to place a hand on Nicole's forehead. "She doesn't appear to have a fever, but she is sweaty. You're right about the shock."

He took Nicole's pulse and smiled. "Strong and steady."

Nicole spoke up. "I can hear you, you know."

Liesl smiled. "It appears our patient is finding her way back to her usual sarcastic self."

Dennis took out his phone and turned on the flashlight. He checked her pupils for a response. "Your eyes are good. You remain on the ground here, and I'll pull a blanket out of my patrol car. You should stay warm."

Marc, who had hovered nearby, approached. "I can get a blanket out of my car. I always carry several."

Dennis looked up at Marc. "Are you well enough to do that?"

Liesl said, "I saw no signs of shock with him."

"Then go get all of your blankets. Thanks, Marc."

Dennis turned his attention to Liesl. "How are you handling this?"

"This is easy-peasy compared to escaping a murderer intent on killing me." Dennis had been one of the first responders to her house in that situation.

He shook his head. "Some things aren't funny."

"No, but experiences like that give you perspective. This is a shock, but not nearly as bad as someone trying to burn the house down around you."

Marc returned with his blankets. They covered Nicole from toes to her nose.

Dennis turned to Liesl. "Wait here with her. I'm going to check out this discovery."

"I'm not leaving."

Marc piped up with, "Neither am I."

Dennis stood and walked to the bones, examining them from a distance for a moment. "Those are definitely bones. Appear to be human, but I can't guarantee that. I haven't had much training in this area."

He returned and kneeled beside Nicole. "Fresh bones are usually white. Those are a dark brown. I'll bet they've been in the ground a long time. I understand bones buried in dirt pull in minerals from the ground. That makes them darker than bones not exposed to soil. We'll know more after the experts examine them."

Dennis stood as the ambulance arrived. "I'll let these experts help you now, Nicole. My job is to rope off the area." He pointed to the fence on his left. "Note the neighbors gathered over there since my arrival."

Liesl called out as he walked away, "Thanks for your help, Dennis."

When the paramedics reached Nicole, Liesl and Marc moved aside. Liesl's phone rang as she stood. It was Lee.

She explained the events to Lee, adding that Nicole was shaken but was improving. She promised to update Lee on her condition and let him know if the paramedics were going to release her or take her to a nearby urgent care facility. Mexico's hospital was temporarily closed due to financial problems.

Marc stood in a spot with a view of the police working to protect the bones. Liesl approached and asked, "Was there ever a cemetery near here? Maybe the headstones crumbled away or were moved, but no one moved the caskets."

"It's possible," he said. "I can review the results of the title search made when we bought the place."

"I'm looking for a legitimate explanation for the bones." She didn't understand all the details about titles but was confident Mark did. If he found anything that might explain the remains, he'd tell the police.

Marc shifted his weight and gritted his teeth. "There may not be a legitimate explanation. It could be a murder scene."

"I hope not." She spotted more officers milling around the site. One of them was Hector. She didn't approach him. Had he been called in to work this as a detective, or did he respond off-duty to the call for help?

A moment later, Hector walked over to her. "What kind of adventure are you involved in now?"

Liesl grimaced. "I came to admire Nicole's new flip house. That was all the adventure I wanted today."

"Did you find these bones?"

"No, Marc used that thing." She pointed to his small excavator.

"That's a skid-steer loader," Hector said.

"Whatever. He used it to knock down a shed. That part went really well. It was while he was clearing away the debris that Nicole screamed.

She immediately recognized what the bones were. It took the rest of us much longer."

Hector pulled out a notebook and pen. "I'm going to need a statement from you."

"Of course you are. It's that kind of day."

When she finished her statement, Liesl checked on the patient. The paramedics agreed to release Nicole to her residence for bed rest. She refused their offer of a ride in the ambulance by saying her *dear friend* would take her home.

Liesl called Lee and advised she was taking Nicole home. He said he would meet her after he arranged for a substitute, so he could take the rest of the day off.

As Liesl helped Nicole to the car, she found it comforting to hear the voices of all the emergency responders and their radio chatter. Was that God's way of soothing their frayed nerves after finding those bones? Maybe it was His way to let them know they never faced a crisis alone. She prayed that the soul who had belonged to those bones had found its way to heaven.

Chapter 22

Kurt

Kurt pulled up to the front of Nicole's house and smiled when he spotted Liesl's car in the driveway.

Hector had called him about the bones. When he mentioned Liesl left the scene to take Nicole home, Kurt scrambled to get to the Smith house.

It didn't surprise him when Liesl opened the door. Nicole should be lying down.

"You beat Lee here," Liesl said. "I expect him any moment." She stepped back to give him room to enter.

"I have an inside source with the police . . . and a siren."

They shared a grin.

"Is Nicole okay?"

"Yes," Liesl said. "She had a shock, but she's better."

"Hector said you helped her. I'm glad she had you there."

He took in her dirty jeans and stressed appearance. "You okay?"

"I'm good. All I need is a shower and a change of clothes. I sat on the ground with Nicole after she showed symptoms of shock. Otherwise, I'm fine."

"Is she okay with me saying hi?"

"Probably. She's lying on the couch in the living room. She's too stubborn to get into bed."

Nicole called from the living room, "I can hear you, you know."

Liesl called back, "I'm not saying anything that's not true. And I would say it to your face."

Once he'd eyeballed Nicole, Kurt felt relief. "You look good, Nicole. I'm sorry I missed all the excitement. It might interest you that I reviewed the security footage from Donnie Davis's place this morning."

Liesl asked, "Did you find anything?"

He debated whether he should discuss it, but decided he would. "I might have found something interesting in the footage."

Nicole asked, "What?"

"It was from the camera covering the employee entrance. I went back an entire month. Nothing unusual happens until the night before the Ag Museum break-in."

Liesl tugged on his arm. "Spill! What does it show?"

He smiled at her impatience. Tugging his arm was proof she'd softened toward him.

"Someone went inside Mexico Security Service the night before the break-in, stayed thirty minutes, and then left. Didn't capture any vehicle on the footage."

Liesl asked, "Can you tell who it was?"

"No. Donnie has excellent cameras on his building, but the footage is still grainy. I could only get an idea of size. Nothing related to gender or other details of the person who entered. I checked with the only employee on duty that night. She was already at her monitoring station working with client needs when the unidentified person walked in, but she didn't see him."

"How could you confirm that?" Nicole asked. "Maybe she's in on it."

"Donnie pulled up information on a call that came in during that time. Her keystrokes on her computer verified she was working during the call, which was concurrent with the entry. It's possible she could be in on it, but she was where she claimed to be for at least most of the time the other person was inside."

Liesl pointed at Nicole, who was attempting to sit upright on the couch. "You lie back down. Lee's going to be here any minute."

"Bossy boots."

"And proud of it." Liesl turned to Kurt. "No internal cameras picked up the intruder?"

"Donnie doesn't have internal cameras. That's why he verified his employee was working by confirming it through her computer."

"So you don't know who it was, but could you tell what they wanted? What they went in for?"

"Not exactly. I speculate they were looking

for the security code for the Ag Museum. The night employee works in a room behind Donnie's office. If you remember the design of the building, there is the reception desk, computer, and two monitors near the entrance."

"Yes," Liesl said.

"The official employee was in a room down that long hall, past Donnie's office. Someone could go in the back door, access the computer in the front, and leave through the same back door. It's possible the night shift worker could be unaware someone else was in the building."

From the couch Nicole said, "That sends shivers down my spine. I'd hate to be in a building that allowed access like that."

"I called Forensics and asked them to accelerate the request for a review of that reception computer. Thanks to Donnie's cooperation, I didn't have to get a warrant. They should be able to examine it and determine if it was used that night. Also, they should be able to tell what information was accessed."

"Good deal," Liesl said. "What about fingerprints?"

"Too many people have used that computer keyboard. Best info is on the computer itself."

"Is there a code to access the information on the computer?"

"Yes. An employee code. They're checking for that. Also, a code has to be used to get in that back door. Someone had access to the code for that door."

"That should narrow it down."

"You would think so, but that's not true. Donnie hasn't changed the code for over a year. A former employee would have the code. We're checking on former employees now, in addition to current employees."

"Does this implicate Donnie?"

"Not exactly. He's been cooperative. But until we figure this out, he's still a suspect."

"Are you serious?" Nicole revealed anger in her tone. "Donnie has been a mess with wives and girlfriends, but he's trying hard to turn his life around. He's been going to AA meetings and to counseling with his second ex-wife. Not to remarry or anything, but to work on having a friendship while they co-parent their little girl."

"I'm aware of all that, Nicole." Kurt held both hands up in surrender. "He and I were never close in high school, but I don't want to add any more problems to his life. He understands I have to investigate. You're more upset about it than he is right now."

Nicole blew out a breath. "I'm sorry. It's been a tough day. It's hard to have my friend be a suspect in this investigation."

"I feel the same, but with a twist," Liesl said. "Aunt Suzanne was killed by one of her best friends; it hurts to suspect another friend in another crime. This hits close to home."

Kurt held up an index finger. "No more talk about the case. We still have an investigation to complete. I promise we'll get to the truth by being fair and diligent."

When Lee came in the back door of the house, Kurt saw it as saving him from further inquisition. *Thank you, Lord.*

Outside Nicole's house, Kurt opened the door of his assigned vehicle as Dr. Johnson pulled up and parked behind him. He sighed. Dr. Johnson remained a viable suspect in the Ag Museum investigation. He was also a highly respected physician, and Kurt considered him a friend. How awkward was this?

Kurt strode toward the doctor, hoping he wouldn't convey any concerns. "How are you doing, Doc? Here to see Nicole?"

They shook hands.

"Liesl thought it might be a good idea for me to examine Nicole after her shock today." Dr. Johnson turned and looked at the house. "I hope she'll be back to her normal self soon."

"I was in there for just a few minutes, but she seemed less energetic than usual. Other than that, normal, but I'm not a trained medical professional."

Dr. Johnson snagged his medical bag off his

back passenger seat. "I'd best get in there and do my job. I'm later than I intended to be, but I had to stich up a resident at the homeless shelter. Good seeing you, Kurt."

Kurt drove away pondering the fact that Dr. Johnson's volunteer work on the board and at the homeless shelter was what made him a suspect in the case. How could a good man like that be wrapped up in criminal activity?

Kurt skipped lunch to be on time for his scheduled appointment with Mrs. Sizemore. Although Mexico was a five-minute town, meaning it only took five minutes to cross from one side to the other, he couldn't risk being late.

Mrs. Sizemore was a significant and formidable part of the community. If he got on her bad side, she could whisper into the ears of powerful people and get him tossed off the police force.

He also doubted she'd forgiven him for breaking Liesl's heart years ago. She could wipe away all the current progress he'd made with Liesl. With the passing of Liesl's aunt, Mrs. Sizemore was more influential than ever to Liesl. He couldn't risk getting on her bad side.

When he arrived at the woman's palatial home, he sat in his cruiser to straighten his tie and check for debris in his teeth. The situation made him feel like a boy on an errand, begging her for a favor.

With a deep breath, he tried to relax. He needed to do three things to come out of this successfully: ask his questions politely, listen to any pearls of wisdom she might deem to share, then thank her profusely for her time and cooperation. He could do it.

A housekeeper ushered him in and led him to a sitting room adorned with a wall of windows, suggesting he take a seat. The room had a beautiful view across the rolling hills of the former Green Estate. The all-white décor reminded him of Mrs. Sizemore herself: sterile, devoid of color, chilly. He eyed the white couches and remained standing.

Five minutes later, Mrs. Sizemore breezed into the room. As usual, her hair was immaculately arranged and clothing expertly tailored. The diamond-encrusted watch on her wrist also caught his attention.

"Thank you for meeting with me, Mrs. Sizemore."

She peered down her nose at him and offered him coffee or tea. He declined, afraid his sipping skills would not rise to her high standards.

She gestured for him to take a seat and he gave in, choosing a chair across from the white couch. At least with a chair, there was less fabric for him to ruin.

"Thank you for agreeing to see me, Mrs. Sizemore."

She harrumphed. "Am I a suspect in something, Detective Hunter?"

He smiled. "Oh, no ma'am. We are contacting every Agricultural Museum board member for his or her thoughts and impressions about the break-in. Since you play a critical part in the museum's success, I'd like to gather information you may have about its operation. You've generously donated your time and efforts to make the museum as strong as possible."

Mrs. Sizemore seemed pleased with his remarks. Flattery might be a successful tactic if he didn't overdo it.

"I'm glad you've evaluated my efforts correctly, Detective." She stared at him, adding no further comment until she said, "Go on. I don't have all day for this."

"Yes, ma'am. Please tell me about the other board members. Is there someone who gets under your skin? Someone who makes you question their motives for serving on the board?"

"Yes. When you asked to talk to me, there was no doubt in my mind that it was associated with this situation you've been handling at the Agricultural Museum."

"Yes, ma'am."

"There's an upstart on the board. I've been wondering about her motives since she arrived back in town."

Kurt asked, "Who are you describing?" even

230

though he understood who she was throwing under the bus.

"That woman from *Moberly*. She left many years ago. Now she waltzes in from California and thinks she's *it*. That we should all kowtow to her. I'm clueless as to why she's on the board. What does she know about agriculture?"

Kurt held his face steady while clearing his mind of comments, such as, *Mrs. Sizemore, what do you know about agriculture? You have a gardener.* Instead, he said, "Let me clarify, Mrs. Sizemore. You're talking about Mrs. Constantine, correct?"

"Of course I am." When she was satisfied she'd expressed her displeasure, she continued. "Ask yourself, what does she know about this community?"

"This is information I'm interested in. You mentioned she's from Moberly. That's about forty miles from Mexico. Has she ever lived here before this?"

"No."

"Any idea why she chose to move here?"

Mrs. Sizemore pulled a face. "When Wonneman's House of Flowers closed, she heard about it and moved here to open her own florist's shop. It didn't last long. She didn't understand customer service then and still doesn't. She shouldn't be on the board."

"Do you think the other board members share your concerns?"

"I know they do." She ran her hand across the couch material. "William Van de Berg and I have had numerous conversations about her. According to the museum director, Dr. Barnes, that woman promised to make a sizable donation to the museum. It was an absolute bribe to get on the board, but she's made no contributions."

Kurt reached for his notebook and pen. "Do you mind if I take notes? These are important points you're making."

She waved a bedazzled hand. "Be my guest."

After he pulled out his notebook and pen, Kurt asked, "Can you speak about her actions on the board? Besides the fact she hasn't made the promised donation?"

"She's voted against several proposals and did that soon after her investiture. I'm going to make a new proposal at the next meeting to upgrade our security. I'm worried she'll vote against it."

"I'll be happy to come and talk to your board about the need for increased security if you'd like."

She clasped her hands together. "What a wonderful idea. Thank you, Detective. I'll take you up on that."

"I value your thoughts on this more than you realize." He scribbled on his notepad for a moment. "Is Dr. Johnson a concern to you at all?"

"Dr. Johnson." She stiffened. "What about Dr. Johnson? He's an exemplary physician in this community. He's one of our own."

"I meant related to the break-in, of course."

"You're wasting your time investigating him."

"He helps at the homeless shelter and the Butterfly House," Kurt said. "This exposes him to people with a criminal past. Is there anything you question about his behavior or associations?"

She looked at him askance. In a sarcastic tone, she said, "*No.* You shouldn't either. He's an excellent doctor. He does his best to keep this community healthy while struggling with the current lack of hospital facility."

"The town has suffered from the closing of the hospital. It's causing citizens some rough patches."

"To say the least," Mrs. Sizemore said.

"He wouldn't assist a thief to break into the museum or give anyone information that would help someone with nefarious intentions?"

"Absolutely not." She pressed her lips together into a thin line. "Let me save you some time, Detective. Without question, Liesl is aboveboard. Same with Mr. Van de Berg, Barbara Burson, and Dr. Johnson. I am also above suspicion."

"Of course, Mrs. Sizemore."

"Those I've listed, including me, work hard for charities in this town. Spend your time investigating museum volunteers and the cleaning staff, or following up with someone like Mrs. Constantine. She's not originally from this community, and she's made promises to the board chairman on which she has not delivered." Mrs. Sizemore rose from the couch.

"Yes, ma'am." Kurt shut his notebook. He wondered if Mrs. Constantine made other undelivered promises. Something else must have happened to create the strong feelings experienced by Mrs. Sizemore.

He stood, realizing his time at the Sizemore home had abruptly come to an end. "Thank you. Your help with the investigation has been invaluable. I appreciate your time."

He all but bowed to her as he made his escape.

Chapter 23

Liesl

Liesl reached the back door of her house ready to kick off her shoes and kick off the sadness she'd carried home. The bone discovery had emotionally drained her and left her physically wrung out. Inside, the fragrance of fresh paint and freshly cut lumber greeted her, but there were no sounds from the construction crew. It must be after five o'clock.

Her phone rang, and she saw it was Justin. They were supposed to have dinner this evening. All she really wanted to do was curl up with a good book.

She took the call and told Justin about her day. Then she begged off their dinner date. Although he wasn't pleased, he understood she wasn't up for an evening out.

A few minutes later, she spotted Mrs. Zimmerman exiting Joey's apartment with her hands full of cleaning supplies. Liesl set down her coffee cup and went outside to help her.

Mrs. Zimmerman spotted her and smiled.

Liesl took the bag of cleaning supplies out of the housekeeper's hand, leaving her to juggle the broom and mop.

"Welcome back, Liesl."

"Thank you." Liesl held up the bag, and the scent of lemon cleaner greeted her. "I'm guessing Joey won't allow you to leave these in his apartment?"

"You are correct. He says they're unclean. I can't disagree with him, so I carry them back and forth from the house."

Liesl frowned. "What about the vacuum cleaner? Are you hauling that as well?"

Mrs. Zimmerman nodded.

"Not anymore," Liesl said. "I'm going to do something. That Joey. He's something else."

Mrs. Zimmerman grinned. "A humdinger."

"I'll talk to the contractor. I'm sure they can build a storage closet for you inside the garage. I don't want you carrying this stuff back and forth."

They reached the back steps of the house. Liesl opened the door and held it for Mrs. Zimmerman to pass.

"You should've mentioned you were carrying the supplies back and forth. It's too hard."

Mrs. Zimmerman turned to her, still holding the broom and mop. "You're paying me to care for your place and Joey's apartment. I'm not going to whine about his refusal to store cleaning supplies."

"Mrs. Zimmerman, you're the hardest worker I've known besides Aunt Suzanne. Nose to the grindstone until the job is finished. I would *never* consider anything you mentioned to be whining."

"Being compared to your Aunt Suzanne is a compliment."

Liesl smiled. "It is, isn't it? I'm being truthful. I'll have a solution for you as soon as possible. In the meantime, take your debit card for the household accounts and buy everything you need to clean Joey's apartment, including another vacuum."

"Thank you."

"I'll figure out a nice place for all that equipment soon. In the meantime, store it inside the garage. In a corner or something."

"That's very nice." Mrs. Zimmerman beamed.

"I apologize for not realizing earlier that you had to slog everything over there and back."

The housekeeper stood holding the mop and broom while she studied Liesl. "Is something wrong?"

"Nothing related to this matter." Liesl hung her jacket on the hook and picked up the bag of cleaning supplies to move them to the pantry. "At least the updates in the pantry have been completed. I'm sure you're happy to have that area back again."

"I certainly am." Mrs. Zimmerman snaked her way past the workmen's tools in the center of the kitchen. Liesl followed her.

After they deposited their loads, Mrs. Zimmerman turned to her. "Now, tell me what's happened."

"I've been told before that my face is easy to read."

"It sure is."

Liesl explained what happened that morning. When she came to the part about believing the bones were tree limbs hanging from the teeth of the skid-steer's bucket, Mrs. Zimmerman's eyes bulged.

"Are you kidding?"

Liesl sniffed. "I wish I was. It was gross to see those bones. Whether they turn out to be old or new, they belonged to someone who used to be living and breathing."

Mrs. Zimmerman clicked her tongue in sympathy. "That is sad. Those bones could belong to someone reported missing, or killed and dumped."

"The speculation was that the bones had been there awhile. If they belong to someone who's been missing, it was a good thing we uncovered them today. If the bones can be identified and returned to their family, that will be a blessing."

"You said the house is over behind Moser's Grocery Store?"

"Yes," Liesl replied. "You turn off Highway 22, onto Kentucky Road and then take a right off Kentucky. It's one of the roads that curves back behind Moser's."

Mrs. Zimmerman pursed her lips. "That's the area where the Union Army had a camp."

Liesl perked up with this information. "I've never known the location of the camp."

"The Union was in Mexico throughout the Civil War—1861 to 1865. They were here to maintain control of the railroad routes that supplied all northern Missouri."

Liesl frowned. "A housing development caused the loss of history."

"I remember the work they did to make that area suitable for building," Mrs. Zimmerman said. "Heavy machinery was used to clear the trees and brush, to grade it flat. *The Colonel* reported they found Civil War era items."

Liesl nodded. "Some of those items may be part of the collections at the Ag Museum and the historical society."

Mrs. Zimmerman nodded. "I'm sure that's right."

Liesl frowned. "If they were digging out there, why didn't they find the bones?"

"Well, in preparing for houses with basements, they'd dig space for the basement foundation and pile the dirt behind them. My guess would be they didn't see the bones then."

"Eventually someone built a shed on that dirt, once it settled. Makes sense. How do you know so much?"

"I was a teacher." Mrs. Zimmerman smiled and

added, "Also, my ancestors met during the Civil War. Here in Mexico."

"Really? You've traced your ancestors that far?"

"The first thing I did when I retired was research my family history."

"If an opportunity ever presented itself for you to teach classes on genealogy, would you be interested?"

"Sure, but I don't understand."

"Just an idea. I'll fill you in later. Okay?"

Mrs. Zimmerman nodded.

"Now, back to the bones. I'm aware Grant was a frequent guest at Graceland. Rumor has it he went there to relax, talk to Mr. Clark, who was the owner of the home, and smoke his cigars."

"There's a historical marker in the parking lot of Moser's Grocery Story that tells all about the Union camp. It's near the highway."

"I'll locate it and read that marker. There's a chance those bones might be that old. Maybe a soldier died in the camp."

"It would be interesting if they were from that era. Even though I'm retired, never forget, a teacher knows everything."

Liesl blinked at Mrs. Zimmerman for a moment before she understood she was teasing. After a chuckle, she said, "You've certainly taught me something today, and I'm grateful."

• • •

Later that night, Sam Apple called Liesl.

"How's it going, Liesl?"

"Your call is the bright light of today's events."

"What happened?"

"Let's take care of business, then I'll explain."

When the discussion about financial matters was a wrap, Sam asked, "So what made your day so dark? Anything I can do to help?"

"I witnessed an accidental discovery of bones. Human bones."

Sam gasped. "Really? Ew. Were you hanging out at a graveyard or something?"

"A house that's being flipped. They tore down a shed and uncovered bones. A haunting surprise."

"You have the most interesting adventures in that small town of yours."

"You're right. There's never a dull moment here. On days like today, I wonder what city folks like you do for entertainment."

"I'm going out on a limb here, but I doubt I'll witness any bones being uncovered later this evening."

"Lucky you."

Chapter 24

Liesl

A week later, the day was sunny and mild. A perfect spring day, Liesl thought as she made her way to her destination. *Am I going on a picnic? Or some other fun outdoor activity? No. Nicole and I are meeting Hector and Kurt at the police station.*

Upon arrival, Liesl was ushered into an interrogation room alone. She played on her phone until everyone gathered for the talk, searching for sources of scrumptious baked goods for the nonexistent nonprofit. If this deal of buying a city block didn't happen soon, she'd have no excuse not to work on her next book.

When Nicole scurried in, she was apologetic. "So sorry to be late. I had a showing. The couple spent more time at the house than I expected."

"Are they going to buy it?"

"They seemed pleased with it. Fingers crossed."

"Then you made good use of your time." Liesl eyed Nicole, noting her color and energy. "Feeling back to normal?"

Nicole smiled. "I am. Thanks for asking. And thanks for taking care of me."

"It's what besties do."

Hector entered the room at a clip, followed by Kurt. Both held file folders and had an air of anxiousness about them.

"Sorry we're late," Kurt said. "An interview dragged on longer than it should have." He gestured to Hector. "You go ahead."

Hector took a seat opposite Liesl and Nicole, tossing his file folder on the table. "This is a planning conversation about our proposed meeting with the Graceland board of directors."

Kurt interrupted Hector as he settled in a chair beside him. "We need the meeting to include the board, staff, and volunteers."

"If you were to approach Mr. Arnold, the historical society's director, I'm sure he would cooperate with you," Liesl said. "He's delighted I offered the coins for display, and that delight should extend to gathering everyone you want."

"Okay, we'll do that," Kurt said. "Is there a room with enough space to hold that many people at Graceland?"

Nicole spoke up. "Their classroom area is often used as a meeting room. I've attended several meetings there."

"I agree," Liesl said. "That classroom was included when they added the modern kitchen. It has plenty of space."

Kurt was pleased with this information. "What I'd like to do is set up several hidden cameras to be used during the meeting. We'd need this done before the meeting, to capture the attendees' reaction about the value of the new display."

Liesl frowned. "Is that really necessary?"

"We should get interesting reactions when we announce our plan to supply an officer to guard the display. We can put the cameras in old books. If we took an old book off the shelf and replaced it with an old book we've rigged with a camera, who would notice?"

Liesl smiled. "No one."

"The plan is to tell them the police guard will be there during open hours," Hector said. He folded his hands. "We want the thief to assume there will be no extra security after hours. If they don't realize they're being recorded, someone involved with the criminals might send a text, get on the phone as they walk out, or seem pleased about the arrangement."

"You'd be surprised how often people react to news that way," Kurt said. "Especially if they believe no one is watching." He turned to Liesl. "I'd like you to stay in the back of the meeting room. We'll rig you with a body camera so you capture the movements of everyone in front of you."

"A body camera?"

"A tiny one. No one will discover it. Sometimes it's easier to spot someone acting nervous, shuffling, or reacting to news when you capture them from behind. They've trained their faces not to react, but the excitement about it comes out in the movement of their feet or hands."

Hector turned to Nicole. "We want you to be inside the museum, but outside of the classroom. We'd like you to ensure no one who's not invited comes into that meeting. We'll outfit you with a body camera too. If someone approaches, we'll have it on video."

"I can do that," Nicole said. "Mr. Van de Berg will be late. I assume you'll want me to let him in the meeting."

Kurt smiled. "Sure. We'll have a list for you."

Liesl asked, "What about Mr. Miller? He's the groundskeeper. Do you want him in the meeting?"

"Adam Miller?" Kurt and Hector shared a glance, then Hector said, "No."

Liesl frowned. "You don't suspect Mr. Miller, do you? He's a wonderful man."

Kurt glanced away from her.

Hector cleared his throat. "We cannot eliminate Miller as a suspect. That's all I can say right now."

"Are you serious?" Liesl's anger rose, and she speared Hector with death ray eyes.

"Yes." He shifted under her gaze and looked away. "Back to the topic. Once we've made the announcement, we believe the thieves won't hit Graceland until your coins are actually there."

"I'd have to agree with your logic," Nicole said.

"If anyone asks you about the security of the coins, you need to tell them you're uncomfortable about it," Hector said. "Blame your uncertainty on what happened at the Ag Museum. Something like, 'the police aren't taking this seriously' and such. Then report to us as to who approached you and what they had to say."

"Why would I say that?" Liesl asked.

"To make the thieves feel more comfortable about breaking in."

Kurt jumped in. "We want both of you to tell everyone you know about the display. How exciting it will be. Build interest. You have connections to media sources. Tell them you want to talk to them about it."

Nicole asked, "If you think this is an inside job, why tell everyone about the display?"

"So the thieves will believe we're not expecting them to hit again."

"I'm happy to talk to the press most of the time," Liesl said. "The negative times are when they give me a harsh review about my book and chew on me like a dog toy."

"An announcement about the coins should be good," Nicole said. "Do you want this out right away?"

Hector smiled at her. "Like yesterday."

"On it," Nicole said. "I'm going to call my sources, starting with Matt Pilger at KXEO. Maybe they'll announce the coin display on the air today or tomorrow. I'll also reach out to *The Colonel* newspaper. It's possible they'd do a feature."

"Excellent," Hector said, "but let us tell the board about it first. That will be the initial announcement that we'll have valuable coins on display. We want the insiders to know first and be surprised, while we can get them on camera."

"Okay. What are you going to say about stationing me outside the meeting?" Nicole asked.

Kurt said, "Liesl can say you offered to watch the museum and help with anyone who comes in while everyone else is in the meeting."

Liesl added, with a growl in her tone, "Everyone except Mr. Miller."

Kurt held up his right index finger. "All inside staff." Then he grinned. "As far as my hiding place inside Graceland, I need to be there from closing until it opens the following day once the coins are in place. It doesn't have to be comfortable, but I'll need to sit down."

"I have an idea for a hiding place," Liesl said. "If I can access it ahead of time, I'll make it comfortable." She turned to Hector. "When was the last time you were inside the museum?"

His face reddened. "Never."

She spun to Kurt. "And you? You toured it in high school."

Kurt squirmed in his chair. "I haven't been back since."

Liesl rolled her eyes at Nicole, then turned back to the men. "Remember the beautiful curving staircase that winds its way from the first floor to the second?"

"Yes," Kurt said. "I remember that."

"There is also a staircase on the second floor that leads to the attic. It's steep, with narrow steps. There's a wall on one side, but no handrail on the outer edge. As you walk up the second staircase, you have to squat due to a low ceiling. The attic door is in the ceiling at the top. You nearly have to crawl into the attic. Then from the attic, there are six or seven steps to get outside, to the widow's walk. That's on the roof."

Kurt frowned. "Are you hiding me in the attic or on the roof?"

"The attic. It's the roomiest area. I think the roof would be too windy." She smiled as she teased him. "If you aren't interested in the attic, you'd have to stand inside a closet or wardrobe until everyone leaves."

"The attic it is."

"It's rather spooky. It made me scream when I first went up there. They had mannequins stored there. For a second, I thought they were ghosts."

Everyone chuckled about that.

Liesl continued, "The wooden door to the attic has a pulley system of ropes and weights to help you push it up, to access the interior. I find it's easier to turn around and use my back to push it open."

"I'm confused." Kurt turned to Nicole and Hector. "Are you all confused?"

They nodded in agreement.

"I'll show you how it works when I'm hiding you there. I suggest you bring a mask and gloves. It's dusty up there."

"Who uses that attic?"

"No one. It's for storage, and only when you're desperate for storage. It was a servant's bedroom when the house was built. Then it was a child's playroom. The walls still have old pink wallpaper on them."

"Can I get out of there quietly?"

"Sure. You pull on the door from the inside. The weights help you pull it up. It doesn't make much noise. Then you walk down. It's easier to go down than up, thanks to the ceiling space."

Hector asked, "How are you going to get people away from the area and have time for him to crawl up there without being discovered?"

"We'll have to ponder that and get back to you," Liesl said. "Nicole will likely need to make a diversion." She grinned at Nicole. "Give us time and we'll come up with some acceptable options."

Nicole asked, "Where will you be, Hector?"

"Outside in a van," Hector said. "I'll be monitoring the feed from the interior cameras.

We'll have you two place the inside cameras."

Nicole frowned. "Place cameras? What does that entail?"

Hector held up his hand. "The hidden cameras we're using for the classroom meeting will need to be moved by you and Liesl after the meeting. We don't want anyone involved with the historical society to know cameras will be in place once the coins are displayed. We'll need them set up in whatever room the director wants the coin display, across from or pointed at an angle toward the exhibit. Video of thieves attempting to steal the coins is what we need."

"What about Donnie?" Liesl turned to Kurt. "Are he and his security business involved in any of this?"

Kurt and Hector exchanged a grimace. "Absolutely not," Kurt said. "They are still under consideration as suspects."

Liesl was curious about the progress Kurt and Hector made with Donnie and his staff. "You said someone entered his business the night before the incident at the Ag Museum. Any update on that?"

"We're checking former employees. The current employees appear clean."

"What about that Vo-Tech student?"

"She was filling in for lunch the day we were there," Nicole said. "I remember her."

"I imagine she'd have the same access to computers and entry codes as a regular employee," Liesl said. "Anyone check her alibi? High school kids like to mess with drugs sometimes. That costs money."

Kurt scribbled a note. "I'll check."

"Back to the historical society," Hector said. "Those interior cameras will have a direct feed to me outside in the van."

Liesl furrowed her brow. "You're aware the director of the historical society is going to get suspicious if I'm hanging around every day at closing time."

"We should only have to do this a few nights," Hector told her. "Greed and the media buzz we'll build should make them strike quickly."

"We want everyone—staff, board members, and volunteers—to know we're setting up on a specific day," Kurt said. "We'll get the exhibit up and invite photographers from *The Colonel* to take pictures."

The room was silent as they stewed in their own thoughts.

"We want them to believe they'll have the run of the place at night," Kurt said.

Nicole arched her eyebrows at Liesl. "How about we go over to the museum right now and figure out the best place for the display? We can take pictures and send them to these guys to figure out the camera placement."

"I've got the time," Liesl replied. "My guess is the director will display them on the second floor.

The room they call the Collections Room, where they have the medical supplies and the three-face stemware."

Nicole nodded. "Works for me."

Liesl turned back to Hector and Kurt. "Any information about the bones?"

Kurt smiled. "Is it safe to talk about bones in front of Nicole?"

Nicole laughed at his teasing. "As long as I'm not staring at them, I'm good."

"The medical examiner sent the bones to a forensic anthropologist in St. Louis."

Liesl sat up straight. "So there's some debate about the age of the bones?"

"Yes and no. They've listed them as undetermined right now, but the ME feels they are old. A forensic anthropologist can tell us their age and a lot more information. At least with more accuracy than our local sources."

Liesl pondered on this information. "So the coroner called in the experts?"

"Tony sent his pictures to the medical examiner, and they discussed it. They both agreed it was best to involve the anthropologist. I believe the remains went to Saint Louis University for review in their Department of Sociology and Anthropology."

Liesl took great pleasure in this. "That's good. I hope they're old. If they are, we need to have a ceremony or church service before sending them off to a museum. In honor of the person who died."

"I'm not having anything to do with those bones," Nicole stated with grit in her tone. "Beg me all you want, but I've seen enough of them."

Everyone laughed.

Kurt scooted out his chair, signaling the end of the meeting. "Thank you for coming and helping us with this."

Liesl nodded and stood up, "Are the bones male or female?"

Hector gathered his file folder and also stood. "The experts agree on the gender of the bones. They feel strongly it's a male."

Nicole grabbed her purse and joined Liesl as they headed toward the door.

"Those boots were leaning male," Liesl said. "Any indication of how he died?"

Kurt opened the door and held it open for the women to pass. "Not yet," he said. "Nothing obvious is what Tony told me."

"Interesting," Liesl said.

"You may have to write about it," Kurt suggested.

Chapter 25

Lieutenant Cormac O'Malley

Cormac was making his nightly tour of the camp. The men seem to have grown used to his tours, allowing him to eavesdrop in plain sight.

Every night, the men who were off duty gathered around their fires. They laughed, told stories about hunting and fishing, and shared their sorrows. They included him in their discussions whenever he was within conversational distance. He didn't know the exact reason. Maybe it was due to his quiet demeanor or the fact that he was a fellow soldier.

The music played at night comprised a variety of songs. Most of the instruments at the men's disposal were fiddles, mouth harps, spoons, and some brass instruments. Several of the tunes were unique to his ear. Other songs stirred memories from worship or his home in southern Illinois. Those songs made his heart sting with the pain of homesickness. It made him sorry this war wasn't the short-term commitment he'd initially believed it would be.

Tonight's composition was a special treat. An accordion—some of the men called it a squeezebox—had arrived by train for one of the men. The soldier could play it well. When a slow tune made the gathered men melancholy, the musician kicked up the rhythm. Cormac stepped away when those gathered started toe-tapping and off-key singing.

A corporal, often used as a runner for the camp, caught Cormac's attention. Runners had the easiest access to information and opportunity to deliver it to the enemy. They left camp alone and went to town. No one in the town or the camp would think anything about this corporal appearing anywhere and everywhere. He could meet someone, pass information, or hide notes in town or along the road to camp.

Cormac added the corporal to his mental watch list.

So far, his nightly rounds had offered little in the way of information. Yet he kept an eye on all the nocturnal activities of the camp. He hoped this would pay off in helping him discern something abnormal in the future.

Moments later, Captain MacTavish stepped from a nearby tent. His jet-black hair and enormous muttonchop sideburns made him easy to identify. What was he doing here?

Cormac was well acquainted with the men who occupied that tent, and they were not under the captain's command.

Why was Captain MacTavish there? Did he have a legitimate reason for being there? Or was his reason more nefarious?

Earlier, he'd seen MacTavish in another place that was unusual. Why couldn't he remember where that was? It would come to him.

Then it hit him. MacTavish was the officer who'd pulled Cormac's squad out of church several weeks ago. He had been the leader of the squad sent to remove them from services to report in aid of another squad.

Did MacTavish's presence at the church make him a suspect? Or did his duties clear him from suspicion? Until he could make that determination, Cormac added MacTavish to his list.

The physician used by the camp was another person with complete access to everything within the perimeter. Every time Cormac spotted him, he was unescorted. Cormac believed his name was Bradley. Doc Bradley.

The camp had no physician, so they used the town's doctor when their infirmary corps needed help. Doc Bradley had free rein to come and go, night and day. Did he have Southern leanings? He would ask Enid about him.

All physicians, including Doc Bradley, worked under constant threat of being shot by the army if appropriate care was not provided. Yet Cormac was aware of nothing in place to stop him or try to prevent him from passing information about the camp. The threat of death only extended to medical treatment.

Doc Bradley was added to his watch list.

As he made his way through the rest of the camp, Cormac deliberated about another suspect. One he trusted implicitly. The only one who was aware of his clandestine activities. Captain Oliver.

Could he consider him another possibility for the spy? He'd insisted Cormac's investigation remain secret. Could the captain be behind the leaks?

Cormac's heart was heavy as he completed his intended observations. Captain Oliver, a spy? To do his investigation justice, he must consider this dreaded idea and keep an open mind.

Four days later, Cormac and Captain Oliver worked together to test Cormac's theory of a spy inside the camp. Captain Oliver planned a mission related to the repair and security of a railroad bridge in a nearby county. All the usual officers were included in the planning.

Cormac observed every officer during the meeting, searching for any questionable activity, gesture, or facial movement. When the meeting concluded, he'd made no progress.

As was his duty, Colonel Michaels announced the mission to the squads selected to execute the assignment. Captain Oliver would command the mission, with a lieutenant leading each squad. O'Malley was chosen as one of the lieutenants.

Captain Oliver ensured they would follow exactly all standard procedures, as in previous missions. Colonel Michaels related the times, individual squad assignments and tasks, and the places involved in the mission.

They marched out of camp the following morning with only Cormac and Captain Oliver aware of their plan to test for an internal spy. When the squads had marched over two miles from the camp, Captain Oliver faked an injury to his ankle by rolling down a ravine.

Cormac chased the captain to the bottom with manufactured concern. To stabilize the "wound," he crafted a makeshift splint. Cormac grimaced and looked skeptically at the ankle as the men peered down at the scene they'd created.

Some men tossed items to Cormac. They offered bandages and sturdy branches cut down to be used for splints. Two of the men climbed down the slope to help bring the captain back to the top.

Once Cormac declared Captain Oliver too injured to proceed with the mission, the captain ordered Cormac to get him back to camp. Then he selected a sergeant and the other lieutenant to take command of the mission.

With the loss of their original mission commander, Captain Oliver ordered the remaining squad to reconnoiter and make some previously noted repairs to a different railroad bridge several miles to the west. No one questioned the change of mission. This bridge was closer and already considered secure. The men moved on without comment, as these things were to be expected.

After waiting fifteen minutes to ensure the men were gone, Cormac and Captain Oliver proceeded to the original assignment location. It took several hours to arrive at the intended destination.

After a moment to rest and chew on some hardtack, they walked around the area and selected a tall, well-leafed tree. Then they built a platform high in its branches that gave them a good line of sight on anyone approaching the area.

By evening, they'd finished the platform. Shadows were lengthening and the music of the woods reverberated around them. Occasionally, their peace was shattered by a passing train along the railroad's northern route.

Several hours into their wait, Cormac sighed. "I can't believe it. No one's coming."

Captain Oliver chuckled at him. "We've only begun. These things take time, Lieutenant. Count your blessings. It could be raining."

Through the evening hours, they took turns observing the surrounding area.

On Cormac's watch, he identified a rustle in the grass. He shook the captain awake. "Listen," Cormac whispered. "I hear something."

Captain Oliver sat silently, scanning the area. "I don't hear anything."

"Something is out there, I tell you." Moments later, a raccoon wandered into view. The presence of such a creature wasn't unusual, due to their proximity to a stream.

After a pause, Cormac said, "Told you I heard something."

"Don't make me laugh, Lieutenant."

As night turned to dawn, Cormac and the captain huddled under their blankets. Both were miserable with the cold and damp, catching sleep when they could.

On Cormac's watch, tendrils of fog entertained him as they rolled across the land. Soon the sun would erase the fog and he would have to face his disappointment about this undertaking.

A sound. Had it been something metallic? Whatever it turned out to be, it was out of the ordinary and caught his attention. Cormac nudged the captain.

When the captain's eyes flew open, Cormac held his finger to his lips.

Through the foggy mist, they spotted a unit of armed men approaching on foot. Not soldiers. They were spread out, creeping across the area.

Neither Cormac nor the captain recognized the men. Whoever they were, someone had outfitted them with pistols, bayonets, and some rifles—weapons necessary for successful hand-to-hand combat.

Cormac and the captain remained silent as the

raiding party searched for signs of their squad. Both had been careful to remove any sign that might give away their presence.

Eventually, the raiding party called off its search.

Cormac and Oliver watched them leave with bitterness. Their secret mission had been to verify or disprove there was a leak inside the camp. Up to this point, an internal spy was a hypothesis. Now, it was proven true.

When this mission was put into motion, Cormac had watched for vendors. No peddlers or service providers came to camp from the time the mission was announced until they marched away. The only conclusion was confirmation of an internal spy.

This information weighed heavily on them as they made the long trip back to the camp. Captain Oliver, with his makeshift splint reattached to his ankle, limped past the pickets and into camp. Cormac, an arm around the captain to support him, watched for any overt signs of surprise from the men and officers.

Cormac's search would continue.

The enemy was one of their own.

Chapter 26

Enid Connolly

On her first afternoon off after the lieutenant's visit, Enid offered to go to Dawson's Mercantile and place the order for the Clark house. Normally her mother handled this duty, but it was the perfect reason for Enid to be inside the mercantile so she'd have an excuse to talk to any townspeople there.

Although her mother hesitated to harness her with ordering duties on her afternoon off, Enid convinced her. It was her argument that she needed things inside the store and would make the trip anyway that won over her mother.

Jeremiah dropped her off in front of the store, reminding her that his errands would take most of the afternoon. They agreed to meet at the only cafe in town, a place where Enid could sit and sip a cup of tea until Jeremiah returned.

Inside the mercantile, she scanned the interior and was disappointed to find only the Dawsons in the store. The elder Mr. Dawson was behind the counter, and his grandson, Young Johnny, worked at stacking flour sacks. No shoppers occupied the store.

"Good afternoon, Mr. Dawson," Enid said. She handed him her mother's list of items. "I offered to bring the list today, as you can see. Jeremiah will be by later to collect everything."

Mr. Dawson welcomed her. "It is a delight to have such a pretty young lady visit the store."

Enid smiled. Mr. Dawson complimented every female who entered his store, regardless of whether she deserved any type of compliment. Enid presumed he found it good for business.

"I hoped to catch George making his delivery."

Mr. Dawson's face drooped. "I'm so sorry. He won't be making a run until later in the week. Thursday or Friday, but I'm never told exactly when. It's part of his safety plan. To keep from being kidnapped again."

Enid was well aware of the kidnapping. If Mr. Dawson was allowed the freedom to speak unfettered, he could go on for hours. To focus him on her topic of interest, she asked, "Has anyone besides George made deliveries to the camp?"

Mr. Dawson took a deep breath.

Enid braced to receive a bushel of words from him.

"You are aware the leaders at the camp insisted my deliveries be made by a 'loyal Union man.' They all but threatened me with closing down my business if I failed to comply with their demand. George saved me, is what he did."

She smiled at Mr. Dawson. "George is a hero."

"Indeed. A true hero. He was a Union soldier

and is still loyal to the Union, even if he can't fight anymore. I was forced, almost at gunpoint, to find someone to make the deliveries. Mind you, I was not trustworthy enough to do it myself, they said. George agreeing to do the deliveries was a godsend."

"Who else is allowed to make deliveries to the camp?"

Mr. Dawson paused for a moment. "The farrier who is mostly a hermit, Duncan Wilson. Heard tell he gets called to the camp frequently. When the army first came, they bought over half of his horse herd. He made them take geldings. He refused them his stallions and brood mares. Told them they'd ruin his business."

Enid nodded. She was familiar with his reputation. He was the strongest man in the county. She didn't know if he leaned Southern or Union in the war. She figured a man like him had no strong opinion either way. He would likely aspire to be left alone with his animals.

His brother, Angus, attended her church when he could. The brothers were as opposite as they could be. Angus was tall and stick thin. He needed glasses to read. She made a mental note to talk to Angus as soon as she could. He was a bookkeeper at one of the banks. She might be able to hunt him down today.

Enid tried to obtain information a second time. "If the Union camp doesn't trust locals, then who are the people who go there? Like Duncan Wilson."

"Emil Thompson be another that's allowed."

"The blacksmith?"

"Yes, missy. Rumor has it he could lean either North or South in his politics, but he reports out at the camp when they send word. Seems they've only picked at me about finding a 'loyal Union man' and not anyone else."

Enid hid a smile that teased her lips. Mr. Dawson had the reputation of a man who freely waggled his tongue. If those in charge of the camp found out about that, they wouldn't want Mr. Dawson relating all of his activities at the camp to the townsfolk. He'd be inclined to tell the whole town what he did, what the soldiers were doing, and what equipment he saw out there.

"What does Mr. Thompson do when they call him out to the camp?"

"That's a good question." Mr. Dawson adjusted boxes of matches on his counter. "I understand they are building their own forge out there, but it isn't finished. At least that's what I've been told. Emil has a sizeable forge at his place. He's mighty skilled too."

She added Mr. Thompson to her list. Was he called out there enough to be the spy? She'd find out.

"Mr. Thompson has six daughters?"

Mr. Dawson nodded. "Right. No sons."

Enid prided herself that she was proof a woman could act as a spy. She tasked herself to find out which way Mr. Thompson's daughters leaned in this conflict.

The front door of the store opened, and Mr. Dawson rushed to help Callie Conway, leaving Enid to gather a few items she needed. Her mother always wanted to make all their candles, but Enid believed store-bought candles provided more light. She selected a small one for her own use.

When she had a bolt of white cotton for a shirt, a needle, and the candle, she returned to the counter for Mr. Dawson to cut the material she would need and then pay for her purchases.

The shirt material was a possible Christmas present for Green Eyes, even though he might be gone, along with the rest of the army, by December. If he was still here, she wanted to give him something special.

Enid opened the front door to leave and spotted Sarah Fairchild, the wife of the town cooper, making her way from the street to the store. She held the door for Mrs. Fairchild and engaged her in conversation.

There were two reasons to converse with the sweet woman. One was to enjoy her company. The second was that her husband had to be one of those craftsmen who frequented the encampment.

Everyone needed barrels and buckets, and her husband made them all.

Mrs. Fairchild was also skilled. She was a seamstress, and people from far and near requested her skill for their gowns and suits.

After they exchanged pleasantries, Enid asked, "Have you enjoyed any call for your sewing skills at the encampment?"

Mrs. Fairchild's smile faded. "No. They made it clear my skills are not welcome there, due to my Southern leanings. My husband, who views politics even more stridently than I do, has been told to stay away from the camp. If they need his services, the camp sends the order through the mercantile. George delivers everything."

"Oh, with those restrictions, I wouldn't want to help them at all."

Mrs. Fairchild arranged her skirt and kept her head down. In a whisper, she said, "I'd like to have my husband refuse any request for his creations by the army. But he says it would be too dangerous for us to make our opinions so widely known."

Enid replied with her own whisper, "I understand. Who makes deliveries to the camp? Besides George, of course."

"Scots MacTavish has been seen coming and going out there."

With wide eyes, Enid stared at Mrs. Fairchild. "What could he possibly do for the army? He barely speaks English and is a trapper. Do they use a lot of fur?"

The ladies giggled at the idea of the bearded man with such a heavy brogue in business with the army.

Enid spotted Mr. Dawson making his way to them. Their giggling must have alerted him to the gossip he'd missed. "I must go, Mrs. Fairchild." She reached out and squeezed her friend's gloved hand. In a whisper, she said, "Don't tell Mr. Dawson anything."

Enid dropped her hand and in a normal tone added, "It's been a pleasure conversing with you today."

"Yes. I hope to see you again soon." Mrs. Fairchild turned and allowed Mr. Dawson to fawn over her as Enid made her escape.

Enid cornered Angus Wilson at the bank after she inquired about opening an account with them. Maybe one day she'd have enough money saved to have need for a savings account. Until then, it was an excuse to see Angus. She brought up Duncan by saying there were rumors he was fond of the Union camp.

Angus was quick to explain what Duncan did at the camp. "With all the horses and other animals at the camp, he helps treat various ailments. He wants to keep their animals healthy. To be accurate, he wants all animals to be healthy. Pain free."

Enid smiled and encouraged Angus to continue. "Sounds as if he's out there all the time?"

Angus frowned. "Quite a bit. But they pay him well."

"Does he do anything else?"

"He makes horseshoes and deals with hoof rot and other conditions related to their hooves."

"I am not familiar with animal ailments. Jeremiah handles them at the Clark house."

"It's nothing I've ever been interested in, but Duncan prefers animals to people."

"Is he pro-Union?"

"More like pro-animal. It breaks his heart when he can't fix them and they have to be put down. I'm not sure he feels as sorry for people."

Enid smiled. "Jeremiah likely feels the same way."

As she turned to leave, she remembered to ask about Scots MacTavish. "Angus, do you know why Scots MacTavish would be seen frequenting the camp?"

"I understand he has a cousin there."

"A cousin? Didn't he come here directly from Scotland? How does he have a cousin in the army?"

Angus shrugged. "We're a country full of immigrants. It's not unusual for cousins to find each other here."

"Is Scots pro-Union? His cousin must be if he's fighting for them."

"As a Scotsman, Scots hates the English. With the English leaning toward support of the South to get their cotton, Scots is fit to be tied. I'd say he is pro-Union."

Enid chuckled. "Take care. It's been a pleasure."

Once outside, she crossed the road to avoid talking to the Widow Harney who, like Mr. Dawson, had a habit of speaking in a never-ending river of words.

Please forgive me for my rudeness, God. I don't have time for the widow today.

On their ride home, Jeremiah and Enid discussed the success of their errands. Jeremiah, in typical fashion, teased her about her new beau.

"Do you like him?" Enid watched his face. She wanted to know the truth, not what she wanted to hear.

"I do," Jeremiah said. "He seems to be a trustworthy fellow, and he's smitten with you."

She blushed. "He teases me almost as much as you."

"Good man."

"Even though he has a sense of humor, he's serious about loyalty to the Union, like George. I admire that in George and in Lieutenant O'Malley."

Jeremiah rubbed his left wrist, which was swollen. "I hope the potion that Mr. Jones fixed up for me today will cure this ache. He said it's probably rheumatism." He frowned. "I took offense that someone my age could have rheumatism, but he said there was a soldier at the camp younger than me that suffers from it."

Jeremiah prattled on, but Enid's mind was elsewhere. In her search for those from town who frequented the camp, she'd forgotten about the chemist. Farley Jones had several employees who made deliveries to the camp.

When Jeremiah was silent again, Enid asked, "Mr. Jones does poultices for your horses, doesn't he?"

Jeremiah nodded. "He treats both people and animals."

Enid felt an urgency to tell Mr. Green Eyes about this. She surmised the soldiers would use the chemist, in addition to Duncan, to treat their animals.

Now that she had information, how was she supposed to get it to him?

Chapter 27

Liesl

Liesl pulled into the parking lot near Graceland and was surprised how many people were there. The coin reveal meeting wasn't slated to start for another hour.

A good crowd would please Kurt and Hector. They'd have more people's reactions to capture with the clandestine cameras.

Liesl's first stop this morning had been the police station so they could fit her with the body camera. Earlier in the week, she and Nicole had placed the hidden cameras in the classroom.

Roxy, the desk sergeant, was the female body camera expert, and she helped them rig the system. Liesl couldn't believe how tiny the camera was. Roxy fixed it to peek out a buttonhole on her suit jacket. The battery pack was also miniscule and easily placed to be invisible. With no need for audio, Liesl didn't have anything in her ear.

She was "live" from the moment she stepped out of the station, but no one captured the images yet. An unmarked police van would collect her video feed once they'd set up in the parking lot of the Show Me Credit Union, across the street from the complex.

Walking toward Graceland, Liesl spotted a lone figure clipping shrubs near the old schoolhouse on the grounds. With a quick diversion from her intended target, she strode over to say hello to the historical society's groundskeeper and general maintenance man.

When he spotted her, a smile lit his face. "Good morning to you." He put down his hedge trimmers and wiped his brow with a handkerchief. "You sure look pretty in that suit. An agreeable change from your usual casual clothes."

She matched his smile. "Always a pleasure to see you, Mr. Miller. I figured I'd better dress up today."

"That meeting's happening today." He winked at her. "I've been ordered to stay away from the house. Told me it's no business of mine."

"I'm sorry."

"No worries," he replied, his smile never dimming. "They try to keep me in the dark, but I know more than they think."

"Any words of advice before the meeting starts?"

"The administration has been in a tizzy about some new display. They have everyone who works here, outside and inside, rushing around, crazy-like, preparing for all the visitors coming. Today will be the first of a lot of fuss, I figure."

"Thank you, Mr. Miller. That's good to know. Has anyone been hanging around more than usual? Board members? Staff? Volunteers?"

He reflected for a moment. "The director held a volunteer meeting a few days ago. Told them he'll be needing them to volunteer more time after the special announcement."

Liesl frowned. "Did he tell them anything about the announcement?"

"No. A couple of them came to me after, to ask if I'd tell them about it, but I have no idea what's happening."

"Call me if you hear anything that causes you to worry. I'd appreciate it."

"Will do. You do the same for anything you might need."

Liesl spotted other people arriving. "I've got to get in there. Talk to you afterward?"

"It would be my pleasure. I also want to ask you about your car. Mrs. Miller is searching for a new one, and I'd like to get your opinion about yours."

"Good. See you after the meeting."

He tipped the bill of his Cardinals baseball hat at her and returned to his work.

She entered Graceland through the one-story annex added several years ago to the original structure. The meeting was being held in the classroom there. It was the building's only space that would hold the amount of people expected. A couple of volunteers were setting up chairs and removing tables that normally dotted the room.

They asked her to wait in the original house until they had the room ready.

Liesl smiled and spoke to several people clustered in the house's hallway. Its wide area accommodated the first arrivals, with an option for more people to spill into the library as numbers increased.

Whenever two or more adult Audrain County residents gathered, a required topic of conversation included farming concerns. Due to the rural, farm-based economy in the area surrounding Mexico, residents cherished good weather, good crops, and good livestock news.

In the summer, subjects discussed included such things as, "Even though we're experiencing a drought, the corn sure looks great," or "That rain last night helped my tomatoes. I've been worried I was going to have to water them by hand."

Since it was now spring, one popular topic was feeder cattle. She overheard, "The price of feeder cattle keeps dropping. We can only pray an adjustment will happen by fall sale time."

Kurt came in the front door of the original structure dressed in a suit and tie. He tipped his head to Liesl, but otherwise did not acknowledge her, which was part of their plan.

Hector entered a moment later, also dressed in a suit and tie. He walked to the assistant director of the historical society, Annette Grayson, and spoke to her. Liesl couldn't hear their conversation. She turned away, so no one caught her staring.

Ms. Grayson handed Hector a tape dispenser. He made his way outside again, but Liesl couldn't follow him without causing suspicion. What were they doing out there?

In a moment, Mrs. Sizemore waltzed through the front door as Hector struggled to tape some type of notice on the moving door. Mrs. Sizemore was dressed, as usual, in impeccable clothes. Her hair was swept up in a chignon, flattering her handsome, unlined face.

The whole town often gossiped about her. Tongues wagged with such questions as, "Did she convince herself she was a natural beauty as an older woman, like Sophia Loren?" Or "How many plastic surgeries has she endured to look that good?" No one had any proof how she maintained her looks.

Liesl approached her. "You look beautiful, Mrs. Sizemore. Nice to see you again."

Mrs. Sizemore gave her a quick glance from tip to toe. "I must say, Liesl, that suit is fantastic. Your heels too. Did you go shopping with Nicole?"

Liesl almost choked, covering up her laughter. You could always count on Mrs. Sizemore presenting a backhanded compliment, if she deemed you compliment worthy.

"Ah . . . thank you. I'm glad you like the

suit." She chose not to relate that Colette from her investment group had recommended the small boutique in St. Louis where she purchased it. Her lack of style and pizazz was part of her personality, and Liesl refused to allow Mrs. Sizemore's comments to make her feel bad.

Mr. Arnold, the director, saved Liesl from further conversation when he called out to the attendees. He advised them that they could gather in the meeting room. When he spotted Liesl, he waved her over to him as he directed traffic toward the classroom.

"The entire board of directors will be in attendance," Mr. Arnold said, smiling. "Mrs. Sizemore is already here."

Liesl nodded. "Yes, I've had the pleasure of speaking with her a moment ago."

He gestured to his assistant director, Annette Grayson. "Annette, will you update us on the rest of the board members?"

She walked over and began reading from a page attached to her clipboard. "Celia Prendergast will attend the meeting via Zoom, as she's out of town. Mrs. Sizemore and Mr. Van de Berg will attend in person. Dr. Johnson will be here as soon as he finishes his last morning patient. Mrs. Constantine will arrive a few minutes late, but should make a majority of the meeting."

"That's wonderful," Liesl said.

Annette glanced up from the clipboard. "Do

you want an update on the staff and volunteers?"

"I don't believe that will be necessary." Mr. Arnold stepped away to greet someone.

Liesl said to Annette, "Nicole should arrive any moment. She's volunteered to be at the front door, to handle any unexpected tourists."

Annette nodded. "Mr. Arnold briefed me about her earlier. I appreciate her doing that. It's impossible for me to take minutes at the meeting if I have to leave and deal with walk-ins."

Mr. Arnold beckoned to her. "We'll be starting the meeting momentarily."

"You need to hold off starting until I can attend," Annette said. "I'm waiting for Nicole Smith to arrive. It shouldn't be long."

"As you wish," he said, clearly exasperated, and led the remaining people toward the classroom.

Annette leaned over and whispered, "He can't start without you. They're your coins. Pay him no mind."

Liesl smiled. "Thanks."

The front door opened, and a harried but beautifully dressed Nicole stepped into the hallway. "I'm so sorry. I had to park on Hisey Street. Did you know so many people were coming?"

"I didn't. I figured it took time for you to get ready." Liesl raised her eyebrows, invoking the secret code, since Annette was within hearing distance.

"No, I had no problem with my attire." Nicole returned the eyebrow statement.

"Good. The meeting is about to start."

Nicole stepped closer to Annette. "Is there anyone in the rest of the museum?"

Annette shook her head. "Shouldn't be, other than the two detectives who are roaming around. They've been trolling inside and out for a couple of days. I assume they're checking into security issues. Everyone else should be in the meeting."

Nicole raised her eyebrows at Liesl. "Okay, Liesl. Off you go. I've got it from here."

Liesl took her place at the very back of the classroom and watched as several people stumbled in late. Mr. Van de Berg was always late, so his tardy entrance was expected. He swooped in, all smiles, with the style and air of an elderly dandy. The smile he gave Liesl was genuine, and she returned it with genuine affection.

In her heart, she was aware this man had no connection to the attempted theft at the Ag Museum. When Aunt Suzanne was killed, she'd wondered if he was a murderer, but she'd vowed never to be disloyal to him again. Liesl's plan, if the stars aligned, was to have Mr. Van de Berg handle all the lease and contract paperwork associated with the city block purchase. If only that purchase would magically occur.

Mrs. Constantine had reported she'd be late,

but it turned out she was only tardy by a few minutes. The big announcement hadn't started when she arrived.

Liesl watched the woman as she made her way through the crowd to sit near the front. Mrs. Constantine was different in appearance from everyone else in attendance. Modern. California in style, especially her spiked hair. In this little town, it was rare for teenagers to have such a daring "do," much less someone of her age. She was on the short side but was in great shape. Her short-sleeved dress showed off the tone of her arms.

Liesl's acquaintance with Mrs. Constantine was only through their board service. She'd withhold any opinion, negative or positive, until she became more familiar with her.

Dr. Johnson slipped in so late, he nearly missed the actual announcement. He squeaked in the door, just in time. He'd done his best to save her Aunt Suzanne when she was poisoned. Therefore he was not a suspect, in Liesl's opinion.

So, who remained as a viable suspect? The staff? Mrs. Constantine? Dr. Johnson? A volunteer from both the Ag Museum and this museum? Liesl was clueless.

The actual announcement went well. Mr. Arnold spoke about the coins with great pride in his voice. His declaration caused the attendees to murmur with excitement.

"Although we will have several coins on display, I can assure you the gold coin is the most valuable. It has a karat gold weight value of over twenty thousand dollars."

Even more murmuring occurred. You could always count on monetary value to rev up a group.

Liesl stood in the back of the room and hoped her camera captured what they needed. During the announcement, there had been lots of movement among the crowd.

Kurt followed Mr. Arnold at the podium and announced the police would guard the display during the museum's working hours. He made no further elaborations, and no one asked questions regarding his statement.

Scattered chatter involved questions about where the coins came from, even though the subject was addressed earlier.

Mr. Arnold handled all questions with aplomb. He told the gathering that once the provenance of each coin was established, they'd update the display with that information.

"Such things take time," he said. "These coins are new to the coin market, so there is no previous research into their history we can use."

Someone asked whether the coins were authentic.

Mr. Arnold smiled at the attendees. "Trust me, an expert has appraised them. They have established the gold coin as a nineteenth-century coin and the others are Civil War coins minted by the Union. With each coin, we will display its value as a rare coin and its value in the material's weight used to mint it."

The attendees squirmed in their seats. Money talked, and they were listening.

CHAPTER 28

LIESL

When the historical society meeting ended, Hector and Kurt scrambled away to review the video footage. Nicole remained inside to eavesdrop on comments people made as they headed out.

When the crowds had gone, Liesl stopped in the powder room and turned off the miniature camera. She would return the camera at the police station on her way home.

It was her plan to examine the exterior of Graceland with fresh eyes before she left. Their plans for displaying her Civil War–era coins left her anxious, but she reminded herself of all their preparations, inside and out.

She stepped outside the mansion through the recent addition. The original Graceland structure was a two-story home. It featured horizontal wood siding painted a pale apple green, with white trim and dark green plantation shutters framing each window. The rafters were exposed to the edge of the roofline, which was usual for that design. A two-story portico with six columns at each level graced the front of the home. Overall, it was a beautiful representation of Classic Greek Revival design.

The crème de la crème was the haunting widow's walk, which was a balustraded platform built upon the roof. Originally, these were popular in New England homes for providing a view of the sea. With a coastline hundreds of miles away, Liesl could only speculate that the builder of the home, John P. Clark, was fond of the style. The only view the house had when he built it would have been farmland and trees spanning the forty acres he owned.

She glanced around, imagining what the property would have looked like in 1857, when the structure was built. A separate kitchen had been attached to the main house with a covered walkway. The builders designed it that way for fire safety. In modern times, the separate kitchen was removed and replaced with an updated kitchen and classroom addition on the back of the house.

With Mr. Clark opposed to slave labor, had only free men built this home? If so, what a statement and accomplishment in a state that would be a part of the War Between the States four years later.

The sound of an approaching lawnmower brought her out of her musings. Another grin split Mr. Miller's face when he spotted her as he rode atop the machine. Without hesitation, he drove to her and turned off the engine.

He tugged on the brim of his Cardinals baseball cap. "You're as good as your word."

"And here you are, still hard at work keeping this place fantastic." She gestured outward with both arms. "Your efforts reflect all the beauty of spring."

He pointed to a row of small shrubs lining the back of the primary structure. "The plan is to add plants and flowers that require little maintenance. Sadly, many with vibrant colors require a lot of care."

"It's lovely, Mr. Miller. I can never find fault with your work. It's artistry, actually."

He turned to her with a serious expression. "I wish those in charge of this museum were like you." With a shrug, he added, "It would be a nicer world."

Liesl frowned. She could sense something was wrong. "You're not telling me something. Are you and Mrs. Miller okay?"

"It's nothing like that. We're fine." Adam lowered his voice. "It's the people here. Everyone has ears. It's the way small towns are."

She nodded. "That's right."

"Well, the museum staff seems even worse than the general population. They're being nosy and secretive. I'm sure it's related to the meeting you were in."

She yearned to find out more, and an idea came to her. "Are you and Mrs. Miller free this evening? I'd like to have you over for dinner. We can have a conversation about my car, and Mrs.

Miller can drive it while she's there too. That way, she can experience the feel with no sales pressure."

He smiled. "That's so nice, but unnecessary."

"I'll run by DeAngelo's and pick up a lasagna casserole to go. Or, I can pick up a Mexican feast. Whatever you prefer."

"Let me check with the boss to find out if we are, in fact, free tonight." He pulled out his phone and had a brief conversation. "We're in."

Liesl grinned. "So, what am I picking up?"

"Jeanne adores DeAngelo's."

"DeAngelo's it is. What's her favorite there?"

"She likes it all, but the manicotti is her most frequent order."

"Manicotti casserole it is. I'll also get salad and garlic bread." Not only would she be able to talk with him about what concerned him, but she might get his opinion about the museum staff, volunteers, and board of directors.

"Jeanne reminded me she has choir practice tonight at seven. Is that a problem? I get off at five o'clock."

"No. The construction workers at my house are all gone by five. I'll expect the two of you at five thirty. That will give us plenty of time to eat. We'll send Mrs. Miller off in your car for choir practice. Then you can stay with me for a private chat. Just you and me. Then I'll drive you home."

"That would be real nice of you, Liesl. We

might be a few minutes later than that. I'll need to shower before coming over."

"No problem. That settles everything but . . . do you prefer tiramisu or cannoli for dessert?"

Mr. Miller laughed. "Both."

Later that evening, after their meal, Mrs. Miller excused herself to go to choir practice. Liesl led Mr. Miller into the library, turned on the electric fireplace, and invited him to sit down in front of the fire.

"Please, make yourself at home."

He grinned at her. "You don't want me to do that. I'd have to kick off my shoes and fall asleep in the chair."

Liesl laughed. "Okay, scratch that. How about make yourself comfortable?"

He settled into one chair and sighed. "Perfect."

"May I get you some coffee? I have regular and decaffeinated. Or a soft drink?"

"No, thank you. But I warn you that I won't be able to keep my eyes open for too long tonight. What was it you wanted to talk to me about?"

Liesl frowned. "Am I that obvious?"

"Known you a long time. We first met when you came to live here with the Schraders. Besides, your face is an open book."

Liesl shook her head. "I've been working on the part about being less obvious to people."

He chuckled. "You need more time. Don't worry, it's one of the things I like about you."

"I'll keep at it." She laughed. "What I need is some insight into the staff of the historical society. Could you give me your input about the director and the associate director? Maybe some of the frequent volunteers too."

He frowned. "What's going on?"

"I'm putting some coins that belonged to Uncle Max and Aunt Suzanne on temporary display at the museum. I need to trust they will be safe there."

Mr. Miller sat back for a moment. "That's why they've been so secretive. Whispering behind closed doors and all. Makes sense now."

Liesl said, "That was what the meeting was about today."

"They don't trust me. Even after all the years I've been there."

Liesl straightened in her chair. "Well, I trust you."

"I'm glad you say that." Mr. Miller smiled and turned his brown eyes to hers. "Do you know the story about how I became friends with your Uncle Max?"

"I don't believe I do."

Mr. Miller wet his lips. "I met Max when I needed to get back on my feet. In retrospect, God must have put him in front of me. He was an angel sent to rescue me. I'd fallen into a rough crowd, got arrested, served my time. When I got out of prison, no one would hire me."

"I had no idea," Liesl said. This was why Mr. Miller was on Kurt and Hector's suspect list. With a criminal history, even decades ago, they would remain suspicious of him.

"To be fair, it was a long time ago. Max needed men to work on the cattle farm. It was hard work, tough work. Lots of guys turned it down. But Max gave me a chance."

Emotion welled up in Liesl's chest. "Hearing that makes me so proud of him, Mr. Miller."

"You should be proud. With this opportunity, he gave me a purpose for my life. I was good with the cattle, but he noticed I loved the land. So he let me dig in the dirt, landscaping, building trenches for irrigation for the cattle, and other things. Then he brags about my green thumb."

"And?"

"Suzanne listens to him talking about my abilities with God's flowers and trees. Before long, she's got me working here, at almost double the pay, designing and planting her landscaping around the house, carriage house, and that back shed."

Liesl smiled. "I remember you working here. You always let me dig and plant with you. I loved that."

"It was fun to get you to smile. You were so sad when you arrived."

"I was. An orphan at such a young age."

"But God put you into the arms of the best people He could find on this earth."

"Yes, he did, didn't he?"

"It was Suzanne who got me the job at the historical society," Mr. Miller said. "When she found out about their opening for a groundskeeper, she made me go talk to the director. There were other candidates with a higher education, some with a horticultural degree, but I can fix most anything. When they grasped hiring me would get them a handyman and a groundskeeper for the price of a groundskeeper, I got the job."

"I'm grateful you shared your story with me, Mr. Miller. I wasn't aware of your connection to Aunt Suzanne and Uncle Max, other than being friends."

"You're like them. You treat everyone with kindness and respect. Whether they are homeless or millionaires, black or white, old or young. Neither of them would treat someone different due to their money or lack of money or their social status."

Liesl couldn't hold back her tears. They rolled down her cheeks as she chased them with a tissue. "You and Mrs. Miller were what I needed tonight."

"I'm glad. You helped my wife decide about her car. Now how about I give you my impressions of the people who work at the historical society?"

"That would be great. I need information on frequent volunteers, too."

"You got it." He narrowed his eyes. "Some people can't resist temptation. I've been there before. You must be cautious about your coins and stuff there. No matter its value, your health and wellbeing are much more important."

"I understand and agree wholeheartedly. Thank you."

He brushed off his cautionary face and smiled. "Where should I start?"

"Let me get a notebook and pen."

After Liesl took Mr. Miller home, she made a nest on the couch with Barney beside her. She intended to finish the last few chapters of a romance novel.

When Nicole called, the ring of the phone startled her awake. She must have nodded off after all the events of the day. She cleared her voice and answered, but Nicole was not to be fooled.

"I woke you up! So sorry."

Liesl smiled at the distress in Nicole's voice. "Not a problem. What's up?"

"The rumors were true."

"What rumors?"

"Jim Dye is the listing agent for the city block for sale."

"It's really on?" Liesl let out a whoop. "That's

fantastic. Now you're going to have to be the agent for the buyer."

"In my dreams, girl. If I did that, I'd be able to buy a house in your neighborhood. For my family."

"You underestimate your abilities, my friend. You are a Wonder Woman when it comes to selling real estate. What block is being sold?"

"It's one block off the square. There is a small building and the rest is paved for parking. The 300 block of North Jefferson that intersects with the 100 block of East Anderson, and borders the 300 block of North Coal, and the 100 block of East Love." Nicole chuckled. "I've got to run. Talk to you later. But I had to take a minute to tell you about that."

"I'm so glad you did."

The minute Nicole hung up, Liesl speed-dialed the office of the St. Louis attorney handling the nonprofit creation. At this late hour, she was forced to leave a voice message, but that was fine.

When Liesl hung up, she did a happy dance. *Thank you, God. There are many good things we're going to do with that city block. Plenty of space for more buildings and businesses! Show me the way.*

CHAPTER 29

AN UNREPENTANT THIEF

Success! Sweet success.

I hung up my phone and congratulated myself on getting my business back on track. Hiring a criminal smart enough to carry off the new plan was imperative for the success of this new mission. It will pay off in the end.

It took time to find a new participant for the upcoming heist. Finding him keeps me from having to do it personally, which is the best way to stay in the clear. Out of the cops' line of sight. With an alibi.

The interviews took place at a bar in a different town. I watched each candidate to spot any problem with alcohol or drugs. For the job, I needed someone with enough intelligence to *accomplish* what had to be done, unlike Big T. But they needed to be skilled enough to pull it off. They also had to be motivated by the payoff offered.

The right candidate had to handle and collect items of value and be trusted to turn them over to me. I'll pay him and pass the required percent of the profits on to my boss.

So many candidates were eliminated within

moments. One was an obvious alcoholic. Bye-bye, buddy. When another candidate arrived, he seemed to be hyped up on something. I showed him to the door.

After clearing out the pond scum, this left a couple of acceptable recruits. Consequently, I had to wait to see if one or both would agree to my offer and requirements.

This mess started when an employee, prior to Big T, absconded with the valuable items he was supposed to obtain for me. It forced me to put Big T, who was loyal but not smart, in a position too complicated for his miniscule intelligence.

My upper network wouldn't tolerate being late with my obligation. They're not known for "taking a joke" about money and debts owed. I could skate on the Big T problem because I had money in the bank. But now it's gone. The next job has to be successful.

An effective heist will ensure thousands of dollars come to me . . . in cash. Some go to the thief, but most will repay my empty saving account.

It would be nice to walk into a bank and steal all of that exquisite cash. However, that is out of the question. Bank robberies always get the Feds involved. I'm happy to keep the local yokels looking into our work. No reason to open the door for the resources available to federal investigations.

I spotted today's newspaper where I'd thrown it on the floor in frustration. The news coverage of Big T's death has been vague. Deliberately so. The police are being tight-lipped about the whole thing. The actual cause of death hasn't "officially" been reported yet, but one article stated there was no criminal aspect to his death.

What does "no criminal aspect" mean? Are they saying that he wasn't murdered? Did he merely fall over dead with a heart attack? Or die from some other health issue?

Why were the cops being cagey with their information? They were holding it too close to the chest for comfort. Did they suspect there was more to Big T's attempted theft?

An event is coming up that will be the perfect test for my new employee. This new job must go off without problems. I hired someone who embodied all of the criminal qualities needed. He's ready to pull off the next theft. Successfully.

I will be there, watching him every step of the way from among the crowd. I'll make sure he doesn't blow this, the way Big T did. It will be exciting. How fun to pay attention to dirty dealings while pretending to be baffled by the crime.

I moved back to a small town on purpose. They have inexperienced cops, and the people who live here are too trusting. Small towns are perfect for the dark undercurrent of crime and criminals ready to take advantage of their innocent ways. Criminals and shysters spread smiles, compliments, and reassurance, all efforts to trick honest people out of their money.

There's a particular fundraiser on the horizon that will have mountains of cash available. Due to some of the board members being resentful of paying fees to credit card companies, they voted to take only cash and personal checks at this fundraiser. The planners failed to consider how vulnerable a fundraiser can be when they're dealing in cash.

They don't realize criminals like me are plotting to steal it.

Chapter 30

Liesl

Justin surprised Liesl by suggesting their date on Friday night should be to attend the silent auction fundraiser for Simmons Stables. Before he could complete his suggestion, she interrupted him and accepted.

He grinned at her. "You didn't let me finish."

Liesl hugged him. "I'm so proud of you. Getting all hometown-acting with me. You're leaving city life behind and embracing this small town."

"The life has a lot of appeal to me." He ticked each off with his fingers. "No traffic jams. Affordable houses. Many churches to choose from when seeking a church home. Friendly citizens. Organizations you can join that are devoted to helping the local community."

"You're right. All of that's true."

"Let's figure out where you want to grab a bite to eat before the fundraiser starts."

"There is one downside to small-town living. Fewer restaurant choices than cities. Honestly, I'd prefer to go to the fundraiser first and then eat afterward. That way, we don't have to rush through dinner."

Justin agreed to her wishes without a blink,

making Liesl grateful for his easygoing nature. It had been a long time since their last date, and that was her fault. She needed to make up for her procrastination tonight.

The now stunningly refurbished stable on West Boulevard was the setting of the fundraiser for the Simmons Stables Preservation group. Named for world-famous horse trainer Art Simmons, the stables originally included several buildings, but they were in bad shape when the preservation group acted to save as many as possible.

They'd been able to refurbish the main stable, and it was a masterpiece. The historic structure was a beautifully renovated venue for parties, receptions and other gatherings.

Justin parked along the boulevard, and they walked through the new iron gates framing the entrance to the parking area. They took a moment to admire the ironwork and decorative horses adorning the fence.

Inside the stable, colorful twinkle lights decorated the interior areas of the expansive wooden barn. The lights created a festive glow in the hayloft, plus they were wrapped around the ceiling joists overhead.

The chatter of the attendees mixed with lively country music piped in through speakers in the loft. When Liesl stepped onto the stone floor lining the barn's interior, she was glad she'd worn boots instead of high heels. Her midi-length skirt, made from a pastel spring print, danced around her calves as she walked.

Justin held her hand as they moved through all the people. She was proud to be his date tonight. He was handsome in a shirt and sweater, perfect for showing him off to the crowds.

With pride in her voice, Liesl asked, "Did you know this is the oldest known structure in the United States continuously devoted to boarding and training champion American Saddlebred horses?"

Justin chuckled. With a theatrical tone, he answered, "I did *not* know that. What a delight to have such a beautiful and knowledgeable tour guide. Please tell me more."

Liesl grinned at him. "What burning questions do you have about this beautiful stable?"

"Ah . . . How old is it?"

"They built it in 1887. The preservation society, which sponsored the fundraiser tonight, formed to preserve it. The members continue to work hard for its bright future. I appreciate you bringing me here to support their efforts."

Justin put his arm around her shoulders and gave her a squeeze. "I have to admit, being here wasn't actually my idea. Someone suggested you'd be delighted to come here."

Liesl chuckled. "I'd guess such a suggestion came from your beautiful and professional real estate agent, who is my bestie."

"Ding. Ding. Ding. You answered correctly. What would you like as a prize?"

Spotting a table with baked goods on it, Liesl pointed toward it. "I believe there is a homemade pie over there with my name on it. Maybe one with your name too."

Justin and Liesl waved at Dr. Johnson, who was seated at a table talking to Mrs. Sizemore, his doctor bag in front of him.

Justin turned to her. "Is he always on duty at these kinds of events?"

Liesl nodded. "He volunteers at all of them. Many people have been bandaged and splinted by him at festivals and public events."

When they'd added their bids to the silent auction paperwork for several pies, Justin led her to the snack area, where he purchased soft drinks for them. While they waited for their order, Liesl spotted her cousin Gretchen. She sat at another table situated toward the back of the stable.

Liesl tugged on Justin's coat sleeve. "You remember my cousin Gretchen?"

"Of course. I met her on our first date. Short, with red curly hair? Has an accounting business?"

She applauded. "An *A* for the student." She gestured toward Gretchen's location. "It's my guess they've put her accounting skills at work for this fundraiser. Let's go say hello."

Justin handed her a soft drink bottle and

loosened the top for her. When he'd opened his drink, he said, "Lead the way."

When they arrived at Gretchen's table, they skirted the line in front of her and stood off to the side. Gretchen was calculating someone's payment. Her bouncing red curls shifted every time she glanced from the bid sheets in front of her to the customer standing nearby.

They waited until the customer paid his obligation and Gretchen counted out his change. When she placed the bills in the nearby cashbox, Liesl observed multiple denominations stacked in tall mounds. After the customer moved away, and before the next person in line approached, Liesl stepped closer.

"Hey, pretty lady," Liesl tilted her head toward Justin. "You remember Justin, don't you?"

Gretchen gave him her full attention. "How could I forget this handsome man?" She batted her eyelashes at him. "Good to see you again, Justin."

Liesl tried not to roll her eyes at her cousin's flirting. Gretchen was a happily married woman, and flirting with Justin was a prank. To end the teasing, Liesl said, "You're hard at work tonight."

"It's part of the joy of being an accountant. You're always tapped to help with the money end of things."

Liesl scanned the area. "Isn't Cameron here?"

Gretchen smiled. "No. He helped me to set

up and get everything arranged. Afterward, I sent him home so he could watch sports and fall asleep in his chair."

Gretchen gestured to the next person in line, who handed Gretchen her bid sheets.

Liesl smiled at her cousin's remark, but when Gretchen had reviewed the paperwork from the customer, Liesl's smile faded. "Is anyone else helping you with this?"

"No." Gretchen continued to tally the bid sheets.

Liesl leaned in and lowered her voice. "You're sitting here, alone, with all the money? Is that wise?"

"It's been fine. They're pulling the bidding sheets at various times, so those who won the bids aren't caught in a long line trying to pay me all at once." She spoke to her customer. "Sixty dollars, please."

While the woman counted out three twenty-dollar bills, Liesl said, "I'm not concerned about your customer line. I'm concerned about you being by yourself with all this money." She waved her hand toward the cashbox atop the table.

"Oh." Gretchen shrugged off Liesl's concern. "Not a problem." Then she placed the twenties in the cashbox and began writing out a receipt.

"Do you want us to sit with you?"

Gretchen pulled a face. "Really? Why would you want to do that?"

Liesl made light of her suggestion. "Do you need a break or something?"

"I had one a few minutes ago. Right before they pulled another round of bid sheets." Gretchen handed over the completed receipt and greeted the next person in line.

Liesl gave up her mission and smiled at Gretchen. "We'll talk to you a little later."

Justin led Liesl toward more auction items on display. Once they reached them, he leaned down and asked, "Is everything okay?"

Liesl shrugged. "It bothers me. Gretchen is sitting alone, surrounded by a pile of cash. If someone wanted to make a grab for the cashbox, it would be easy. They could snatch it in front of everyone, or when Gretchen was heading to her car. She has no one to protect her."

"I agree. Are you acquainted with the people in charge of the fundraiser?"

"I am. One is a classmate of mine."

"Why don't you make a suggestion for someone to sit with her?"

Liesl mulled this over, then said, "I'm going to go one step further. I believe the police should be here."

Justin frowned at her. "Isn't that too much? Two people sitting with the money should be fine."

Liesl spotted one of the stable preservation members, but he scurried off before she could catch his attention. It wasn't her place to explain to Justin about the elevated theft concern in town. Before she could decide whether she should text Kurt, Justin pointed toward the front entrance.

"Nicole and Lee are here. They even brought Claudia."

Liesl smiled and waved at them. "I'll bet they're not staying long. Claudia's going to be all over the sweets."

Claudia darted through the crowds to reach Liesl and gave her a hug.

Liesl ran her hand through Claudia's brown curls that bounced around her pretty face. "Between your curls and this beautiful pink dress, you're the most beautiful ballerina in town."

Lee cleared his throat and grinned. "I believe tonight this is Princess Claudia. Her outfits determine her occupation."

Liesl made an exaggerated bow to Claudia. "My princess. Please forgive me for being such a fool. I beg your tolerance for my mistake, your majesty."

Claudia giggled.

Nicole rolled her eyes at Lee and Liesl. "She's this way because you both encourage her."

Liesl grinned at Lee. "Has your wife forgotten I make my living spending hours hunched over a computer writing make-believe?"

Nicole chuckled. "Give it a rest. How much time have you spent writing recently?"

Liesl frowned. "Not enough. It's time for me to have some looming deadlines in my future."

Once the men fell into conversation, Liesl pulled Nicole a few steps away from them.

"What's up?"

"I'm worried about Gretchen." Liesl gestured with her head toward Gretchen's table. "She's over there by herself, dealing with an enormous amount of cash."

"Yes. She's obviously alone. If she's taking in a lot of money, then she's too alone for comfort."

"There's no one standing guard or even sitting with her. I offered to sit with her, but she said she was fine. She doesn't understand the situation our law enforcement is facing right now."

"Do you want me to talk to her about it?"

"You could, but I doubt you'd have any better luck. We can't tell her the reasons behind our concern without violating our agreement with Kurt and Hector."

"True." Nicole observed Gretchen for a moment. "We could take turns staying close to her."

"Maybe, but I sense she needs an official protector. Someone with law enforcement. Maybe even someone with a gun." Liesl wrung her hands. "If our town has a problem with thieves right now, we can't stand around and let her handle all that cash alone."

"I agree. Reach out to Kurt."

"You think?"

Nicole nodded. "Yes, I do."

Liesl gave Nicole a quick hug. "You're the best."

"And don't you forget it!"

Justin was still talking to Lee. With him distracted, Liesl fished her phone from her purse but hesitated to send a text. Figuring it was easier to explain the situation over the phone, she called Kurt and launched into an explanation of the situation.

"You're worried someone will try to steal from Gretchen?"

"She's alone, surrounded by pots of cash. If I were a thief searching for a quick hit, she'd be my target. There are so many opportunities. When she's helping a customer or distracted by packing up to leave, or when she's walking to her car with the cashbox tucked under her arm, she's extremely vulnerable."

"I agree. With what happened in the museum, we'd best not take a chance. I'll grab Ross. He's awake and always up for an adventure. We'll head your way in a second."

"Why you? I figured you'd call a patrol officer. Someone already on duty."

"It's possible the person or persons stealing the money could be associated with my case. I'm not going to let something happen without me being there."

"Now I feel guilty for getting you involved."

Kurt laughed. "Good." He hung up.

A weight lifted off Liesl's shoulders when she slid her phone into her purse. Kurt would handle it. Now she could relax and enjoy the rest of the evening.

When Justin and Lee finished their conversation, Liesl offered to do something of Justin's choice. "What items do you want to peruse next?"

"Can we check out the bridles and saddles over there?" He gestured toward them.

She spotted the table full of horse gear he indicated. "So, besides shopping for a house, you're considering livestock? A horse?"

Justin laughed. "No horseflesh for me. But I admit to loving beautiful leather. The smell of it. The look of it. Everything. It brings out my inner cowboy."

"Lead on, John Wayne." She slipped her hand into his, and they made their way to the table filled with beautiful leather craftsmanship and aromas. It didn't disappoint either of them.

While Justin continued surveying the leather goods, Liesl had a short but sweet conversation with Mr. and Mrs. Miller. They told her they were supporting the fundraiser for one of their grandchildren who was a horse lover.

Justin and Liesl were still at the display when Justin scanned the crowd and stiffened. He spun toward Liesl with a scowl. "Did you ask Kurt to come?"

His reaction surprised her. "I talked to him about the situation with Gretchen. He offered to come."

He kept the scowl. "Is there something going on between the two of you I should know about?"

The question took Liesl off guard. "Ah . . . He's a cop. I was concerned about Gretchen being alone with all that money. He came to check it out. Why would that make you believe something is going on between me and Kurt?"

"The two of you have a long history. Does the romance continue?"

Liesl blinked at him for a moment, speechless. Was the romance rekindling? Kurt wanted that to happen. What did she want?

Apparently, she'd taken too long to answer because Justin stalked off, leaving her confused and miffed. Was jealousy a flaw in Justin's character? Or was he right to envy the sparks between her and Kurt?

Nicole approached Kurt and Ross. "Hey there, Mr. Ross. Would you like to join Claudia at the snack table?"

Ross smiled. He was adorable in his blue jeans and western-themed shirt. If anyone was taking the cowboy attire seriously tonight, it was Ross. All he needed was a child-sized Stetson to cover his white-blonde hair.

Ross turned to Kurt. "Can I go with them, Dad?"

Kurt made a solemn face and pointed a finger at Ross. "No caffeine, buddy." Then he smiled and dug out his wallet and pulled free a ten-dollar bill. "Why don't you be a gentleman and treat these pretty ladies?"

Ross squealed and grabbed the bill.

Princess Claudia and Cowboy Ross set off toward the snack table with Nicole scurrying close behind them.

Kurt called to Nicole, "Thanks, Nic."

Nicole shot a hand in the air and waved, never taking her eyes off the rushing children.

Liesl waved at one of the painters who'd helped with her recent remodeling. Frank LaMotta. He appeared to be alone. *Why was such a cute guy here without a date? Maybe he had a date and she'd failed to spot her.*

With a glance around for Justin, who was nowhere to be found, Liesl approached Kurt. "Thanks for coming."

"No problem. Your call was a good excuse for Ross and me to get out tonight." Kurt lowered his voice and leaned in. "Can you point me toward Gretchen? I haven't spotted her yet."

Fighting the distraction of Kurt's awesome cologne, Liesl gestured with her head. "Over there. Toward the rear of the barn on the right-hand side. They've got her tucked into a corner by the back barn doors."

Kurt rolled up on his toes and scanned over the crowd. "Got her. I'll talk to you later." He strode away, leaving a wonderful scent in his wake.

Liesl stood alone in the crowd. She couldn't spot Justin anywhere. Had he left? Did she care? She wasn't sure.

She was alone. She felt free to peek through the crowd to witness Kurt approaching Gretchen. Although she couldn't hear their conversation, she watched his actions. Within a moment of reaching Gretchen's table, Kurt pulled up a chair next to her and sat down. Maybe the secret was not asking if he could join her, but to simply move in without consent.

Liesl shook her head. *That guy. He sure is a charmer.* In this case, she was grateful he could charm himself into a seat next to Gretchen. *Bet his awesome cologne helped.*

It was good that Gretchen had no idea how much planning had gone into this maneuver. She might have resisted the protection if she'd known the plotting that had made it happen.

Liesl stood and studied her and Kurt for a moment. Gretchen was hard at work, counting money and providing smiling customer service to buyers. Kurt, on the other hand, was the picture of relaxation. He was draped sideways in the folding chair, his right arm resting on the table, his left arm hanging by his side. Few people would pay attention to his alert eyes, scanning the crowds for trouble.

His eyes and left arm gave him away. Although hidden from view, Kurt's pistol was on his left side, in a shoulder holster under his sport coat. He always carried his service weapon when working, and tonight she'd called him out to work.

With Kurt appearing to have the situation under control, Liesl turned her attention back to finding Justin. When she swiveled, she bumped into Mrs. Constantine.

Liesl reached out to steady Mrs. Constantine, her face flaming at the faux pas. One glance at the older woman revealed she wasn't happy about the collision.

"I'm so sorry, Mrs. Constantine. I'm such a klutz."

After a pause, Mrs. Constantine said, "No worries." She backed up and lifted both palms in a "hands off" gesture.

Liesl scurried away and had no trouble spotting Justin because of his height. He was at the leather display table again. While in conversation with another man, he saw her and nodded.

After the fiery reaction he'd had earlier, she wasn't sure what their future would be. Until she decided, she thought better about talking to him and decided to play with Nicole and the kids.

When Liesl glanced over at Kurt and Gretchen

again, nearly thirty minutes had passed. Kurt remained by Gretchen's side.

She also looked around for Justin. He was still at the fundraiser, but he'd never come and talked to her again. Was it a standoff between them?

She decided to stay with Nicole, and they rotated as a tag team with entertainment ideas for the kids. Eventually, however, they were getting desperate for new material.

Nicole dug into her purse and pulled out a set of car keys. "Between the kids and the sniping I keep overhearing from Nancy Jo and Paul, it's time we headed home."

Liesl turned to get a glimpse of the nearby couple Nicole mentioned. Both Nancy Jo and Paul were in their fifties. They'd been married for over twenty years and had three beautiful children. He was a contractor, and she was his accountant, which might be the reason they disagreed. Didn't every couple need time away from each other? "I guess being out in public makes them testy about things."

Nicole narrowed her eyes. "I hear they argue at the office too. I'm glad Lee and I have different occupations and work separately. Working together and living together would be too much togetherness."

"Justin and I may have had a little too much togetherness tonight," Liesl said. "He was angry I called Kurt to chaperone Gretchen."

"I'm sorry," Nicole said. "He's probably picking up on all the vibes you and Kurt have."

"Are we so obvious?"

Nicole rolled her eyes. " 'Fraid so. Call me. We'll talk about it later." She strode to Lee and rattled her keys near his ear. "Time to go."

Lee turned, distracted. "Go find Claudia, and then we'll head out."

"Okay. She and Ross are around here somewhere."

Liesl pointed toward the children, who were hovering over the snack table. With no money in hand, they admired the offerings.

Farther to the right, a tall, thin man lingering about twenty feet from Gretchen's table caught Liesl's attention. She didn't recognize him. In a small town, a stranger was rare. He looked about fifty to fifty-five years old and stood alone, another red flag in her evaluation of him. If he didn't accompany anyone, why was he here?

At a fundraising event, she would expect to see people she didn't know. Yet, as she studied this man, her instincts told her to be cautious. With all the criminal happenings in town, her "spidey senses" were on alert.

Liesl waited for the man to join a group or approach someone else. He didn't. He gazed at Kurt, or the money box in front of Kurt, and that made her even more nervous.

She pulled out her phone and sent Kurt a text about the man.

Kurt reached into his pocket and pulled out his phone. He read the message. When he finished, he didn't turn in her direction, but let his gaze wander to the man she'd identified.

Nicole was gathering Claudia and Ross near the man in question. Liesl's stomach sank.

Kurt, now standing, had the "cop look" adorning his face.

Without a moment's hesitation, Liesl bolted toward Nicole, Ross, and Claudia, pushing her way through the crowd.

Nicole spotted Liesl, assessed her panicked approach, and responded with her own fear. She made a grab for Claudia as Liesl barreled in on Ross.

When Liesl reached Ross, she swept him up with her right arm and headed straight for the back barn doors. She pushed her weight against them, but they were latched.

Nicole threw up the latch, then Liesl pushed against the doors again, and they swung open.

In the crisp air outside, Nicole and Liesl ran around to the front of the stables, still holding the kids. Luckily, with all the games they'd been playing inside, their foray outside made the children believe this was another game. They laughed and squealed as Nicole and Liesl ran with them.

"I've got my keys," Nicole said. "Let's put the kids in my van."

"Good idea. Then I'm going back in there."

"No, you are not." Nicole used her don't-even-think-about-arguing-with-me voice.

Liesl asked, "Where are you parked?"

Nicole moved quickly, Liesl right on her heels. Nicole hit her remote opener. The van chirped, and the lights flashed.

When the kids were in the van, Nicole dragged Liesl inside with them. She hit the automatic close button, and the van door slid shut.

Nose to nose, Nicole said, "Let me repeat. Don't even think about going back in."

"I get it. Accepted. But shouldn't we let the guys know where we are?"

"Yes."

Nicole pulled out her phone, but her hands were shaking so much Liesl said, "I'll call Justin. He was with Lee the last time I saw either of them."

Justin answered on the first ring. "Where are you?"

"In Nicole's van with Nicole and the kids. Get out of there."

"Why?"

Liesl grunted. "Is it over?"

"What do you mean?"

Liesl turned enormous eyes to Nicole. "Has anything happened in there?"

"Like what? Someone eating too much cake?"

"Nicole and I rushed the kids out of there when I believed Kurt was getting ready to take some guy down."

"Hold on . . . I see him and another guy sitting with Gretchen at the money table. Everything appears fine there."

"Describe the other guy, please."

"My guess would be he's a cop. He's tall, fifties maybe. Balding on top."

Liesl's cheeks flamed. "They're both sitting there?"

"Yep. Talking."

Liesl frowned. "My mistake. I'd say it's time for us to get dinner."

"Sure. Let me check if we won any bids, and then I'll be out."

"Okay. Thanks." She hung up and closed her eyes. To Nicole, she said, "I'm so embarrassed. Appears the guy that scared me is a friend of Kurt's."

Nicole patted her. "Better safe than sorry, girl. I'm sorry it scared you, which scared me. But no harm done. You believed you were doing the right thing, and it was definitely the best thing for the kids. If there had been any danger back there, the kids would have been safe because of what we did. They considered it a game."

Liesl glanced at Ross. "Speaking of kids, what's going to happen to Ross? He doesn't need to stay here on a school night and be out late."

Nicole pulled up her phone and tapped out a message. "I'll take him home with me. Kurt can pick him up there later tonight. You have the rest of your date to finish."

"I doubt if it will be much of a date, since Justin was upset I called Kurt."

Nicole reached over and patted her hand. "Don't be too hard on yourself. Couples disagree about things."

"What should I do about Justin?"

"Nothing right now. You've finally discovered he's human, like the rest of us. Cut him some slack. Give the situation some time and thought."

"You're the best."

"And don't you forget it."

Chapter 31

April, 1862
Audrain County, Missouri

The Spy

My contacts had requested a meeting at our usual place near Davis Creek. The old shed served our purposes well. It was a forgotten structure but lent itself to use when we needed to pass more information than we'd want to put on paper.

Thanks to the failure of the information I'd passed to them, this visit was going to be contentious.

Once inside the shed, the anger and resentment from the three secessionist leaders already gathered was palpable. They were the only ones who knew my identity. I didn't know their followers. Didn't want to know them.

I held up my hands in surrender. "I'm sorry about what happened. The details I gave you about the mission were correct when they left the camp."

"Correct?" The unofficial leader of the gang spoke first. "You got it all wrong. The whole thing was a waste of time."

The rest of the men mumbled their displeasure.

"Hear me out. It was good information when I passed it to you. The squad's commander got hurt and had to be brought back to camp. That put them two men down. He ordered the remaining squad to work at a different location, one more secure."

Another man spoke up. "All that time and effort for nothing. Because of you."

"Hold on. I have no control over a change of plans that occurred after the squad left camp. The commander was injured. Plans change when that happens."

They exchanged looks among themselves. Not pleased, but resigned to move on. "What about the future? Got anything to pass on to us?"

"The next mission will be to make repairs on the railroad bridge that didn't get repaired when the commander got hurt. Same place. In the next couple of days. I don't know exactly when."

The leader all but growled at me. He stepped close enough for me to smell the whiskey on his breath.

"Now you're telling us to go back to the same place where they were supposed to be last time? Is this good information? Everything we do is a risk. We put our necks in a noose, risk dangling from a hangman's knot."

My anger rose to the surface. "I'd face a firing squad or a noose if they caught me. You're not the only ones risking your lives." I turned and left the shed.

The rebels were upset about a failed mission.

I was upset for an entirely different reason.

I'd expected someone to get suspicious about me eventually. After weeks of successful spying, that time had come.

Had they spotted me going about my nocturnal business? Or was the information passed to the Confederacy too precise, thus making the camp's officers suspicious of an insider?

With my rank, I'm noticed everywhere I go, but no one questions where I'm going or where I've been. My commander trusts me. That's due to the paperwork that brought me here. He doesn't know I killed a man to get those papers and his uniform.

As I made my way back to camp, I reached into my pocket and rubbed my gold coin. The gold piece brought me luck. It was a talisman. A lucky charm of my mission to do everything I could to bring down the Union Army.

Although my spy connections worked well, I decided to step back from further actions for a while. It would allow those angry men to cool off. Better to be cautious and pause my actions than to proceed.

Being a spy is hard work. You're lying to everyone, and no one is your friend. You have to keep track of all your lies and make sure you repeat them to the right person. Death is a daily risk.

The sound of steps nearby put me on alert. I grabbed my knife and dove into nearby brush.

Within seconds, I spotted the unofficial leader of my spy connections. He must be looking for me. I spotted a pistol in his right hand.

He was alone.

If his desire was to kill me, I had a surprise for him.

I waited until he passed me, then silently came up behind him and slit his throat with one quick slice of my sharp blade.

The man had been out of control. With that kind of temper, he could talk. He had to die.

When his body's found, his buddies will know the same fate waits for them if they don't keep their mouths shut. But why should I wait for that? Maybe it would be better to set them up and get them all killed.

I could report receiving information about a rebel raid planned for our next mission. Send the report up the chain of command. No one would know where it originated.

I could start over with different contacts. I'd be safer that way.

This is war, after all.

Chapter 32

Lieutenant Cormac O'Malley

The evening was dark. While the enlisted men relaxed by their fires, the officers gathered for a meeting. Cormac was deep in thought, surrounded by other lieutenants and captains in their sometimes heated discussion of plans to protect a railroad bridge.

The general received information about a raid planned for the next night to sabotage the bridge. If damaged, it would halt supplies and troop movements to their encampment and to other army battalions. Now the lower-ranking officers scrambled to assemble an acceptable plan to ambush the raiders.

Sergeant Samuels pulled open the tent flaps and entered. He saluted the highest-ranking officer, Colonel Michaels. "Permission to speak, sir."

Colonel Michaels returned the salute. "Granted."

"I've an urgent message for Lieutenant O'Malley."

Cormac turned to Captain Oliver. "Sir, request permission to speak with Sergeant Samuels."

Captain Oliver said, "Granted."

Samuels led the way toward the main gate with quick steps. "It's George Hunter, sir. Says he has information for you. Something critical. He's at the main entrance."

"You trust this man, Hunter?" Cormac asked.

"Yes, sir."

"There's no question of his loyalty to the Union?"

"No, sir."

"All right. Go back to your duties now. Say nothing about this. If anyone asks, you and I discussed supplies. Don't say a word about George. I'll handle this."

Samuels nodded.

"I'm obliged to you," Cormac said.

Samuels veered off toward the valley area, to the tents of the enlisted men.

Cormac proceeded to the main gate. Two sentries were on duty. Beyond them, in the silvery light of the half-moon, he spotted a man in the shadow of a tree. He stood, shifting his weight from foot to foot. George. Even from this distance, in low light, he recognized the way George leaned down when his weight transferred to his injured hip.

Cormac approached a guard. "I have supply business with this man. We'll stay out of the camp."

The guard saluted and moved off.

Cormac walked toward George. When he reached the shadows beneath the tree, he asked, "How can I help you?"

George's nervousness showed with his shaky words. "Is there somewhere we can talk? Privately?"

Cormac beckoned to George to follow him. They headed to a grove of trees out of view of the sentries. Farther away from the gate, they'd also be beyond the guards' ability to eavesdrop.

At the trees, Cormac looked back to reassure himself their distance was sufficient. Satisfied, he turned to George. "Good enough?"

"It is." George removed his hat, clenching it in his hands, while he wiped his brow with his sleeve. "I have two pieces of information. The first involves a Southern sympathizer who was found in the woods this morning with his throat cut."

Cormac grimaced. "What was his name?"

"Robert Anderson. He was a local hothead. Part of the gang who kidnapped me a few months ago."

"Do you think he could be connected to the spy?"

George shrugged. "He had enemies. The sheriff is trying to track his killer, but cutting his throat from behind is not a country boy move. It's a soldier's move."

"Agreed. I'll see what I can find out. What's the other information?"

"I overheard something. I was out in the blacksmith's yard. Emil Thompson's the blacksmith. He sent me outside to search for a piece of steel. Then a man came into his forge, unaware I was out there. He was bragging about planning a raid."

"What?" The shock hit him hard. The intelligence they'd received was true.

"A raid against a squad from this camp. I stayed out until he left. As soon as I could, I headed here." George kicked at the dirt at his feet. "I feel God put me at the smithy for a reason."

Cormac was confused. *There's a voice inside camp telling them about our missions, and now the army has information on rebel raids. What's happening here?*

"This conversation," he said to George. "Did it seem the leak was from someone inside the camp?"

"Yes."

More proof of an internal spy and a gang of rebels. "Tell me everything you overheard."

"I caught only bits and pieces. What I could hear caused me concern. A group of them are meeting tonight. To plan for a raid tomorrow. The man was trying to convince Emil to join the meeting."

"Where's the meeting?"

"Didn't get that. I'll follow him later tonight. I'll track him."

"I need more details." Cormac's stomach roiled. He didn't like being right about a camp spy.

"He mentioned a bridge. Don't know which one or where."

Cormac grimaced. "How could they know so much about what we're planning right now?"

George shrugged.

"We've been told one of our railroad bridges was a target for tomorrow night," Cormac admitted.

"It's a good source, then."

"You never saw who it was?"

George shook his head. "Didn't need to. Recognized his voice."

"Friend of yours?"

"Nope. Some Southern sympathizers captured me a while back. Won't ever forget their voices. That sticks with you when you're blindfolded and all you can do is listen. I listened real good."

Cormac frowned. Sergeant Samuels had mentioned this incident when they discussed George's character. "I understood this group was arrested."

"They were. Did jail time too. But they're out. They're even worse now. I would have claimed some as friends before this war, but not now."

George's sincerity was obvious. Cormac cast away any further doubts about him. "My captain and I recently obtained proof there's a spy inside the camp."

George nodded. "The way the raid was talked about, there's no doubt you have a spy."

Cormac blew out a breath. "Even with proof, it's hard to accept."

"I understand. Their actions kill and injure your soldiers." George patted Cormac's shoulder. "You're doing what you can to stop it. Anyone reported sneaking in or out?"

"No."

George pulled a face. "So, either someone is really good at getting past your pickets or there's another way in and out of the camp. There are some caves in this area. You reckon there's a cave nearby they use?"

"Could be," Cormac said.

"What about a stream? There's running water everywhere around here. When you wade through a stream, you don't leave footprints. The noise of the water covers your footsteps."

"I'll go outside our perimeter and search for streams and caves tonight. I'll also see if I can catch anyone leaving the camp."

"I'll do my best to find this meeting," George said. "Knowing the guy talking about it, he'll start his evening in the saloon. I'll follow him without much trouble."

"I'm obliged to you. Anything else you can tell me? I'm fighting the enemy in a fog."

"If I can't follow the guy, my best friend and I will put together a group to search secluded barns and outbuildings around town. We'll find those Southern sympathizers tonight."

"Is your group made up of loyal Union men?" Cormac asked.

"Not necessarily, but they're loyal to me. I can trust them. My best friend, my father, my sweetheart's father, and a few others. If I ask them to help me, they will."

"If they catch you or your men, they'll kill you."

George locked eyes with Cormac. "I'm prepared for that. Enid Connolly told me you were a man of God. If you are, then put your faith in Him. I do."

"That's good advice."

"If I obtain information, how do you want me to tell you? I'd better not risk coming back here."

Cormac hesitated, then said, "Tell Enid. She can bring the information to me. But I don't want her in danger."

George's face darkened. "You'd risk her being hurt?"

"Never. That's why I don't want her writing anything down. Many of the men are aware I'm sweet on her. They won't think twice about her visiting me."

"You're sweet on her?"

"Smitten."

George smiled. "I understand. My affection for Alice has taught me about feelings I've never previously experienced."

"The men have seen Enid and me talking at church. Some know my hope is to court her. If she came here with a message, the men would just tease me. They'd never suspect she was delivering information."

George's eyes narrowed. "You're not playing with her affections, are you?"

"No." Cormac met George's eyes.

"She's aware of it?"

"She knows I care for her. I'm doing my best to impress Miss Mary to earn her trust and gain additional time with her daughter." Cormac shrugged. "Never expected to fall in love in the middle of a war."

"Part of God's plan. Not for us to know, but to accept. If I may be so bold, I caution you not to underestimate the intelligence of women. Alice and my sister have shown they can be my greatest allies."

"Enid's already helping gather information on possible spies and contacts."

George stuck out his hand. "She's a fine girl. Pretty, fun, brave, and hardworking. A woman of God."

Cormac shook George's hand. "She's too good for me, but I'm hoping she'll overlook that."

"I feel the same about Alice. Don't know what they see in us."

"I've got to get back to the meeting. I'm obliged to you."

They exchanged nods and went their separate ways, both aware a new friendship had formed.

Chapter 33

Liesl

Liesl spent the day side by side with Mrs. Zimmerman, cleaning the completed kitchen. Then they unpacked and washed all the dishes she'd put away before the remodeling.

Once she'd convinced Mrs. Zimmerman to head home, Liesl went grocery shopping to restock the canned goods and other food she needed to restore the kitchen to a functioning, joyous space.

When she'd unloaded the food, she sat down to congratulate herself, and her thoughts turned to ice cream. It had been such a long time since she'd had a bowl or a cone.

Did she buy ice cream? A frantic search of the freezer revealed a flaw in her recent restocking efforts. How could she have forgotten her favorite treat?

Without a moment's hesitation, she grabbed her raincoat and purse. The sky was overcast, but not dreadful enough to make her rethink her mission. She walked to Joey's apartment and knocked on his door.

Within seconds, he greeted her wearing jeans, a nice white shirt, and a sport coat.

"Are you going somewhere, Joey?"

He smiled and glanced at his watch. "In seventeen minutes, the Millers are picking me up for a fellowship dinner at First Baptist Church."

"Excellent. Tell them I said hello. Need anything from the grocery store? I'm out of ice cream."

"I can loan you my vanilla swirl, if you'd like."

She almost laughed at his concern. "Thank you, Joey. It's nice of you to offer. I'm going to buy several varieties. Need anything?"

"No, thank you." He looked past her shoulder.

She turned, spotting a car pulling into the driveway. "I guess your ride is early."

"No," Joey said. "That's not the Millers' car. They either drive a 2022 Kia or a 2015 Chevrolet."

Liesl puzzled over the strange car until a tall, gray-haired man stepped out of it.

"Oh, it's Mr. Hunter. Kurt's father." She turned to Joey, but he was gone. He'd slipped back into his apartment.

"Hello, Liesl," Mr. Hunter called out. "Did I catch you at a bad time?"

She walked up to Mr. Hunter and gave him a quick hug. "I was headed to the grocery store, but you've saved me."

He reached out and patted her arm. "Could I have some time to explain something?"

Liesl tried to hide her mystification. "Is everything okay with you and Mrs. Hunter?"

"Yes, fine. But I need to talk to you. Privately."

"Of course, Mr. Hunter. Come on inside." He was one of the nicest men she'd ever met. Whatever he needed, she would do her best to provide it for him.

"Thank you. But only if it suits you." He hesitated. "This is a private, personal matter, and that's why I'd like to discuss it face to face."

"Of course." Liesl beckoned him to follow her and headed to her house. She was confused as to his purpose, but pulling from her training in social graces, she asked, "How about I make us some tea or coffee?"

"Either is fine. Anyone else in your house?"

"Not a soul. My kitchen remodel is finished, praise the Lord. They did good work, but I'm glad to be rid of all the noise and aroma of fresh paint. We can cozy up to the fire in the library or sit on the couch in the formal living room. Joey's getting ready to leave for the evening, so there's no one else to disturb us. Except Barney."

His brow furrowed. "Barney?"

She opened her front door, and the beagle came bounding to greet them. "This is Barney. My dog."

Mr. Hunter smiled. "I forgot about him. Ross talks about this dog all the time. That boy does a lot of talking, and I listen to about half of it."

"That's expected."

"When he's with me, I remind him God gave us two ears and one mouth, but he doesn't understand what I'm trying to say."

"He will," Liesl said. "One of these days, you'll be begging him to talk to you. Let's hope he never turns into a surly teenager." She chuckled and led Mr. Hunter to her new kitchen. "How about I choose coffee? On a rainy night like this, coffee appeals to me."

"Fine."

She led him into the library and gestured for him to take a seat in front of the fireplace. After fumbling along the mantel, she found the remote for the electric fire and turned it on. Then she left him to bring coffee.

When she returned, she carried a small tray.

"I brought cookies. Coffee and good cookies are always welcome, aren't they?"

"Perfect."

He reached out and picked up his cup. "I apologize for being so mysterious about this, but once we have a chat, you'll understand why. You need to understand things from the past."

Things from the past? She launched a silent prayer.

Dear Lord, Please help me receive this information Mr. Hunter wants to share with grace and kindness. Guide me to help him in any way I can.

She studied Mr. Hunter, then took a seat and tried not to fidget while he gathered his thoughts.

"This is about Ross. Back when he was conceived." Mr. Hunter stopped, turning concerned eyes to her. "This is painful for you, I know, but some recent events make it necessary for me to tell you more about that situation."

"Thank you for understanding. Go ahead."

He sighed. "It's all the coverage about those coins you inherited. I need to tell the truth about how they came to be yours."

She was deeply confused. How could he know such a thing?

"The coins came from my family," he said. "My great-great grandfather, or maybe it's great-great-great grandfather, was a local hero during the Civil War. They gave the gold coin to him for services he rendered to the Union Army as a civilian. The other coins were his own keepsakes. He figured coins minted by the Union during the war would be valuable."

"What a heartwarming story. What was his name?"

"George Hunter."

"Where did he live?"

"The family farms were off what is now Highway 54. The east end of town, in what is now Vandiver Village. He'd enlisted as a Union soldier, was injured and sent home to die. He fooled them by living through the injury. Then he did this service for the Union encampment here in town."

"How could you part with the coins? They are

a precious piece of your family history. I'll return them to you after the exhibit."

"Let me explain, then we can talk about it. Okay?"

"I'm sorry. I have no patience."

Mr. Hunter grinned, then it faded as he started talking. "When Kurt told us what happened between him and that girl, I wasn't sure he'd survive the consequences of his actions. He knew when he admitted it, you'd walk away. Likely forever."

"I was so broken when he told me." Liesl's chest tightened. "My faith in him was destroyed."

Mr. Hunter nodded. "Exactly how anyone would feel in that situation. He knew he'd lose you. What I feared was that he wouldn't want to live anymore." He hung his head.

Liesl had no idea Kurt's parents had been concerned about that.

"We were in high school. We thought we knew everything." Liesl gestured outwardly with her arms. "We were clueless back then."

He lifted his head.

Liesl spotted tears filling his eyes, and her own began to well up.

"Every plan he made, every dream he dreamed, everything he wanted, involved you and a life with you. He lost you, and it crushed him."

Liesl swiped at the tears running down her cheeks.

"When he told us the girl was pregnant, you'd think that would be the lowest point of the whole situation, but it wasn't. His lowest point was losing you."

"I understand." Other than the deaths of Uncle Max and Aunt Suzanne, her breakup from Kurt was the lowest point in her life.

"As a parent, I couldn't make everything go away and get you two back together. However, I prayed about the situation. We all prayed about it. My belief that God has a plan for our lives helped us get through it."

"He has a plan. I believe it with all of my being." Liesl smiled at him in reassurance. "Then what happened?"

"When Kurt told me that girl didn't want to have the baby, he was beside himself with grief."

"What?" No one had ever told her this before now. "You mean, not only did she not want to raise the baby, she didn't want to give birth?"

"Exactly. We were as horrified as you. She was considering terminating the pregnancy. We were helpless. This was our grandchild. But the mother wasn't our daughter, and we couldn't insist she have the baby."

"What did you do?"

"I talked with my wife, and we approached the girl. We decided not to tell Kurt unless it was necessary. The girl agreed to talk to us, so Mrs.

Hunter and I asked God to help us with what to say and do. God guided us to listen and not speak."

"So what happened?"

"The girl's parents had not been very involved with raising her. They weren't interested in helping her raise the child or helping support her while she raised the child."

"I was unaware of that. Lots of teenagers face the same issues."

"I asked her what she really wanted to do with her life. She responded bitterly, saying she wasn't going to have a life unless she got rid of this baby. After some coaxing, she eventually opened up."

"You and Mrs. Hunter are kind people," Liesl said. "My guess is she could sense it in both of you."

"She wanted to go to cosmetology school and become a stylist. To eventually work in an upscale spa and beauty salon. My wife understood what she was saying better than I did, but it involved skills with cutting and coloring hair. Maybe one day having her own shop."

"What did you do with this information?"

"God helped us hear the thoughts of a girl who wanted to make a life for herself. To accomplish it, she needed help. I offered the option of sending her to a school of her choice while she was pregnant and after. She would sign away her parental rights and be free to pursue a career she'd received training to do."

"A reasonable request."

"She also wanted to get out of town, so the wicked tongues wouldn't reach her ears. My wife has a widowed sister in Colorado. My sister-in-law agreed to let her move into her house and take her to her classes and medical checkups."

"Your sister-in-law is a blessing."

"Yes, she is. Kurt found out the girl was staying with his aunt until the baby was born. We told him it was to help the situation. He was unaware we were paying for her school and medical expenses."

"You took on all of those expenses?"

"How could we not? We wanted to present Kurt with his child. Kurt needed to have the love. The person he loved the most was gone. His life depended on the love of that child."

Fresh tears erupted from Liesl's eyes. She'd always focused on her own sorrow, her own hurt. She didn't know what Kurt and his family had gone through.

"Kurt was happy she gave birth to the baby. He was ecstatic to be a single parent. He just didn't want the girl around."

"He's a wonderful father," Liesl said. "Since I've been home and experienced his relationship to Ross, I consider it magical. Two peas in a pod."

"When Ross was born, Kurt took him in his arms and smiled for the first time since your departure. The cost to have Ross in his arms was worth every penny."

"But that has nothing to do with the coins. How did they get from your family to mine? I don't understand."

"We didn't have enough money to cover the expenses. Your uncle gave me what was needed. To save my pride, I gave him the coins that had been in my family for over one hundred and fifty years. Sort of collateral."

"But how did you end up with the coins in the first place?"

"I told you about my ancestor, George Hunter. I was named after him. My full name is Stephen George Hunter. As I said, he was awarded the gold coin for service to the United State Army. It was something he did after he was mustered out of the military due to an injury. The family legend says that he delivered supplies to the Union Army and helped identify a spy."

"That's so cool."

He shrugged. "I'm not sure how much of that is true, but the coins passed into my possession, and I was proud. But I had no use for them, other than to admire them. That's when I realized God put them in my care to use them to save both my son and my grandchild."

She nodded, unwilling to interrupt him again.

"Your Uncle Max and Aunt Suzanne were good friends of ours. That friendship never wavered when this crisis occurred. I kept up with you through them." He smiled at her. "I hope you don't mind."

"Of course not. I figured they kept up with Kurt. Nicole did too. Everyone stayed informed but me. I couldn't handle it."

"You had a lot to process. All of us did. I found out you'd left town when, after church one day, Max put his arm around me and said, 'Our Liesl has gone to Houston to begin a new life. I'm not sure she'll ever be whole again.' We sat down on a pew and prayed together."

"Your friendship held up through it all, didn't it?"

"It did. They were aware of how Kurt was taking it. Same for us, we stayed informed about you. When I told Max I needed money to bargain with the mother for our grandbaby, your uncle said, 'What needs to happen? How much do you need?' He said he would take care of everything."

Liesl swelled with pride. Uncle Max always did what was right. Her tears renewed their flow, and she reached for a tissue.

"When Max told me that, I broke down and cried. I hoped this baby would save Kurt. He needed someone to love, someone to care for, and someone who would love him in return.

Replacing all that love and caring he'd lost with you. I prayed this child would give him a replacement future."

"Ross is such a blessing," Liesl choked out. "A loving little boy. We should all be grateful for what you did to save him."

"My pride wouldn't let Max do what he did without payment. I gave the coins to him as collateral. I begged him to keep records of all the expenses. He set up some sort of account to pay for her school, her medical expenses, her maternity clothes, and food. My sister-in-law wouldn't take anything for rent. We argued about him taking the coins, but in the end, he finally took them to save my pride."

"Was Aunt Suzanne aware of this?"

"I don't know. She was never involved in our discussions."

"She didn't tell me anything about this, and neither did Uncle Max, but they wouldn't."

"It's a personal and heartbreaking matter for all of us." Mr. Hunter smiled. "I can tell you these things because you can keep a secret, like your aunt and uncle."

Liesl wondered if he also referred to her inheritance. She'd certainly kept that secret.

"When Ross was born, the girl signed the papers. He's never known anyone as family but Kurt and us."

"He's lucky to have you all. Kurt's done a

fantastic job raising him, and you and Mrs. Hunter help out a lot."

"We love him so much." Mr. Hunter studied her for a moment. "When news about the coins reached us, Mrs. Hunter and I agreed it was time to tell you the history of them and how they ended up with you."

"Thank you for telling me."

"Please don't tell Kurt."

"It's not my place. But you and Mrs. Hunter should tell him. He has the right to the whole story."

"You are aware he never cared for that girl?"

Not trusting her voice, Liesl nodded.

"He will be upset that we more or less bribed her to give birth. He'll care that we left him out of the decision-making process. But his involvement would not have allowed the arrangement to work. I made a business deal with her, whereas he would have stirred her emotions."

"Please tell Kurt. The story needs to come from you."

"I'll think about it."

"Pray about it too. God will guide you to tell him at the right time."

Mr. Hunter nodded. "I dread it."

"Yes, but it must be done."

When Mr. Hunter was leaving, Liesl gave him a long hug at the door. "Thank you, Mr. Hunter, for trusting me with this secret. I'm also grateful for the wonderful story about my Uncle Max. I was aware he was that kind of man. It's nice to hear the proof of it."

After he left, she realized Mr. Hunter never spoke the name of Ross's mother. She hadn't either.

She decided to add Madison Lowe to her prayer list. For Madison's sake, for Ross's sake, and for herself to forgive and move on. She would also pray for Mr. and Mrs. Hunter to reveal everything to Kurt.

Chapter 34

An Unrepentant Thief

I drank my coffee in an effort to stifle a scream. My perfect plan for fast cash crashed and burned right in front of my eyes.

I blame it on not one, but *two* cops.

We were there, at the fundraiser. Ready to act when the moment was right. Then one of the local yokels pulls up a chair and sits down at the money table.

Does he leave? No.

Instead, he's joined by *another cop!*

They had their touching reunion scene at the money table. So my thief stood and watched. After an hour, I told my guy to go home. If the cops were guarding the table, they would certainly guard the money all the way to the bank.

I was pulled out of my thoughts when my teenaged daughter pounded her way down the stairs. I rose and pasted a smile across my face. Fifteen minutes later, she was out the door.

Now there was only one more heist planned. One. It was going to have to go off without a hitch.

If not, my network was going to come looking for me and take my "pound of flesh" in a way that would kill me.

This last shot had better work or I'm dead.

Chapter 35

Liesl

On the morning of the coin exhibit's opening, everyone was nervous and eager. Kurt insisted Liesl and Nicole meet him and Hector at the police station for a briefing.

Liesl pulled up at the station and watched Nicole pull a box of Ralph's doughnuts from her passenger seat. She climbed out of her car and called to Nicole, "You are a genius!"

Nicole grinned. "I hope I have enough."

Liesl helped her maneuver through the police station, handing out doughnuts along the way, until they entered the interview room. They had only four doughnuts left, but that was enough.

Hector was all smiles, but Kurt drummed his thumb on the table in a fast beat until he grabbed a treat from the box.

Once the doughnuts were consumed, Kurt turned to Liesl. "The cameras on the display are all set. Hector will have a good view of the Collections Room. What's the plan for getting me inside? Unnoticed."

"I've been doing some research in the library at Graceland for several days now. Someone tipped me off about a family legend that might be associated with my coins. So, I've used that as an excuse to be in their library for the past few days."

Kurt looked pleased. "That's a good cover story."

"It's not a cover story. It's the truth. I asked the assistant director, Annette, to pull everything they have from the Civil War era. Diaries, newspapers, that sort of thing. Now I'm reviewing them to verify the family legend."

"You didn't tell me about this," Nicole said.

Liesl gave Nicole the raised eyebrow look. "We'll talk."

"Moving on," Hector said.

"Our plan is for Nicole to come in the back entrance around four thirty this afternoon." Liesl eyed Hector and Kurt. "The last tour starts at four and should be ending by that time. Nicole will ask any remaining staff and volunteers to help her unload some books. These were Aunt Suzanne's books that I'm donating to their library. There's a lot of them, and the boxes are heavy. We loaded them that way on purpose."

Nicole and Liesl shared a smile, then Liesl continued. "While everyone else's attention is at the back of the museum, unloading and carrying in boxes, I'll let you in the front door, Kurt."

"Okay."

"When you're outside waiting for me, remove your shoes," Liesl said. "I'll kick mine off when I'm in the library doing research. That way, we can go silently up the stairs to the second floor and then continue up the dangerous staircase to the attic. We'll have some squeaking boards along the way, but the place creaks all the time. Shouldn't be a problem."

Hector's eyebrows lowered. "Are you concerned about that second-floor staircase?"

"Yes," Liesl said. "There is a wall on one side, but no handrail on the outward side. As you ascend, the ceiling height stays the same. When you reach the top, you're almost crawling. But, if you spin and push your back up against the attic door in the ceiling, it opens easily and without a sound. I got up there yesterday to dust an area for you to be comfortable inside."

"Is that it?" Kurt asked.

"You'd best bring gloves and a facemask to use inside the attic. You don't want to be sneezing up there. I put a stool in there for you to sit on while you're waiting for all of us to clear out."

"Thank you."

Liesl smiled. "A bottle of water might be good too."

"We have a plan for tomorrow too, if we need it," Nicole said. "On Sunday, if the thieves haven't hit, we'll regroup and figure out new distractions for the next week."

Hector nodded. "I hope we won't need any. If they're going to strike, I think it will be during the first night or two."

"That soon, huh?" Liesl frowned. "Any idea who might be connected?"

The men exchanged glances. "We pulled video from businesses near Donnie's security office the night that unidentified person went in. There was a figure who walked from a white Mercedes toward Donnie's business. Too poor of a picture to determine who it was, but we're checking into the car."

Liesl started listing car owners with her fingers. "Mrs. Sizemore owns a white Lexus. Mr. Van de Berg drives a Cadillac but shouldn't be allowed to drive because he's all over the road. Dr. Johnson drives a beat-up truck." She glanced up. "Does that help?"

Hector laughed. "Who needs a computer when we have you as a resource?"

"I wish I knew the car every suspect drives. But guys . . ." Everyone turned at Nicole's serious tone. "I believe Mrs. Constantine drives a white Mercedes."

"I'll check," Kurt said. He scratched a note in his pocket notebook.

A few minutes later, they all went their own ways, to meet again at Graceland.

Liesl found the parking lot of the museum filled but squeezed her car in between the edge of the pavement and a tree. When she grew closer to the house, she waved to Mr. Miller, who was hard at work near the Prairie Grove Church, built in 1889. It had been moved to the Historical Society Complex grounds in 1998.

Nicole called out to Liesl and did a shuffle-run to reach her. "I had to search for a parking place."

"Me too," Liesl said. "I was watching Mr. Miller at work. He impresses me so much."

Nicole tilted her head from side to side. "I agree, but I feel caught in the middle with Kurt and Hector concerned about his criminal career. He may not be trustworthy."

Liesl grimaced. "I don't believe that."

Nicole threw up her hands in defense. "I'm repeating what they said, not disagreeing with you."

"His days of crime were decades ago. Everyone goes through a time when they make mistakes. Lots of people do something they regret that affects the rest of their lives."

"Yes, ma'am," Nicole said. "Mistakes and regrets are part of life."

"Mr. Miller can't erase history. He has to move forward and make the best of the situation."

"You realize the same can apply to Kurt? His one-night dalliance resulted in his breakup with you. He can't undo that."

"I know," Liesl said. "I've been working hard with prayers and conversations with God about Kurt. What he did lost me for him. But that brought the most wonderful little boy into his life. I believe it's time for me to put all of that hurt behind me."

"I'm so glad you realize that. He's never stopped loving you."

"But what do I do about Justin?"

Nicole stood and studied her. "I don't think you've ever stopped loving Kurt, either. If that's true, you need to be honest with Justin. He deserves to know and move on."

Liesl put her hands on her hips. "Professor, we have other things to take care of first."

"That we do."

Liesl led the way to the back entry of Graceland. "Let's keep our focus on what we need to do now."

"Speaking of conversations we need to have," Nicole said as she followed in Liesl's wake, "when are you going to fill me in about the family legend related to your coins?"

Liesl held the door open. "When I'm given permission to do so."

"Okay then." Nicole stopped and gave her a squeeze. "We've got this."

Their plan went without a hitch. Hector was on inside guard duty during the afternoon hours. At the end of the last tour for the day, he left. Once he was out, Nicole made a fuss about needing help unloading the book donations from her car. She wrangled the two remaining employees to help her unload.

Liesl kicked off her shoes and smiled at her preparation. She'd purposely worn a long pair of wide dress pants, so if anyone noticed her going to the lobby, her stocking feet would be covered.

With silent steps, she made her way to the front door, unlocked it, and opened it wide enough for Kurt to squeeze through.

He was still dressed in the clothes he'd worn when on duty earlier—a light-colored sport coat, tan slacks, and a white shirt open at the collar. *He should have put on coveralls.*

Liesl withheld comment about how the dust in the attic was going to mess with his fashion choices. She relocked the door and led him directly up the grand wooden staircase to the second floor.

Once there, she signaled to Kurt to stay at the top of the first staircase while she quickly circled through the second-floor rooms. They were vacant. She blew out a breath in relief.

She beckoned Kurt to follow her up the second staircase. At the halfway point, Liesl turned so her back was facing the entry to the attic and she faced Kurt. She walked backward up the stairs until she was hunched over and her back pressed against the attic door above her.

With gentle pressure, she leaned against the door. It opened easily, thanks to the ropes and pulley system. The musty odor from the attic invaded her nose. She pushed to open the door wider then signaled for Kurt to follow her. At the top, she took a step to her right, onto the attic floor.

Kurt slipped in behind her. He held her waist to help her balance as she stepped back onto the staircase, facing forward this time, and she glided silently down the steps.

When she turned back to determine if Kurt had shut the entry, all she saw was the closed attic door. She didn't slow her steps but regretted being unable to wish him luck.

Back on the first floor, Liesl entered the library. She slipped on her shoes and sat down at the desk covered with research books and her notes.

When Nicole came in with a heavy box of books in her arms, she said in a loud voice, "Didn't you hear me ask for help with these boxes?" She winked at Liesl.

Annette, the assistant director, and Carol Krumb, a volunteer tour guide, followed Nicole into the room. They were all weighed down with boxes.

"I'm so sorry, guys," Liesl said as she raced over to Carol to help with her box. "I missed it."

Nicole said, "You always get lost in a world of books and research."

"Are there more boxes? I'll make up for my mistake." Liesl was well aware of three more boxes in the car but wanted to continue the pretense.

They sent Carol Krumb on her way home while Annette, Nicole, and a humble and apologetic Liesl unloaded the last boxes. Although Annette wanted to unpack them, Nicole and Liesl diverted her attention by pointing out how tired she must be.

"Our publicity for the coin display was a hit," Nicole said. "The crowds were immense. Let's lock up and head out. Those books will wait until tomorrow."

Nicole and Liesl stood and chatted about nothing while Annette checked the lock on the front door. Leaving Liesl to clean up her research area, Nicole followed Annette in her security rounds.

With that completed, they extinguished the lights and the three exited by the back door. Annette locked the knob and the deadbolt. At the parking lot, they said good-bye. Liesl couldn't help but glance up toward the attic when she pulled out onto Muldrow. She prayed all would go well tonight.

As she drove past the front of Graceland, she spotted the white van parked to the side of Show Me Credit Union, which was situated across the street from Graceland. The van had been parked there all day, with a repossessed sign on the windshield displaying the Credit Union's phone number for inquiries. It was the truck that would receive the hidden camera download.

Hector should be in there right now. Again, she prayed all would go well tonight.

Once home, Liesl couldn't settle down. She delivered barbecue from Pig Up and Go to a delighted Joey but had no appetite herself. What was going to happen tonight? Nothing? Everything?

Barney seemed to sense her tension and followed her everywhere she went, his nails tapping on the wood floors. The minutes stretched into hours as she paced.

Her phone rang as she was telling herself to get ready for bed. The noise startled her and caused her stomach to sink. All her worry churned there as she stared at an unidentified phone number. It had a Mexico prefix, so she answered it.

"Liesl?"

"Mr. Miller?"

"Yes, it's me. You said to contact you if I had any information about the museum."

"Yes, I did." She clung to the phone, dreading the information Mr. Miller was about to impart.

"Tonight, I picked up my grandson at the high school. His team had a wrestling match in Jefferson City. He lives in that neighborhood behind the museum. When we were going down South Missouri Street, I saw a white sedan parked near the museum. I think it's a Lexus."

"Really?" Her fingers tightened on the phone. *Mrs. Sizemore drives a Lexus. No! She couldn't be involved in this mess.*

"I suspect someone's messing with the museum."

"Thank you, Mr. Miller. I've got to go now. This is important information."

She hung up and called Hector to alert him that someone may be near or in the museum. When he didn't answer, she sent him a text. Where was he? Had he left the van for some reason? She ran to grab her car keys.

She sent Kurt the same text from the garage.

Liesl said a prayer of thanks that she lived only about a minute from Graceland. Although it didn't give her much time to decide what to do, she'd be there quickly.

She avoided South Muldrow. That street ran between Graceland and Show Me Credit Union, where Hector was stationed in the van. Instinctively, she turned right onto Grove Street and parked in the lot at Centennial Baptist Church.

She checked her phone, but there were no messages or missed calls. She set it on silent mode and scurried toward the museum's parking lot.

It was a quiet night. People were heading to bed, and many houses were dark. Liesl stayed on the sidewalk until she reached the parking lot, then she crossed it to the landscaped area. She strode from tree cluster to tree cluster, searching for signs of anyone outside the museum.

The silhouette of a man wearing a baseball cap approached on foot from South Missouri Street. Liesl stood still until she identified Mr. Miller.

"What are you doing here?" she whispered.

He whispered in return. "Figured you'd try to protect your coins once informed someone was messing around here."

"Not the coins. I care about Kurt. He's hiding inside."

She caught Mr. Miller's stunned expression in the moonlight.

"The coins are bait for thieves," she whispered. "I can't explain now. But I have to get into the museum as quietly as possible."

"No, ma'am. If thieves are in there, they could hurt you."

"I've reached out to both Hector and Kurt. Neither has responded. Something's wrong. You've *got* to get me inside."

He stared at her in confusion.

"Please, Mr. Miller. I need in. *Now.*"

"Don't the police have anyone stationed outside?"

"They are supposed to have someone out here, monitoring the feed from cameras inside the museum." She threw open her arms. "But something has gone wrong. Please. I must get in there. *Now!*"

Mr. Miller reached into his pocket and pulled out a giant ring of keys. "We're going to need tools. Follow me."

Chapter 36

Enid

Enid watched as her mother nodded off in front of the fire. Another dinner party was planned for the following evening, and they'd had a tough day preparing for it. She couldn't bring herself to wake her poor mother just to tell her to go to bed.

After sweeping the kitchen, washing and drying the last dirty pot, and hanging the wet dishtowel, she decided the kindling basket needed refilling for the morning fire.

As she pushed open the kitchen door, someone snatched it open from the outside. Startled, she gazed into Jeremiah's face. He grabbed her arm to keep her upright. His face pulled together in concern as he said, "George Hunter is here and needs to talk to you."

She stared at him. "Is something wrong?"

Jeremiah frowned. "You'll have to ask him. He wouldn't tell me what this was about."

With a glance at her still-sleeping mother, Enid set the basket down inside the kitchen and followed Jeremiah into the dark night.

An apologetic George waited for her in the barn. He pulled off his hat as manners dictated and then gave a brief explanation of the situation. He told her what he'd discovered and that

Cormac wished for her to deliver the information George gathered, to avoid suspicion by the camp spy.

She swallowed. It was unusual for a servant to be out at night. She would need a reason for being on the road. Her missus was sick? Mr. Clark sent her to fetch something from the camp or deliver a message? She'd think of an excuse while she made her way there.

She turned to Jeremiah, who hovered nearby. "Would you saddle up Deborah for me?"

His face clouded. "Absolutely not. If you have to go somewhere, it'll be in Mrs. Clark's gig. I'm driving."

"You could get fired for using it without permission."

"You could get fired for riding Mrs. Clark's favorite horse. They'll be no arguing from you. I won't stand for you to be out at night alone. They'll be no more discussion." He scurried away.

She turned back to George. "I guess that's settled."

George smiled. "I'd best be going." He put his hat back on his head and limped toward the barn door. "Good luck."

Enid called after him, "Thank you, George. Appreciate your help."

Jeremiah had thrown blankets into the gig before they made their clandestine exit from the Clarks' barn. Wrapped in their warmth, they could tolerate the cold night.

He asked where she needed to go, but never inquired about what she was doing or why. He risked his livelihood because she needed him. She vowed to do something special for him if they got away with this undertaking.

When they reached the camp entrance, several guards noted their approach. One strode toward them. Enid turned to Jeremiah. "Let me handle this."

Jeremiah offered her a hand as she stepped out of the buggy.

"Sir, I know it's rather untoward for me to be here at this time. However, my employer, Mr. Clark, has a message he asked me to bring to Lieutenant O'Malley."

The man looked confused.

"I promise you, the lieutenant will be grateful if you send a runner for him." She gestured toward Jeremiah. "You see, he sent his best man to bring me here. It's important."

The sentry hesitated.

"Please, sir." She waved her hand toward Jeremiah. "Mr. Clark would not have sent both of us to deliver a message if it wasn't important. Please summon the lieutenant."

The man nodded. He turned and called out, "Private? Find Lieutenant O'Malley at once and send him here."

"Thank you," Enid replied.

The guard returned to the gate, leaving her to deal with a grumbling Jeremiah.

He glared at her from the buggy. "This had better be important. At least you said I was Mr. Clark's best man."

"I'm sorry to involve you in this, Jeremiah," Enid said. "It is important. You're my hero tonight."

Moments later, Cormac rushed down the hill.

Enid waved at him.

Cormac grinned at her, then fell immediately into the proper role of a gentleman. He swept off his hat and bowed low. "Such an unexpected pleasure."

He held his hat and closed the distance between them. "Did George send you?" he whispered. "Thank you for coming."

She held out her hand, and he lowered his lips to it. In a whisper she said, "The spy was at the meeting place. He delivered a map with the location of the bridge. George came to me and sent his friend to report them to the sheriff."

Cormac straightened and released her hand. Then he leaned toward her. He whispered, "How long ago?"

She stepped back and whispered, "Less than an hour."

He took her hand in his and squeezed it. "I'm most obliged for your visit, even if it must be so brief."

Cormac nodded his thanks to Jeremiah as he helped Enid back into the gig.

Enid waved as he turned and nearly ran back into the camp. *Godspeed, my sweetheart.*

Her smile faded as she turned to Jeremiah.

His stare pierced her as he asked, "Are we through with all this nonsense?"

"Thank you. I'll make it up to you somehow."

Jeremiah maneuvered the horse and buggy toward home. The seriousness of their journey rendered them silent and melancholy. The country was at war, and they were in the middle of the conflict.

Lieutenant Cormac O'Malley

Cormac stood motionless, straining to hear anything like footfalls in the night. Although the moon was nearly full, the cloud cover rendered the night almost black. The clouds also hid stars, leaving Cormac with no heavenly light this night.

Sadly, it was a perfect night for spying. And there was at least one spy in their midst.

At this distance from the camp, no sounds from the soldiers or sentries trickled through. The cicadas moaned, but not as loudly as earlier in the week. The whisper of the wind blew through at random times, but otherwise, the night was still.

Previously, Cormac had made rounds to all the

camp sentries, advising them to be on alert again and reminding them that this darkness brought the potential for enemy attack on any night.

Cormac kept his concern about spying missions to himself. They didn't need soldiers shooting in fear and possibly wounding him or the camp spy. He would rather catch the traitor in the act of espionage than have a guard shoot him. They would never resolve the question of a spy without evidence. He needed to catch the spy with the accompanying proof.

He was grateful to George, Jeremiah, and Enid. The information he'd received confirmed that someone from his unit was meeting with the rebels. Now he waited for the spy to return to camp.

Cormac walked quietly through a thicket of trees. Eventually, he halted and leaned up against an oak's trunk. He listened for any anomaly from the regular night sounds of crickets, cicadas, and the hoot of an owl. All were normal. The rhythms lulled him into comfort.

When the owl took flight, the rustle of wings startled him. Soon after, footsteps approached—the reason the owl changed location. The steps came from the east.

Cormac stiffened, hopeful the lack of light and his position against the tree would keep him concealed. Huddled against the tree, he deliberately slowed his breathing and listened for footsteps or groundcover rustling around him. Nothing.

After a moment, the night brightened. Not a good time for the clouds to part. He feared his own hiding place would be the next thing revealed. *Lord, help me!*

His heart hammered in his chest. Was it loud enough for the man to hear? He tried to breathe silently. Out of the corner of his eye, he saw the flash of a blade. He leapt away and fell on the ground, hard. The fall knocked his breath from him, but he scrambled up and ran, loping into the thicket and then hiding behind some bushes until he caught his breath.

All was silent for a moment, then he made out the man's form moving toward him. Cormac ran, crashing through the brush, heedless of the noise he made.

He wanted to bring the spy in alive, to face the punishment for being a traitor, but he'd shoot him if necessary. Cormac grabbed for his pistol and once more took cover.

After a moment, he spotted a man sliding silently through the shadows. He walked like a hunter. Cormac was the prey. Slowly, he lowered himself to the ground, his pistol ready.

Peeking through the brush, he observed the near-silent stride of the unknown man. When he was within twenty feet of Cormac's refuge, he halted.

What was he doing? Taking in his surroundings? Looking for him? The man stood still for at least a minute, maybe two.

Cormac kept up his silent breathing, not daring to move. His pistol was in his hand, tempting to use. Did he have enough proof against this man to kill him? He debated whether it was time to step out of the shadows and hold him at gunpoint. The spy seemed too far away for that and could make a run for it.

The man turned a circle. He reached into his pocket. He turned over the object he held, then flicked it away from Cormac's hiding place.

Cormac stretched to keep his eyes on the object. It shone in the dim moonlight as it arched up and then descended into the brush.

When Cormac turned his gaze back, the man had disappeared.

Oh, no! He'd been spotted after all. The man threw that object to distract him, and it worked.

After a moment of hesitation, he scrambled toward the camp. This spy would try to get back into camp undetected. Cormac had to catch him before he made it past the sentries.

At the same time, he dreaded discovering the spy's identity. Which soldier could it be? Not Captain Oliver. *Please God, not Captain Oliver.* Fear that his captain could be the spy filled him with a dread that pulsed with each heartbeat.

Pushing down his fear of an ambush in the dark, he focused on locating the spy. When he spotted movement again, he ran toward it, gun in hand.

The crash of Cormac running through the brush

must have alerted the man that he'd been spotted again. The shadowy figure fled.

The moon was again hidden by the clouds. Darkness prevailed.

When Cormac believed he was gaining on the man, a sudden yelp filled the air. It was a combination of a gasp of air and a cry for help. Then silence.

Cormac ran to the area but saw no movement. He heard no breathing. No footsteps.

He stopped and listened. His thick dread grew heavier. The only ragged breath he heard was his own.

Could the man be lying down in front of him? Had the specter flattened himself, hoping to disappear?

Cormac searched the area slowly and meticulously. Nothing. No sounds of breathing that matched his own gasps for air.

The man had disappeared into the night. But that was impossible!

How? Where could he have gone? A cave? A trap door to a secret tunnel? Such a feat of engineering would be an advantage for a spy. But how could a tunnel have been built without the camp hearing the work or seeing it being performed?

Silence surrounded him. No stream or creek flowed nearby, and there had been no splash.

Cormac made another circle, searching everywhere. There was nothing to be found. Had the spy escaped into a cave? Fallen into some type of underground waterway? After searching for over an hour, he gave up.

In despair, he made his way back to the camp perimeter. How had the man slipped through his fingers? Perhaps daylight would help him figure out what happened.

Cormac found Captain Oliver alive and well in his tent. He reported the evening events, and Oliver ordered him to form a squad to search the area. The captain then selected a second squad to lead himself, and they headed out at dawn to uncover the truth.

The two squads scoured the area where Cormac lost the spy. They worked with machetes and axes, chopping down the brush to locate last night's tracks.

Early in the search they found a gold coin. Cormac studied it. The coin was the right size and shape to have been the object the man flicked through the air to divert his attention. Its gold would have winked in the low moonlight. Cormac grimaced. He'd lost the spy due to his distraction by this coin.

Eventually, some of the men discovered a hole surrounded by low brush. It appeared to open into an underground spring or creek. As they studied it, one of the men noticed two canals as wide as boot heels cut into the mud, running down the inside of the hole, possibly an indication that someone slid down the opening, into the water below.

"Don't get too close," Captain Oliver said when he saw it. "Step away. This is dangerous. The ground could give way at any time."

The men moved back cautiously.

"Did anyone see a body down there?" Captain Oliver asked. "Either floating or under the water?"

No one admitted to seeing anything but water within the hole.

Captain Oliver then called Cormac over to him. "With no body visible in the spring, it may have floated out some underground waterway. Those arteries could intertwine for miles beneath us."

"But sir, how can we confirm he's dead?"

"It's too risky to send anyone down there. I'm sorry. The search stops here."

Cormac closed his fingers around the coin, hiding the mocking, shiny gold. He vowed to give the coin to George Hunter. George deserved to benefit from his assistance with this matter. Cormac would pass on some coins to Enid, too, for her part in carrying the information. He appreciated George and Enid's loyalty to the Union. And their loyalty to him.

While he stood there, Captain Oliver put a hand on his shoulder. "You did your best, Cormac. That's all you could have done in this situation. Your instincts were right. There was a spy."

"A spy who may have escaped, sir."

"Not the result you wanted, but the spying has stopped. Right?"

"Yes, sir. I believe the spy fell into that spring and drowned, but doubt we'll ever know what happened."

When they returned to the encampment, a search was underway for Colonel Michaels. He was last seen the night before, heading away from headquarters toward "Tent City."

Cormac moved to say something, but Captain Oliver shook his head. When he could, Captain Oliver pulled Cormac away from the other men.

"He's gone. Shakespeare wrote in Hamlet, 'Give everyman thy ear, but few thy voice.' You and I know the truth. The men who helped us search know we searched for someone outside of camp who threatened you. There is no need to officially confirm we've had a rebel among us."

"We do nothing else?"

"We'll report him as a deserter. With his description. The entire army will receive the information. If he somehow survived, we'll have a better chance of capturing him. The important thing to remember is the spying has stopped. You've helped to protect our men."

"Yes, sir." Cormac swallowed hard. "Thank you for believing in me." Then he saluted and walked away.

CHAPTER 37

KURT

In the attic, darkness, tedium, and dust prevailed. Kurt wanted to play with his phone, but he knew this type of duty forbade it. Luckily, he'd brought along a fully charged digital book reader with a glowing display.

The e-reader was the perfect choice. No sounds to distract. Entertainment for the mind. It would be hours before anyone attempted to steal the coins. In the meantime, he had candy for his brain.

Six hours passed. Even with the digital reader, it seemed an eternity.

He shut the device and stood for a stretch. With his eyes used to the darkness, he studied the peeling wallpaper. This had been a child's space. How many children had slept and played in this house since its construction in the 1850s?

A noise interrupted his thoughts.

He held his breath and listened. A voice. Someone was inside the museum. Maybe two people. Would a thief talk out loud to himself?

Silently, Kurt made his way back to the stool. He tapped out a text message to Hector.

Someone is inside. Maybe two. I'm going down.

He didn't wait for a reply. He removed his shoes and socks then tiptoed to the attic entry.

With gritted teeth, he pulled up on the door to the attic, praying it wouldn't make noise. It opened with minor squeaks from the ropes. Nothing audible downstairs.

The museum's night lighting provided illumination as he cautiously made his way down the stairs, his pistol drawn and ready to fire.

When he reached the second-floor landing, he turned toward the Collections Room, where the coins were on display.

He took one cautious step before he was tackled from behind. The force of the confrontation threw him to the ground, his arms out to his sides, forehead whacking the hardwood floor.

It dazed him for a second. Then he turned to face his assailant.

Mrs. Constantine was on top of him, her sneering countenance inches from his, a knife in her hand.

For a millisecond, he stared at her in surprise.

She raised her knife and brought it down toward his chest.

Kurt grabbed her arm with his free hand to fend off the blow, but the knife pierced his upper chest, leaving him gasping from the searing pain.

He turned the gun toward her.

She made a grab for it.

He rolled and held on, trying to take aim at her. But he struggled. She was too close and surprisingly strong. He hit her in the nose with the heel of his palm, and she screamed.

Footsteps approached. He heard a grunt, then felt pain from a blow to his head.

Time seemed to waver as things happened in slow motion. His vision blurred. He lost his grip on the pistol, unable to resist the encroaching darkness.

CHAPTER 38

LIESL

Mr. Miller used construction knowledge to help Liesl. He pried the trim off a small window at the back of the Firebrick Museum addition. Then he unscrewed the window from its frame and lifted it out in one piece.

"The seal on this window is bad. Been meaning to fix it. Good thing I didn't."

He helped Liesl climb through the hole where the window used to be.

"Thank you," she whispered. "Call 911."

She kicked off her shoes then ran silently down the hall, toward the original structure of Graceland.

Nightlights required for commercial structures lit her way. She hurried down the hall of the newer addition, slowing at the director's office. The door was closed. Annette had closed and locked it when they left that afternoon.

Liesl moved into the original mansion.

The hallway from the new addition opened into the house's library. A survey of the room showed the stacks of her research materials undisturbed on the table. Shelves bursting with books and historical items appeared untouched.

She listened for a moment. Hearing nothing, she moved forward.

Reaching the grand hallway, she paused, listening. Nothing but her accelerated breathing. She crossed to the grand staircase, pressed herself against the stairwell wall, and silently climbed the stairs.

Her line of sight rose to the level of the second floor, and she almost gasped aloud when Kurt's sprawled form came into view. He was lying at the bottom of the attic staircase, blood spreading around his head and soaking the front of his shirt.

Heedless of the danger, she ran to him. She reached out and checked for a pulse in his neck and experienced immediate relief. He was alive.

Her eyes overflowed with tears, but she brushed them away. Now was not the time.

God, save this man. This man I love.

Blood oozed from his left shoulder area. At least it wasn't his neck. *Thank you, God.* Without hesitation, she reached into his sport coat pockets until her fingers located the handkerchief he always kept there.

She pressed the handkerchief where Kurt was bleeding, which caused him to moan. Although she regretted hurting him, he remained unconscious. The pressure she applied lessened the flow of blood.

She prayed Mr. Miller had done as she asked and called for help. Meanwhile, they had to hide. Being out in the open like this left them vulnerable to attack.

She couldn't leave him to search for a hiding place. And she had no defense against someone who might discover them.

Kurt's pistol.

With her right hand keeping pressure on his wound, she reached under his jacket with her left hand. The holster was there, but empty.

Did someone use his own gun against him? She couldn't tell what had made his wound, but she and Mr. Miller hadn't heard any gunshots. How long had Kurt been lying here? Where was Hector?

Voices rose from downstairs. What was happening there?

Please, God. Let this be Hector.

Regardless of the commotion downstairs, she had to get Kurt out of sight. To a place of safety. But where? Downstairs wasn't an option.

Liesl turned and eyed the dangerous staircase to the attic. If she could drag him up the stairs, she'd barricade the attic's entrance. They might be safe up there.

Could she pull him up those steps? Without him falling over the side?

The closest option on this side of the hallway was the wardrobe room. The museum staff filled it with enormous wardrobes from various eras representing the home's history. There were also some old steamer trunks in that room. Could she get him out of the hall and drag some steamer trunks to block the door against the attacker? That location was closer and didn't involve any stairs.

She chose the wardrobe room.

Liesl had to abandon holding pressure on Kurt's wound to move him across the hallway. She needed both hands, so she prayed that he wouldn't bleed out.

She hooked an arm under each of his shoulders and half slid, half carried him toward the room's entrance. With his head limp, she supported it with her torso, as she turned and reached for the knob. The door opened with ease.

A trail of blood that snaked along the floor like an angry serpent marked their path. So much blood. How could Kurt survive such a loss? The blood also left a route for the thieves to follow and discover where they were hiding.

She strained to pull him over the threshold. Her socks caused her feet to slide, so she reached around him awkwardly and pulled them off. With bare feet, she succeeded in gaining the traction necessary to pull him inside the room.

His bleeding had increased, likely from dragging him here. His skin was clammy. Had it been that way before?

She maneuvered Kurt to the far side of the room. In the corner, there was enough light seeping through the windows for her to look around for things to improve their situation. She shoved a large trunk in front of him, hoping it would hide him. A bucket crammed with cleaning supplies caught her attention. She armed herself with a rag and a bottle of glass cleaner, then peeked out the door. No one visible.

She tiptoed silently to wipe up the blood left behind. It was risky, but they'd be discovered if it wasn't removed.

As she scrubbed, indecipherable shouting rose from downstairs. What was going on down there? She hurried to finish. Whatever was happening down there could move up here fast.

"Well look at you."

Liesl's head snapped up. Mrs. Constantine stood three feet away, outside the Collections Room. Her nose was puffy and red. One hand pointed a pistol at her. The other arm was loaded with looted items.

"Cleaning up what remains of a stupid cop?"

Liesl leaped to her feet. Without regard to her vulnerability, she sprayed glass cleaner at Mrs. Constantine's face as she closed the distance between them.

When Mrs. Constantine shielded her eyes and screamed, the stolen goods and Kurt's pistol hit the floor with a crash.

Liesl pummeled Mrs. Constantine's stomach, her rage unfettered.

Footsteps pounded up the stairs.

"Stop, Liesl," Hector said. "Step back."

She turned. Hector and another cop stood at the

top of the staircase, their weapons pointed toward Mrs. Constantine.

Liesl said, "Call an ambulance."

Hector replied, "Already on the way. Are you okay?"

"I'm fine but Kurt's hurt. He's in the wardrobe room." Liesl gestured with the spray bottle still gripped in her hand. "He's bleeding." Then she ran to Kurt.

Back in the wardrobe room, Kurt remained unconscious. She applied pressure on his wound again and waited impatiently for the EMTs.

The sound of Hector reading Mrs. Constantine her rights reached Liesl, and she smiled. She was proud to have bested Mrs. Constantine. She vowed never to buy anything but glass cleaner with ammonia from this day forward. You never knew when you might call on that ammonia to save your life.

Moments later, footsteps sounded near their room. From her position on the floor beside Kurt, she could see boots and a pair of uniform pants approaching in the light of a bright flashlight.

"Over here," she said from behind the trunk.

She recognized Officer Howard.

"The EMTs are right behind me."

"Thank you, Officer Howard. Thank you." She sighed with an enormous sense of relief.

"How bad is he?" The flashlight's beam found Kurt, pale and still unconscious.

"I don't know. Bleeding from his shoulder. Pressure helps stem the flow."

Officer Howard squatted down to assess Kurt.

She fought back tears. Now was not the time to cry about this.

The noise of people ascending the stairs diverted her tears. More help. *Thank you, God.*

"Hector has Mrs. Constantine under control. I'm going downstairs to help with Frank LaMotta. He put up quite a fight."

"The painter, Frank LaMotta?"

"Yes, ma'am. He's in on it."

Officer Howard stood. "You've done all you can do. Keep up the pressure."

He and his light moved away as other men came into the room. They flipped on the main lights and went into action on Kurt. One took over applying pressure to the wound while another checked his vitals.

Liesl assured the EMTs she was unhurt. In response, they suggested she leave. She took one last look at Kurt, said a prayer, and began a search for her socks and shoes.

When she made it outside and saw all the police cars, relief filled her. They'd pulled into the circle drive at the front of the house, and one had parked near the rear entrance. Lights were flashing, but the sirens were off. Was every officer in the county here?

Mr. Miller stood at the edge of the parking lot.

He waved when he saw her approaching, then pulled her into a warm hug.

"You all right?"

"It's Kurt. He's wounded." She breathed deep. How could Kurt be hurt like this? *Please, God, heal him.*

Once she was steady on her feet, he asked, "Are you sure you're not hurt? You're covered in blood."

"It's Kurt's blood." Liesl burst into tears. Now was the time to cry.

Mr. Miller patted her back. "Bless him. I hope he's not too bad."

One of the EMTs walked past them and said to Liesl, "I'm getting a stretcher. He's stable." As the responder hurried to the emergency van, he turned and called out, "Good work up there."

Liesl and Mr. Miller gripped each other in another hug.

"Thank you, Mr. Miller. He would have bled to death without our help."

Mr. Miller put an arm around her shoulders as Kurt was loaded into the ambulance.

"You know, he's going to be just fine, Liesl. Just fine."

"From your lips to God's ears."

Soon after, law enforcement began loading up the handcuffed Mrs. Constantine, who walked by with red, watery eyes, a puffy red nose, and her wild California hair askew.

Liesl elbowed Mr. Miller. "I can take credit for her eye injuries, but Kurt must have caused that injury to her nose."

"I can't believe Mrs. Constantine is behind all this," Mr. Miller said.

"Believe it. That woman had a gun pointed at me before I cleaned her up with some ammonia in her eyes."

Mr. Miller grimaced and shook his head. "I should have gone in with you."

"You did everything a hero needed to do."

They watched Frank LaMotta pass by with handcuffs on his wrists and zip ties around his ankles. The zip ties made his stride more like a tiptoe as he hobbled to a separate squad car.

"Why is he trussed up like a Christmas Turkey?" Mr. Miller asked.

"Officer Howard said Frank put up quite a fight when they caught him on the first floor. I missed it but could hear the scuffle on the second floor." Liesl gave a wan smile. "How nice it is to see them taking their first steps to punishment for their crimes."

"Now they need to learn from their mistakes, like I did," Mr. Miller added.

Chapter 39

Liesl

Liesl didn't enjoy visiting in hospitals. Her last experience culminated in the death of Aunt Suzanne. At least Kurt was recovering. She could pull herself together and visit him, couldn't she? It was required if she was going to say what she needed to say.

She could be brave. After all, she'd helped save his life. If she could do that, she could do anything.

At his room, she found his mother and father inside. After a brief conversation, the Hunters excused themselves.

As Kurt's dad walked past her, he gave a slight shake of his head. She assumed he had not yet told Kurt about Madison, Ross's mother.

Kurt looked pale, but several levels better than he looked when she'd last seen him. He motioned for her to take a seat.

The room was warm, so she removed her raincoat before sitting in the chair his mother recently vacated.

"How are you feeling?" she asked.

"Pretty good. Considering."

"You've improved since I last saw you."

"They tell me you saved me." He shifted on the bed and pulled up the sheet.

"Not just me. It took a village. I wouldn't have known something was wrong if Mr. Miller hadn't called me. Then he got me inside quietly. The other police and EMTs took care of the rest."

"I'm grateful. Thank you." He shifted again. "I'll wait until later to ask why Mr. Miller knew to call you."

She smiled a Cheshire smile. "Good plan. We can discuss it when you've healed."

"Hector was here before my parents arrived. I have information about the case, if you're interested."

"Fill me in, please. I have unanswered questions."

"That part-time student at Donnie Davis's office is Mrs. Constantine's daughter."

"No. Really? But her name wasn't Constantine. I'm sure of that."

Kurt nodded. "It's confusing, but her last name is Brown. Courtney Brown. Her father was Mrs. Constantine's first husband. Hector hasn't been allowed to speak to the daughter yet. She's a minor, but Donnie confirmed their relationship with her address and emergency contact information on file at his office."

"No wonder we didn't connect her with Mrs. Constantine."

"Mrs. Constantine's arrest removes any suspicion from our other suspects. When Mrs.

Sizemore told me it was her," Kurt said with a grin, "I should have listened."

Liesl smiled. "Wait until she sees you again. She'll rub that in your face."

"I can handle it. All good cops are experienced in taking a tongue-lashing from an angry citizen."

"Mrs. Sizemore better not ever figure out that Mr. Miller thought it was her car near Graceland that night. She'd never forgive him or me for believing it was hers."

"What happened there?"

"Mr. Miller called me about a suspicious white Lexus. Turns out it was a suspicious white Mercedes."

Kurt grinned. "I'll never tell her."

"What's going to happen to the daughter, now that her mother's been arrested?"

"Hector said her father's flying in to get her to take her back to California."

"Poor kid," Liesl said. "Having a criminal for a mother. I'm glad her father is taking her where people won't know about her mother's arrest."

"Mrs. Constantine appears to be a drug distributor."

"Thank goodness we didn't have a human trafficking network in town."

"DEA and Homeland Security try to stop drugs from getting in the country, but shipments slip in and go out to distributors all over the U.S. With her connections in California, they believe she was a distributor with a network of street thugs selling them."

"I can't imagine her daughter having to live with that information about her own mother."

"By the way, your instincts were right about the money that night at the Simmons Stables fundraiser."

"What do you mean? That guy was your friend. A cop. How did I fail to spot a cop?"

"Not your instincts about Jimmy Reed. I know him from the Missouri State Highway Patrol. Your instincts about the money. Since Hector arrested Mrs. Constantine's accomplice, he's admitted to being at the fundraiser with Mrs. Constantine to nab the money."

Liesl nodded. "I spoke to him there. If you need a witness to verify Frank's presence there, I'm your girl."

"Frank's throwing her under the bus for a chance at a plea deal. They planned to grab the money at the fundraiser. It would have been easy, but you called for someone to protect Gretchen. They could have hurt her that night."

"Glad my instincts were partially right."

"I want to thank you for protecting Ross that night."

Liesl smiled. "You mean, even though my instincts failed me miserably because he wasn't in danger from your cop buddy?"

Kurt smiled. "Don't make me laugh. It hurts when I laugh."

"Sorry."

"I meant, your instincts were to grab him and get him to safety. I'm grateful for that."

"Where is he now? With your mom and dad here, who's taking care of him?"

"Your buddy, Nicole."

"Okay, so tomorrow I'll pick him up and take him to my place for an overnight adventure. That way, your parents can be here tomorrow, too."

"That's nice, but you don't have to do that."

"I want to. He's been asking to stay overnight. With my dog on alert and my alarm set, we'll be fine."

He smiled. "The only thing your dog alerts to is food."

With her indignation over his remark, he held up a hand. "I'm not going to argue with you. You can take him to your place. I'm grateful you grabbed Ross to get him out of harm's way. Again."

"It was pure instinct on my part. Ross was laughing the whole time I carried him to Nicole's van. Thought it was a game." She grinned at him. "I got you out of harm's way too. What is it with me dragging the Hunter men out of danger, real or perceived?"

"I said I was grateful for that. Extremely grateful."

"You should be. You're heavy." She put her hand on the small of her back and grimaced. "My arms and back are still sore from dragging you across the floor."

He placed his hands against his bandage. "Please. Stop being funny."

"Okay. Here's a serious question for you. Where was Hector when everything went down?"

"He got my text saying someone was inside, arranged the team to enter, and then they had a stand-off with Frank LaMotta. Downstairs. Caught him with some of the coins in the main hallway. Or, at least they caught him after a scuffle in the hallway. You must have gotten in right before his team arrived."

"I heard them shouting and scuffling down there after I dragged you out of danger." She clutched the cool metal of his hospital bed's rail. "So, how did you let a woman beat you?"

"I guess you could say that. She jumped me from behind just as I turned the corner to go into the Collections Room. She knocked me down, and I could see she was as surprised as I was. She stabbed me before I could shoot her. But I did get in one good blow to her nose."

"I saw the damage. Bravo." Liesl smiled. "But how did that criminal get on the Ag board and the historical society board in the first place?"

"She lied. She volunteered to serve, saying she had prior board service in California and could help bring additional revenue streams. No director will turn down 'additional revenue streams.' Then she used her inside information in an attempt to steal the most valuable items."

"But you said she was a drug dealer. Why did she need to steal things?"

"My guess is she was a user herself. Those kinds of habits cost money. We'll know more when the investigation unfolds." He coughed and winced. "Coughing hurts as much as laughing."

"You have a serious injury."

"I was lucky you were there. The only thing the doctor is concerned about is possible nerve damage. That's more of a wait-and-see kind of thing."

She frowned, considering the possibility of permanent nerve damage. Could that throw him off the force? He'd be devastated if that happened. "Speaking of bones, any news about the old bones found at Nicole's flip house?"

"They may belong to an officer of the Union Army who disappeared in 1862. They listed him as a deserter in the records. Interestingly, the records don't list him as a disappearance, which means he wasn't on a mission for the encampment when he went missing."

"How do they know that?"

"Not completely sure. The forensic anthropologist found that connection. Also, the emblems on his deteriorated clothing found with the bones seem to put him as the same rank as the officer who deserted. They're running more DNA tests to verify his background. They'll return him to his family if they can confirm his identity."

She studied Kurt. His eyelids were drooping. "I've stayed long enough. Time for you to rest and me to run."

He hesitated, then asked, "Are you interested in spending some time at the Lake of the Ozarks this summer? My parents are using their cabin less and less, and they want me to take Ross there more often."

Liesl smiled. "I'd love to, on one condition."

"What? Name it."

"I want to bring Barney."

He rolled his eyes. "Done. I figured you'd ask for something hard. By the time it's warm enough to swim, I may have a dog for Ross. Would you help me pick one out at the animal shelter? I like your idea of an older dog."

"It would be my pleasure." She stood to leave. It was time for her to gather her courage. She'd come here to say something, and it was time to say it.

"Kurt, I'm going to go now, but I'll come back the day after tomorrow. As you know, tomorrow I have an adventure planned with a marvelous little boy."

"He's going to love it."

Liesl shifted her weight from foot to foot.

"Remember when you said you wanted to be more than friends one day?"

As he stared at her, concern painted his face. "Yes."

"When I was dragging you along the floor, a lot of things became clear to me. I should have told you earlier that I want to be more than friends. Now. Today. Always."

He grinned as she spun on her heel and walked to the door.

He called out, "Good," as she crossed the threshold into the hall.

She smiled. *Thank you, God, for letting him live.*

Author's Note:
Historical Information

The only existing museum mentioned in the book is the Audrain County Historical Museum. All museum employees included are fictional. The primary structure of the Audrain County Historical Museum Complex is called Graceland, an Italianate, Classic Revival style home, built by John P. Clark in 1857. It is on the U.S. National Register of Historic Places and is located in the eleven-acre Robert S. Green Park.

Graceland Museum includes many fascinating items, including the Cauthorn-Stribling Library. They built a modern-day addition to Graceland to accommodate the American Saddlebred Horse Museum and the Fire Brick Museum. Also within the Robert S. Green Park is a Country Church, a Country School, and stables built by Robert S. Green.

Information included in this book regarding the home of Mr. and Mrs. Clark is as historically accurate as possible. We found no records related to servants for the Clarks, other than they did not believe in slavery and owned no slaves. All the servants in this work are fictional.

Although Missouri did not secede from the Union during the Civil War, it was a "border state," which left it divided between Union loyalists and secessionists. The Union army occupied Mexico, Missouri, from the spring of 1861 until the end of the Civil War because the town's railroad lines were key to the control of northern Missouri.

Colonel Ulysses Grant, a regimental commander stationed in Mexico, was a popular leader. He received orders to transfer to Ironton, Missouri, and was informed of his promotion to brigadier general upon arrival. He later became the Commanding General of the Union Army and was elected the 18th President of the United States.

The citizens in and around Mexico appreciated Grant because he halted the forcing of locals at gunpoint to swear their loyalty to the Union. He also stopped the military from seizing local property and supplies. Although George Hunter's mercantile deliveries could have happened because of Grant stopping supply and property seizures, both he and his deliveries are fictional.

General John Pope was commander of North Missouri for the Union Army, headquartered in Mexico, Missouri in 1861. He commanded the Army of Virginia until defeated by Confederate Generals in several battles. After the war, they appointed him to commands involving the reconstruction of Atlanta and the Indian Wars.

All Union soldiers are fictional except for General Pope and Colonel/General Grant.

Acknowledgments

I am grateful to the staff of the Audrain County Historical Society for the history and tours of the home of Mr. and Mrs. Clark, also known as Graceland. Thanks to Audrain County Historical Society's former Executive Director, Lori Pratt, for everything she did to assist with information for this book. Many thanks to Assistant Director Janice Robinson for all the information she shared. Pam Singleton should win an award for her patience with all the questions I asked during our tour. Thanks to Consuelo Baum, for her loving care of the flowers, bushes, and all other flora, which contribute beauty to the grounds surrounding Graceland.

I dedicate a special thank you to Morgan. I appreciated the tour of the Old School House and Church during our exterior grounds tour, but special kudos for crawling up into the attic with me with a heavy-duty flashlight so I could personally experience the attic and the view from the Widow's Walk.

Heartfelt thanks to Dana Keller and Penny Rutherford at the Mexico Area Chamber of Commerce for the excellent services you perform for me as a writer and member of the Chamber. You ladies ROCK!

My sincere appreciation goes to Matt Pilger, KXEO radio, and to the Mexico Ledger, for the publicity about my books. This writer appreciates the hometown support you provided.

To my friends and family: Thank you to Helen and Larry Glick, who sent flowers and were "over the moon" about *Show Me Betrayal*. Thanks to "Cousin Bruce" Oliver, who bought a "million" copies and handed them out all over Mexico, Missouri. I appreciate Susan and Alan Atkins and Laura and Steve Erdel for their interest in my books and providing a place to stay when visiting my hometown. Thank you to Ann and Bill Berg, for the beautiful flowers that adorned my table at A Walk Back in Time. Special thanks to Top of the Rock Chorus for your unflagging support and enthusiasm.

About the Author

Ellen E. Withers is a retired insurance fraud investigator, which helps provide the realism and intrigue found in her new dual-time mystery series, *Show Me Mysteries*. Set in Ellen's picturesque hometown of Mexico, Missouri, each book features a historical structure, a dual-time plotline, and intriguing mysteries.

Ellen has earned over 90 awards for her short stories, including a prestigious Pushcart Prize nomination for published short fiction. She is a columnist for *Writers Monthly PDF*, a guide for professional writers, about writing for contests. As a freelance writer, Ellen has written over 75 nonfiction articles published in local, regional, and international magazines.

She is one of three contributors to *A Gift for All Time*, a Christmas novella collection, published by Scrivenings Press. Her guide to winning writing contests, published in 2024, is *Magic Words: Enchant Judges & Conjure Contest Wins for Novels, Short Fiction, and Nonfiction*. This book provides writers with the craft technique needed to win contests and catch the attention of publishers. It educates writers to win contests and provides a tremendous resource for contests to enter—in one publication.

Ellen serves as an officer of the Pioneer Branch of the National League of American Pen Women and is a board member of the Arkansas Writers Conference. She is a member of White County Creative Writers, Sisters in Crime and Tornado Alley, a local chapter of SIC.

Center Point Large Print
600 Brooks Road / PO Box 1
Thorndike, ME 04986-0001 USA

(207) 568-3717

US & Canada:
1 800 929-9108
www.centerpointlargeprint.com